"THIS IS MADNESS!"

"You know as well as I that you are only marrying me so that Granbury cannot! And now you want me to hide like a frightened child while you take care of the man."

Valentine scowled in frustration. "I cannot put you in danger."

"And why not? You will allow my maid to help—to risk her life. But I cannot? I am tired to death of being treated like a pretty package that must be petted and primped, sold to the highest bidder, or gather dust upon a shelf. I will bring him down myself, if you cannot help."

"I am sorry, I do not mean to treat you—"

"Of course you do!" Just as quickly as she had interrupted him, Emily bit back her tirade. It would do no good to point out to him that he seemed to believe her as brainless as her mother did. Did he think her incapable of living a life without luxury? "We have little time, as you have so often reminded me tonight. Do we marry and return? Or do we return unmarried."

Dear Romance Reader,

In July, we launched the Ballad line with four new series, and each month we'll present both new and continuing stories set everywhere from medieval England to the American West—the kind of passionate, romantic stories you love best, written by the most gifted authors. At the back of each book, we'll tell you when you can find subsequent books in the series that have captured your heart.

New to Zebra with her fabulous series *The Dream Maker*, Alice Duncan offers **Cowboy for Hire.** Set just after the turn of the century, this quartet chronicles the lives—and loves—of the people behind that intriguing innovation, the moving picture. In the first book, two amateurs learn that their real-life passion is much more compelling than their on-screen roles. Next, talented newcomer Kelly McClymer continues the Fenster family saga in the second book of *Once Upon a Wedding*, as a man caught between honor and passion wonders what do with his **Star-Crossed Bride.**

New favorite Shelley Bradley presents the last offering in the popular *Brothers in Arms* trilogy, with **His Rebel Bride.** For one stubborn knight, choosing an Irish bride seems simple—until he realizes he must scale the battlements around his rebellious lady's heart. Finally, the third book in Gabriella Anderson's charming *Destiny Coin* series crosses the Atlantic once again, where a young woman with a passion for botany discovers a new desire—for a man who cannot be hers. Does love mean more than **A Matter of Honor?**

Kate Duffy
Editorial Director

Once Upon a Wedding

THE STAR-CROSSED BRIDE

Kelly McClymer

ZEBRA BOOKS
Kensington Publishing Corp.
http://www.zebrabooks.com

ZEBRA BOOKS are published by

Kensington Publishing Corp.
850 Third Avenue
New York, NY 10022

All Kensington titles, imprints, and distributed lines are available at special quantity discounts for bulk purchases for sales promotions, premiums, fund raising, educational or institutional use.

Special book excerpts or customized printings can also be created to fit specific needs. For details, write or phone the office of the Kensington Special Sales Manager: Kensington Publishing Corp., 850 Third Avenue, New York, NY 10022, Attn. Special Sales Department. Phone: 1-800-221-2647.

Zebra and the Z logo Reg. U.S. Pat. & TM Off.
Ballad is a trademark of Kensington Publishing Corp.

First Printing: March, 2001
10 9 8 7 6 5 4 3 2 1

Printed in the United States of America

Prologue

"Must we stop?" Emily asked nervously, as the carriage slowed.

"The horses cannot go on much farther unless they are fed and watered—and I cannot let you starve." Valentine smiled reassuringly at her, but she could sense his unease.

"I wish it were done."

"It will be soon enough." His gaze was solemn as he asked, for the hundredth time, "Are you certain of this Emily? I am willing to wait until your father sees reason—"

"We have already waited months as it is." She shook her head firmly. "No, Valentine, Mother will never allow him to consider you. She has a most unreasoning desire to see me a marchioness, at the very least."

"Given time—"

Emily grimaced, remembering the last scold she had received for continuing to encourage the attentions of a suitor her mother did not approve of. "Given time, I will find myself locked away until I do as I am told. My mother has strict guidelines for a dutiful daughter to follow." And a dutiful daughter did not want to marry Valentine Fenster, no matter that he had a title. Viscountess was not a sufficiently powerful title for any daughter of the countess of Wertherley.

His expression was serious, his blue eyes bright with concern for her welfare. "I cannot bear to think of the gossip you will suffer when society hears of our elopement." The way he cherished her made her heart melt, but she could not allow him to love her so well that he lost her—and that was without doubt what would happen if they turned back now.

"It will be for the briefest of times, as you well know. And once we have settled and begun our family, we shall become yesterday's news and quite too boring to gossip about."

He made a little noise of distress deep in his throat. She laughed at his feigned shock, noting all too well the upward curve of the right half of his mouth—which indicated he was anticipating the benefits of marriage as eagerly as she.

Fastening her gaze on his beautiful mouth, she smiled, knowing how to end his argument, as well as any further talk of halting the elopement. Without hesitation, she went into his arms and kissed him soundly. As she had anticipated, the heat of his return kiss was all the reassurance either of them needed that they were doing the right thing in defying her parents' wishes and making a runaway marriage.

To her great disappointment, as the carriage

rolled to a stop, he broke off the kiss to whisper in her ear, "Let's get you fed, my lady. This will wait until we're married."

Eager to get the delay over with quickly so that they could be back on their way, Emily did not wait for the coachman to open the door, but flung it open herself and prepared to leap out. Unfortunately, as she stood exposed to the light of day, she caught a brief, horrifying glimpse of her much too proper cousin Simon.

She turned her head away, praying that he had not seen her, and quickly retreated, closing the carriage door and knocking Valentine—who had been half-risen to follow her—onto the floor of the carriage. His hand tightened on her arm, bringing her down on top of him.

They did not even try to untangle themselves, just lay frozen where they had fallen. Valentine's voice was low and urgent. "What is the matter, Emily? You look as if you've seen a ghost. Has your father discovered us?"

"Worse. Simon is in the courtyard of this very inn."

"The duke is—" His whole body went tense and still beneath her. "Did he see you?"

"I pray not."

But her prayers were not to be answered, as the coach door swung open and her cousin's imperturbable countenance appeared above them. "Emily?" His cold green eyes swept over them lying in a tangled heap and his voice was sharp enough to sliver a diamond. "Fenster."

"Your grace." His voice was as cold as Simon's had been, but in a very different way. Emily could feel Valentine's horror as if she were experiencing it herself. He held Simon as a hero, with good enough cause she supposed, although right now she would happily wish her cousin to the devil.

"My uncle did mention that he was afraid you'd no better sense than to run off with her." Emily twisted to glance at Valentine, hoping that he would show some sign that he did not intend to meekly give her up. A spark of anger flared deep in the blue depths of his eyes, reminding her that any argument between them over such a serious matter could result in a challenge.

For a moment she was afraid that the men would fight each other there in the courtyard of the inn. Then Simon said, with a hint of disappointment in his eyes, "I had thought better of you."

Emily did not need to look into Valentine's face to see the devastating effect of those simple words. He worshiped Simon—the perfect duke, the perfectly saintly paragon of society.

The perfect man to foil all her hopes and dreams of a future with Valentine.

Simon reached in to assist her out of the carriage and she went, numbly. "Come, Emily. I will get you home before your foolishness has been discovered, I hope." He glanced back into the carriage where Valentine had not moved. "Can I trust you to say nothing of this, Fenster?"

She tried to catch his gaze, staring into his familiar and well loved face, but he avoided looking at her.

For one brief moment she dared hope that he might try to persuade Simon that this elopement was not a foolish whim.

"I would die before I would bring harm to Emily." His words broke her heart. He meant every one of them—and he had decided that eloping with her would hurt her. As if her reputation meant more than her heart.

Simon stood silent for a moment and then shrugged lightly. "Your death is not necessary, Fenster. Just your silence."

One

Scotland, 1840

Approaching darkness and the lowering gray of the sky blurred the lines of the stone walls of Eddingley Castle ahead. The castle itself was massive, its towers and walls rising like ghosts in the mist, but for a moment he blinked, thinking that he had imagined it there in front of him. No, he could see lights now, glowing dimly through the growing gloom. For an eerie moment he could not shake the notion that he had traveled back in time four hundred years. Despite the urgency of his mission, he brought Caesar to a halt and simply stared at the sight ahead of him.

He understood, then, what his impatience and callowness had cost her. His own twin sister, Miranda, had a penchant for believing in fairy tales and he knew without a doubt what she would say about this. They had locked Emily in a tower and thrown away the key. But that was not strictly true. They had put the key to her release in the hand of a man whose very soul was corrupt. He only hoped that they had done so unwittingly. And that he was not too late to prevent a tragedy from occurring.

It was late in the day for a social call, but after his hasty journey, he did not want to wait now, so close to his goal. He urged the horse forward as suddenly as he had halted him a moment before. At the end of the drive he dismounted and threw the reins to the willing stableboy, not daring to pause for fear he would lose courage.

Would they let him speak to her? Should he, if they did? No. It was better not to meet, not to see her. It had taken almost these entire three years for him to put her out of his mind, and his heart. Even now, though it was no business of his, he couldn't bear the thought that her family might marry her to a man whose reputation was shadowed by the most vile of rumors . . . and some truths that Valentine would reveal only to her family.

The footman opened the door to him. He felt a little shudder of relief when the door was not summarily shut in his face. Three years had apparently been long enough for the memory of his indiscretion to fade—at least in this footman's mind. He held out his card. "Please tell the countess I've come on a matter of extreme urgency."

The footman placed the card on an ornate salver and then, apparently reading the name at last, blanched. His gaze swept up in horror to Valentine, who spoke in a voice that brooked no dispute, "Tell the countess it is a matter of life and death, or I would never have come."

He wondered briefly if he should have added that

it was Lady Emily's life for which he feared. Would that make the matter more urgent for her mother—or less? But then the footman was back, ushering him into a cold parlor which lacked all but the most haphazard adornment. Obviously, his indiscretion had not been forgotten—or forgiven.

He stood before the cold grate, the sting of the insult not even truly registering except in that it would make his task even more difficult than he had feared.

Lost in thought, the first he knew that the countess had deigned to join him was when her sharp voice cut his thoughts short. "You are fortunate the earl is dead. I do believe he would have whipped you for the insolence of appearing here, despite the fact that your sister married his nephew."

Prepared for battle, what else might he have expected from the countess of Wertherley? Could he soften her? He turned and offered her an unoffended, deferent smile. "I can assure you, Lady Wertherley, I most sincerely regret attempting to elope with your daughter. I can only claim that my feelings for her clouded my reason enough that I did not stop to think how unsuitable the match would be." He dared to meet her eyes, hoping to put this matter, at least, behind them. "I can make you a solemn oath that I no longer believe myself a worthy husband for her."

"And I am simply to believe this change of heart after you have so grievously deceived my family?"

"In the years since, I have had the responsibility of my five younger sisters, my lady. I am now appalled at how badly I wronged you and the earl. I know I would treat any young fool who dared to dishonor any one of my sisters as sharply as you treated me. I would not harm Lady Emily for the world." He willed her to read the truth in his eyes.

There was no softening in her bulldog features. "All well and good, as my daughter is due to wed Lord Granbury as soon as the year of mourning for her father has passed."

"So I have heard. It is about the upcoming wedding that I have come."

"Have you intentions to upset our plans, then, after all? You would do her no favor, she has been unlucky in her last two hopes of marriage. Both men died before they could be led to the altar."

And this was the crux of the matter, then. Would the countess choose another engagement, cut off before the wedding, over her own daughter's welfare? "I do not wish to cause further scandal, my lady, but neither can I wish harm for Lady Emily, or for your family." He paused, putting every ounce of sincerity in his voice despite her skeptical mien. "I have recently been in London on business and have heard disturbing rumors which I felt would alter your feelings toward Lord Granbury as a suitable husband for your daughter."

"And I am to believe you to be a disinterested party?" There was sharp amusement in her high-pitched voice.

"I assure you, my lady, I have no intentions toward Lady Emily myself. I have long wished to make amends with your family. I regret that I could not tender my apologies to the earl himself."

"He would have had you whipped from the house had you dared. You are fortunate that I am more generous in nature than my late husband." Her eyes narrowed to slits that nearly disappeared between brow and cheek. "It is a strange time you choose to make amends, if you ask me. So, if you traveled these many dusty miles to apologize, then I say to you, let your actions show your words to be true. Stay away from Emily; she has had troubles enough these last few years. To be seen with you would finish any hope she has of repairing her reputation."

True enough. It was why Valentine had never sought her out to apologize for humiliating them both, and risking her reputation with a failed elopement. Still, this close he was grateful for the reminder. Society had become more careful of conduct recently, the young queen's new husband did not approve of frivolity, and thus neither did she. "I would lay down my life before I would bring harm to your daughter. I feel I have the method to make amends to you all. That is why I have come."

"Indeed?"

"I cannot think you realize the reputation of the man you have chosen for your daughter—"

"And you are one to judge that?"

"I have heard rumors—"

She interrupted imperiously. "I put no stock in the whisperings of silly persons of no consequence."

Then she had heard them? He wished he could tell from her expression, her movements, anything about whether she would actually risk her daughter's life for a prestigious marriage. And the marquess of Granbury was a prime catch, indeed, if only his heart was not as black as his boots.

He said simply, "I know of three which are true."

Her brows rose. "Indeed. And I am to take your word for it?"

He could not help the flush which crept up his neck. Would he never live down his impetuous mistake? "I did not expect you would. I have brought you proof." He made a movement to remove the letter he had brought, but she held up her hand to stop him.

"No. You have played your last trick to ruin my family. You are not going to cause my daughter to lose her last chance to restore her reputation and her place in society. It is bad enough that she has to endure whispers of an attempted elopement, two engagements in which her affianced died, and an entire year of mourning for her father before she can yet be decently wed. Emily will marry in a month's time, as soon as the mourning period for her father is over. No trick of yours will stop that."

"Emily's life is in danger! Is all you can think of her reputation?" As soon as the words crossed his lips he wished them back. "Pardon me, my lady."

Her eyes narrowed and her hand reached for the bellpull. "Your actions reveal your true nature, my lord. If you are seen here again, your greeting will be harsh, I can assure you."

"I wish only to protect Lady Emily."

Her eyes gleamed with malice. "If that is so, then

I assure you, you must never see *Lady* Emily, nor speak to her again. I am informed by your sister Miranda that Julia has hopes of an engagement to a young viscount. I can assure you that, one word from me into his mother's ear, and her hopes will be dashed. Think of your family, as you claim you have been doing, and let me take care of mine."

Juliet. He met the countess's eyes briefly, wondering if her threat was as badly aimed as her knowledge of his sister's name. But no. She understood power, and she was sure of herself in this. Juliet, who had happily enumerated her viscount's laudable traits only last week, would find him and his mama turned cold to her if he did not leave the castle immediately.

He had muddled things yet again. Would he never be done hurting Emily? The countess would perhaps have listened to another, but not the man who had tried to elope with her daughter. If only Simon and Miranda had not been abroad when he received confirmation of the worst of the rumors. The countess would have heard the duke and duchess out.

In the midst of his desperate casting about for someone who might gain her trust, the butler appeared, but before a footman could be called, Valentine departed. He would hope that the letter he'd dispatched to Simon, calling him back from his travels, would find him and bring him here as soon as possible. It was the only thing he could do now. Pray God he had not left things too late.

He had cantered halfway down the long drive, his anger fueling the length of his strides, before suddenly halting. Her mother would not hear his objections, but could he leave now without at least attempting to alert Emily to the serious danger that faced her if she chose to marry Lord Granbury?

Though it was the one thing he did not wish to do, he supposed he must at least try to see her directly. To give her the letter and let her make her own decision about her fate. To reassure her that he would ask Simon to intervene with the countess. It was his duty, his obligation to her for the disaster he had brought into her life. He dismounted and sent the horse that he had let from the local inn back home with a sharp slap on its rump. He turned back, careful to leave the path and keep out of sight of any vigilant servants.

With a sigh, he climbed a tree which gave a good overlook of the castle and the gardens which Emily had always been partial to. He did not think it necessary to watch the drive, for rumors had reached him that Lady Emily was a virtual prisoner here, though a petted and cosseted one. While she was not allowed off the grounds, the milliner, the seamstress, the bootmaker all came to and fro to prepare her the finest trousseau for this latest wedding preparation.

If she did not show herself in the gardens before nightfall, perhaps he could determine which room of the castle was hers. He would not climb through the window, as Rapunzel's prince had done, but surely he could find some other way of gaining entrance in order to warn her? He remembered the utter venom of her mother's final words to him. Would she truly ruin Juliet's chances? He could not be certain of anything except that he must warn Emily, and he must not be seen doing so.

"Have you taken leave of your senses completely?"

"I have only just returned to them, Mother." Emily had known this would be a difficult interview with her mother, but she could not understand the countess's sudden fury. Usually her temper was slow to build—she rarely expected her only daughter to defy her and it generally took time until she understood that Emily would not be easily swayed to the countess's way.

"You are to marry Lord Granbury in a month's time. He has been unbelievably patient to wait the year of your father's mourning for you, considering your past. Do you believe your reputation can stand another such scandal?"

"My failed elopement is only a rumor, Mother, it was never confirmed. Neither Valentine nor Simon would be so loose lipped! As for the deaths of my former affianced, that cannot be put at my feet. Lord Matterington was, after all, quite elderly, and poor Dibby was in his cups from his first day in long pants—it is only a wonder that he did not tumble from his horse sooner."

"You are a fool if you think the rumors of that foolish elopement are not heeded. And though you may well be blameless in the deaths of those poor men, your connections will never be forgotten. After all, most women manage to get themselves properly affianced and wed the first time they try. All Society waits to find out whether this marriage happens or not. And you want to call it off because you do not like your groom. Nonsense."

"There is something evil about the man, Mother, not just unlikable. I believe he is dishonorable."

"Has he done something to make you believe such a thing?"

That was the problem. Granbury had been nothing but a gentleman. There was no reason for her skin to crawl when he was near. But it did. She could not see that argument swaying her mother, however.

"No. It is a look in his eye. A way of speaking that seems to make things more confusing rather than clear as they should be." She set her lips stubbornly, determined to make her mother understand. "I want an honorable husband. One that I can trust. One that I can come to love." Like Valentine, not that her mother ought to hear her say such a thing out loud, else she'd likely lock her in her room and hold the ceremony tomorrow lest Emily find some way to escape.

"Honorable? My dear, there is no such thing as an honorable man. You are much better off with a title and a fortune." She paused and peered sharply at Emily. "Has something happened . . . recently . . . to make you change your mind so disgracefully?"

Emily squirmed under her mother's gimlet glare, wondering what awful thing the countess suspected her daughter of this time. "No, Mother. I have only just got over my grief at Father's passing." Suddenly, she thought of something that might sway her mother. "I do not think Lord Granbury is half so fine a man as Father was."

The countess sniffed and brought a lacy handkerchief to her mouth. "It is a shame that your father had no son to carry on the line. Your cousin is no match for the late earl."

"Yes. And Cousin Harold seems to have no respect for you, Mother. He cannot be the earl that father was." Emily hoped that this last line would deter her mother from her interrogation as it was her fondest habit to denigrate poor Harold, whose only sin was to have inherited the earldom and it's entailment upon her father's death.

Unfortunately, her mother was not to be waylaid. "Your father, dear man, put all faith in Lord Granbury, Emily. I should think you would be ashamed to second guess his decision now, when he cannot guide you with a father's wisdom."

"But mother, Lord—"

"—your intended," her mother finished with heat. "I am determined to see you do not let this attack of vapors ruin your last chance at a respectable place in society. Believe me, you will thank me later."

She yanked the bellpull with a distracted air. "Soames, send for Letty, please." She glanced at Emily. "Go to your room, child. I will send Letty to you with a hot posset and some cakes. I expect your nerves will be restored by tomorrow and we can discuss this matter more reasonably."

Emily knew her mother's tactics well enough by now. Whenever her daughter showed any sign of disagreement, the countess ignored the fact that Emily had a maid to tend to her needs, and used her own personal maid, Letty, to reinforce Emily's status as child.

It irritated her that she should be treated like a recalcitrant infant instead of a woman on the verge of marriage. "I will not marry him, Mother. I intend to tell him so myself, if you do not."

Her mother's eyes gleamed for a moment, then she bent her head and put a hand to her temple. "We'll see how you feel tomorrow, my dear."

Emily turned away. A hot posset was her mother's solution to all ills. But there was no point in arguing further tonight. Tomorrow morning her mother would see well enough that she meant what she said.

Two

"Here you go my lady." Letty held the noxiously sweet posset to her lips, but Emily took the cup from her and set it back on the tray next to the plate of cakes.

The maid frowned. "Your mother says to drink it all up, Lady Emily."

Emily sighed. "I will, Letty, I will." Her own maid, Nancy, would not have insisted in such a bossy manner. But Letty would report back to her mother, so it was wisest to comply. She picked up the cup and pretended to sip, just so that the maid would leave her.

Letty nodded and departed. Emily felt a moment of relief as she set the cup back down—until the sound of the key being turned in the lock froze her. Swiftly she went to the door and tried to open it. She had not imagined the sound. Her mother had ordered Letty to lock her in!

She lifted one hand to pound the door and demand it be unlocked, but stopped midway. It would do no good. Outright opposition only made her mother more stubborn.

She sat nibbling at a cake and staring at her door, deciding what this new move indicated. Had her mother taken her threat to break her engagement more seriously than usual? Had she already determined to move the date of the wedding up?

It was more than possible. Since her father's death, her mother had become fixated on Emily's upcoming marriage. All her hopes and dreams seemed pinned on it, now that her own husband was gone and she was merely the widow of an earl. Cousin Harold, who had taken over the entailment, had both his own mother and a wife, and Emily's mother had quickly learned what the death of her husband meant to her social status.

But the year was nearly up. Surely her mother could wait one more month in order to avoid the slightest cause for malicious gossip? Any girl who married too hastily would have the gossips counting months. She shuddered at the thought.

Children. Even if one wasn't likely to arrive scandalously early, she would no doubt have them. Lord Granbury's heirs. She had not even been able to make herself use his Christian name, Francis, and she was now to have his children? It was unthinkable.

Emily tossed the cake back upon its plate and began to pace. She would have to escape. But to where? Her parents had chosen Scotland for her exile with good purpose. Her friends were far away. Miranda would have come to her aid, but she and Simon were blithely enjoying a trip through Paris and Germany at this very moment. Who else had the courage to defy both her mother and Lord Granbury?

Valentine.

She wondered at her own daring for a moment, even as she savored the name. He would help her, though she could not, she warned herself sternly, expect him to have the same feelings for her that she still held for him—not after his marriage last year. For a moment she nursed the ache in her heart that remained as painful as it had a year ago, when her mother had told her of the marriage. If not for that news, she would never have been so weak as to have accepted Lord Granbury's suit.

But no, no excuses. She had thought she would not mind a sensible marriage since she could not have Valentine. That did not excuse her failure to recognize that Lord Granbury was not the man for her, despite her father's appreciation for his title and wealth. She was no brainless chit; she should have been more careful, no matter her grief. Once agreed to, an engagement was not lightly broken, even if the groom's smile made the bride wish she had fleas and several missing teeth so that he'd turn his attentions elsewhere.

She wondered briefly if Valentine's marriage had been as poor a match as her upcoming one. She still did not know the name of his wife, even though she had scoured the London papers without her mother's knowledge, looking for any news of Valentine and his bride. No, she had missed the announcement, since it had happened right after her father's death, when her mother had forbidden the paper to enter the house for three months. And she would not wish him a poor bride. He deserved a good wife: he was a good man, no matter what her parents thought.

Valentine would help her, she was sure. With new decision, she stripped the coverings from her bed and set about making a rope from her bedsheets— something that was much harder than it had ever sounded when she read it in a novel. After a few false starts, she had created something sturdy and— hopefully—long enough to reach from her window to the ground below.

Quickly she packed a bundle of belongings and tossed them to the ground below. So that her mother's maid, Letty, or her own maid, Nancy, would not sound the alarm should they check on her in the night, she replaced the covers on her bed, arranging the pillows to serve as her own sleeping shape. Carefully she settled her collection of porcelain dolls back on the left half of the bed.

The dolls, with their pretty painted faces, had kept her company since she was a child. If she could have fit them into her bag, she would have taken them with her for companionship as she traveled.

"Good-bye girls," she said softly, patting the head of the nearest doll, Clarissa. Once at the window, she leaned out and looked down. It was quite a distance and the pit of her stomach twisted at the thought of falling. She looked at her locked door. There was no one in the house who would unlock it without her mother's permission. And she did not dare find herself forced to the altar, now that her mother knew she did not want to marry Lord Granbury. She did not know if she would have the courage to refuse.

She let out the rope, and squinted down to see where it reached. It didn't reach all the way to the ground, but was it ten feet too short? Five? Courage, she told herself, you have jumped farther than that climbing field gates.

Even with the locked door to remind her how awful her future was, she hesitated on the sill. If she fell . . . She'd just have to make certain that she did nothing so silly as fall. Holding her breath, Emily began to climb down. When she had reached the end of the makeshift rope, she dared a hasty peek down to see how far away the ground was. It seemed, at this point, to be much farther away than she had thought.

For a moment she hung there, her arms aching, her eyes closed against her damnably vivid imagination. Would the countess cry to see Emily's broken body upon the grass tomorrow? Would they assume she had tried to kill herself? She shivered at the thought of being buried in unhallowed ground. Would it be better to climb back up? *Could* she climb back up?

Courage, she reminded herself, and released her grip on the bedsheet. She dropped farther than she expected. However, her landing was not on solid ground, but rather into a pair of strong and encompassing arms, which clasped her against a broadcloth-covered chest.

For a moment she thought she was caught and would find herself an unwilling bride before morn-

ing, and then her captor released her with a little
push and a familiar voice whispered, "What are you
doing, you reckless little fool?"

She turned and faced the man who had held her
so tightly for but a moment, and then let her go free.
"Valentine."

"Lady Emily." His face was familiar and strange
all at once. She knew his features by heart, but three
years had changed him. His once ready smile was
tucked away and he had only a stern look for her.
Still, he was here, just when she had determined to
go to him for help.

She could not seem to break her gaze from him.
Or to speak. All she could think of for a moment
was that her longing, her need, had conjured him
from London to her side in a flash of witchcraft. He
couldn't be real. But he was. With no thought to her
resolution of minutes before to expect nothing, with
no thought to his wife, she threw herself at him, arms
tight around his neck, and kissed him full on the
mouth.

Her lips were as soft and sweet as on the day they
had parted. Valentine could not keep himself from
wrapping his arms around her. Hard travel with
sparse food and little rest had left him too exhausted
to fight his need to hold her. His worry as she inched
down the makeshift rope had drawn the tension to
a tight point inside him, leaving him defenseless
against the sensual assault she was making upon him.
But almost as soon as he began to return her kiss,
he came to his senses and pushed her away. "We
have no time for this, Emily. You must climb back

up at once, before someone finds you missing and cries out an alarm."

She stepped away from him, a blush creeping up that he could see even in the moonlight. "How did you know I needed you?"

He shook his head, trying not to laugh at her expression of wonder. Emily had always been most enthralled when Miranda told one of her fairy tales. "I did not. I had news to give you. Urgent news."

"What news? Is Miranda hurt?" Her smile disappeared into a worried frown.

"No. Miranda and Simon are fine." He looked away, realizing for the first time how bold he was, coming directly to her. "I have discovered some information in London that I thought you should know. The marquess of Granbury is—" No. Emily was an innocent. He could not tell her the man she planned to marry was a cold-blooded murderer, torturing and strangling female servants for sport. "Lord Granbury has some unsavory business in his past which could do you harm should you marry him."

She smiled at him, as if he had complimented the color of her eyes. "And you have come all the way to Scotland to tell me so? I do not deserve a friend so loyal—not after the way my family treated you."

He could not let her believe that. "I am responsible for your—" He glanced at the castle tower, the window with its makeshift rope trailing down. "—your imprisonment. It was my foolish attempt to elope with you that has put you in this predicament. I do not think you should count me a friend as much as a peni-

tent soul who needs to make amends for the damage
I have done you."

She blinked away tears and he fought the urge to
comfort her. "And am I so innocent? You did not
carry me away bound and unwilling, after all."

The memory her words conjured was a blow.
Emily, smiling, chattering about the future, about
their daughters, their sons. "I knew I was not good
enough for you, Lady Emily." He remembered again
why he was here whispering in the dark with her.
"And, I am afraid, neither is Lord Granbury."

As if she sensed that he had returned to business
because he did not want to force an unwanted inti-
macy upon her, she straightened and said sharply, "I
have no intention of marrying him . . . that is why
I must run away. I thought to seek you out, but fate
has placed you here on my doorstep—or windowsill
as you will. You will help, will you not?"

He stared at her, trying desperately to absorb all
that she was telling him. She'd had her own doubts
about her future husband. She wanted to break the
engagement. She had been running away . . . to
him. Anger rose more swiftly than he could control.
"Did our misfortune teach you nothing? You cannot
run away, your reputation will be shattered."

He hardened his heart to the tears which started
in her eyes at his sharpness, and to her whispered
reply, "My reputation is nothing compared to what
will happen to me if my mother has her way and I
marry that odious man."

"There is no need to run away. Simply refuse to
marry. It is your right, after all."

"You don't know my mother if you can suggest that, my lord. Although I must confess I am surprised that she chose to lock me in my room tonight. I had not thought she would take my objections seriously until I broached the subject with Lord Granbury himself."

He thought of the countess as she had been only hours earlier. No doubt his own arrival, his own attempt to bring Lord Granbury's evil to the countess's attention had precipitated her concern for her daughter. "Then you must take the matter to your fiancé. But running away is not your solution."

"Of course it is. Both my mother and my fiancé are of like minds—and they are not reluctant to force others into doing what they believe best."

Valentine shifted nervously, only too aware of the night breeze and the danger they courted with every moment they remained here. He did not believe her mother intended a forced wedding tomorrow. No, she had simply taken the precaution of locking Emily in so that Valentine would have no opportunity to seek her out. However, were anyone to discover Emily out here with him, confirming all the countess's worst fears, the wedding might very well occur by dawn.

He examined her set face and remembered, belatedly, that she did possess a stubborn streak. How to convince her to stay? "Emily, I must insist you return to your room immediately. The road is no place for a gently bred young woman."

Her lips pressed into a taut line and she moved a few steps away to pick up the bundle she had dropped to the ground before she climbed down herself. "With you or without you, I will quit this place tonight."

Stubborn or not, her bravery touched him and made him proud of her. But she was still as innocent as she had been when he first knew her. She did not understand what her life would be like were she to carry out her impetuous plan.

Not daring to touch her again, he grabbed hold of the bundle in her arms. "Climb back up to safety now and I will help you. I have already sent an urgent message to Simon. If anyone can change your mother's mind, it is the duke of Kerstone himself. I am certain that, between us, we can find some way to break your engagement that will not ruin you for polite society forever."

"You would do that for me?" Her surprise was obvious, and he realized how harsh he must have seemed to her after she had welcomed him so completely.

"I would do anything for you." As heat kindled in her eyes at his words, he realized belatedly how loverlike that sounded. "I meant nothing improper, I assure you." Her gaze turned from his. "I know how foolish I was and I know I owe you more than simple apologies."

She stood quietly, her eyes not leaving his face. He could not tell what was going on in her mind. Would she believe him? Would she kiss him again?

With a sigh, she dropped her bundle. She reached for the rope, but she was several feet short of grasping it. "I can't."

"Let me help you." He lifted her as high as he could, until she sat upon his shoulders, but still she could not reach.

"My fate is sealed." He could have sworn there was amusement in her voice as she slid down to the ground, warm against him in the chill of the night. "You must help me run away, or I will be disgraced."

He had thought himself a better man than to be tempted by such a prospect, and it took all his willpower to refuse. "Not until we try the kitchen door, my lady." He did not allow himself to show the slightest doubt—he had a feeling she would use it against him and they would both soon end up in ruins.

"Here." He took the bundle from the ground with one hand and her arm firmly in his other and marched her toward the back of the castle.

"If I do not run away tonight, I may be an unwilling bride tomorrow, don't you understand?" Her protests came in hurried whispers as he pulled her forward. "My mother is determined to see the match made." If it wasn't for the shadow-filled darkness he might have run, he was suddenly so certain he must return her to her room before disaster could befall them.

As he had suspected, the kitchen door was unlocked and guarded only by an exhausted and snoring scullery boy. However, the locked door to her bedchamber presented a unique problem. Fortunately, the countess ran an orderly household and the spare set of keys were soon located hanging upon the wall in their appointed place.

In less than fifteen minutes, Emily was once again safely in her room. She was not happy, although she had ceased her whispered protests and now simply stood at the window staring out into the darkness defiantly. He stopped, his hand upon the door latch as he realized that he might have to repeat this performance if he did not convince her to stay put. "Emily."

She did not turn until he said her name a third time. "Have you not left? I thought you anxious to see me locked up once again." Her eyes were fierce with anger, but her lower lip trembled.

"I know it is difficult, but I promise, even if I cannot reach Simon in time, I will stop this marriage—without harming your reputation."

"How?" Emily wanted to believe him, even though he stood in the doorway so obviously eager to go, she knew all affection for her must have fled him long before he took a new wife.

"I don't know."

"I would prefer to hear at least a shadow of an idea, if you truly wish me to put my faith in you." Her jab nettled him, she could see it in the heightened color of his cheeks.

Reluctantly, with a glance into the hallway, he closed the door and settled against it, as if he were afraid she would bolt if he left it unguarded. The truth was, she would stay here in this room, with him, as long as she could. Married or not, he still held the power to keep her by his side.

He sat nervously on the bed, but leaped up when she perched next to him. He looked so tense, so tired. She realized just how long a journey he had made in order to see to her welfare, and it warmed her heart. Her eyes settled on the cakes and posset that her mother had sent up.

"You must be hungry. Eat," she said, offering the plate to him. "Drink the posset if you wish, although it is altogether too sweet for my taste. Mother believes that if she feeds me enough of them they will sweeten me, but I'd rather toss them out the window than down my own throat."

He reached for the plate and cup, holding them almost as if they were a protective barrier between the two of them. "I have not eaten since morning; these will serve me well."

She smiled, watching him demolish the sweets to the last drop and crumb. Valentine was here with her, as she had always wished. Just the two of them, as intimate as lovers. But they weren't lovers, and they never would be now.

She closed her eyes, sadness seeping into the corners of her soul. If only he weren't married. . . . If only he were free . . . and her mother would walk in now, wouldn't she be thoroughly compromised? The countess would *have* had to let her marry Valentine then. She'd have no choice in the matter. But his marriage made that an impossible dream.

"What can we do if Simon does not arrive in time?" She was much too nervous to bring up the first subject on her mind. She could not ask him about his marriage, not until she could bear hearing the answer without tears. After all, she had no idea if he loved the wife waiting patiently for him at Anderlin. Perhaps, she shivered, even a child. A year was long enough, and he was keeping great care to maintain a respectful distance from her.

Or was it a loss of affection and respect? A disdain for a young woman who had once, foolishly, agreed to elopement as a solution to their troubles? She searched his face, looking for a sign that he thought her a silly girl in need of rescue from herself.

But his face was grave and still, his thoughts tucked deep inside, no matter how they might churn within him. At long last he left the solitude of his thoughts and looked toward the window. "We must get the sheets back in and tidied up. The servants should notice nothing amiss in the morning."

"Leave it. I can manage on my own."

She was surprised to see doubt cloud his eyes. "You cannot run away, Emily. You must trust to me to fix things for you."

She tried to mask her own nervousness in a strong and steady reply. "I do."

He caught her gaze with his own. "Promise me."

She made herself look back steadily. "I promise. I will wait for Simon to arrive." At least, I will wait for a while, she added silently.

As if he had heard her amended promise, he leaned forward, his words slow and careful. "If necessary, I will think of something to delay matters until Simon can arrive, and send word to you, Lady Emily. But I cannot risk your reputation. I still shudder at the disgrace I nearly caused for you three years ago."

Torn by the fact that he would soon be gone, she did not keep the pain from her voice. "That was not our fault—it was Simon's. If he hadn't caught us, we'd have been safely wed long ago."

His eyes widened in surprise at her honesty, but he recovered well enough to say slowly, "We'd have regretted it. You'd not be wearing such fine silks now." He eyed her gown and she wanted to shred it in front of his eyes. As if he thought she cared for the quality of the silk she wore more than the quality of the man she married.

"That was not important then, it is not important now."

"I cannot argue with you—" He rose to leave, but stopped, staring at her in puzzlement, almost as if he didn't know who she was. His voice slurred as he said, "What have you done to me?" His movements were slow and his eyes confused as he sank back on the bed.

Emily looked on in horror for a moment, but then suddenly realized what she had unwittingly done to him. Laudanum. She glanced at the empty posset cup. "My mother had Letty dose the posset! I am so sorry, Valentine."

But she wasn't really. He wouldn't be leaving yet, after all. She would have him to herself for a few hours longer . . . asleep, she realized, as she watched him fighting, and losing, the battle with Morpheus. "Mother does not do anything half measure, I'm afraid," she whispered, drawing the covers around him and pressing a kiss to each eyelid.

Three

He was suffocating. Worse still, his arms and legs would not obey his commands to move so that he could remedy the situation. Muffled voices made him fear his hearing was going as well, until he regained just enough of his wits to realize that he was underneath the covers of Emily's too-soft feather bed. The weight of her porcelain dolls pressed down on him, threatening to spill to the floor if he dared to move.

He heard Emily's voice, and her mother's sharp reply. And then Emily's hip nudged his and he realized that she was in the bed next to him. He could feel the outline of her hip so warm and firm that he had no doubt she was clad only in her nightgown. Apparently her mother did not yet know that he was also in the bed, because, although her tone held irritation, there was little shock or anger. He fought his own personal dismay and shame for a moment—he had not intended to disgrace Emily yet again—before giving in. He must do the honorable thing, he must marry her, there was really no question about it.

He wondered if she had drugged him on purpose for this very outcome? But the puzzlement and dawning horror in her eyes when he had begun to behave so bizarrely told him otherwise. Besides, she had had no idea he was even here in Scotland until she fell into his arms.

Her mother had meant to drug Emily, not him. The woman had no scruples at all. But she had locked Emily in securely. Why, then, had she also drugged her drink? He bit back a groan as understanding hit him. Of course—because Emily was unstoppable when she had the bit between her teeth. Hadn't she intended to run away when he caught her outside her window? Which was why he himself had wondered for a moment whether she had intended to compromise herself with him.

Emily's distress conveyed itself to him through the restlessness of her limbs beneath the covers, and he heard it in her voice as well. He stopped the whirl of his own thoughts and struggled to hear the low-voiced conversation taking place next to him.

"Mother, it is not even dawn. I will not see him here. It is not proper. Please, my lord, you must leave."

Valentine tensed at the sound of an unmistakably male voice. "Of course, my dear. Give me just one moment to explain myself, if you will."

Granbury, Valentine thought. What was his business here?

"Your mother sent a note telling me you are having doubts about our wedding. I came immediately, knowing that my presence would help to reassure you about the suitability of our match."

Emily's body had stilled its restless movements as she answered her fiancé, but Valentine could feel the tension in her nevertheless. "You traveled from London? In the darkness? You must be mad."

Valentine grimaced. Ever the diplomat. He expected any moment that Emily would whip the covers down, revealing her indiscretion and putting an end to her engagement. He shifted a little, unwilling to be caught with an arm beneath his head when he knew the ugly reputation of the man, but her hand came to his shoulder and stilled him with urgent pressure. She did not want him exposed. At least not yet. What game was she playing?

"I was not in London, as it happened. I was nearby and the journey was nothing compared to easing the mind of my beloved."

Beloved? Valentine tensed. He had thought the match made for practical reasons, not ties of the heart. The man he had heard about in London would be dangerous to a wife he adored. Perhaps he should have taken Emily away when she asked. But how could he have known that Granbury considered her more than a mere blue-blooded vessel for his heir?

"You are too kind, my lord. And that is precisely why I am worried that I am not the right woman to be your wife. I am star-crossed, after all."

"You?" Granbury let out a harsh sound that might

have been meant as a laugh. "You are talking non-sense, my dear."

Emily shifted restlessly in the bed, but kept her hand against his shoulder as a reminder not to reveal himself. "Nonsense? When I do not seem to be able to get to the altar with a live groom?"

Granbury laughed, apparently richly amused. "My dear, that is in the past. I will take you to the altar in health, I assure you."

"I—"

"Star-crossed, indeed!" the countess put in indignantly. "What a notion, girl. It was not *you*. You come of good stock and could never be at fault."

He heard a scuffling noise as she spoke. "So good of you to come and ease her mind, my lord. As my note said, it is just an attack of nerves. I know that your presence will ease her. I can see that she has already begun to regain her head. Please, retire now in comfort and we will talk more of this in the morning." The door snapped closed on Granbury's sound of protest.

Emily began to tremble next to him and Valentine wondered what was upsetting her, now that her mother was ridding the room of Granbury. "I—"

"You wicked, ungrateful child!" The countess's voice was not loud enough to carry into the hallway where the marquess might still lurk. But as she was standing directly over the half of the bed where Valentine huddled, he heard her clearly. "Why are your sheets hanging out the window?" His heart began to thud. Would Emily reveal him now, now that Granbury was gone? But no, her hand was pressed hard against his shoulder.

"I—"

"You were trying to escape. Do not deny it. Where did you think you would go, you foolish girl?"

"I—"

The countess practically snarled, her rage had grown to such a fevered pitch. "Never mind, I can guess who has encouraged your selfish inclinations to ruin yourself. I will have the grounds scoured for that reprobate and have him whipped out of Scotland."

"No! I had no help, Mother." Emily's voice was sharp with fear, and her hand clenched tightly upon his shoulder. His muddled mind tried to make sense of her panic. How much worse could it be that Valentine might have helped her escape if he were found here now?

Emily continued quickly, "It was my intention to escape, Mother, I do not deny it. I . . . I could not, however. It is too far to the ground. I was afraid of falling and so I remained here, as you can plainly see."

The countess was silent for a moment, but Valentine could imagine the searching gaze pinned upon Emily. "You had no help?"

"No, Mother. I swear it. Please do not think any of the servants would have—" Emily's voice shook, as if she were close to tears. Her body trembled against his, as well, and he realized that she was terrified of her mother and had no intention of revealing his presence.

"Servants! They wouldn't dare help you. No, I thought . . ." The countess left her sentence unfinished, apparently unwilling to speak his name. At least, she seemed suddenly to believe her daughter.

Valentine's arm was fast going numb, but he was not about to destroy the scenario that Emily had cleverly set up. She had her mother believing that she had tied her bedsheets together and then had not been daring enough to risk breaking her neck in a fall. As well, she had neatly disarmed her mother's suspicions that Valentine had encouraged her escape.

"Star-crossed." The countess had returned to Emily's earlier topic. Her anger was still explosive. "I tell you that you will not know the meaning of the term as intimately as if you go haring off with the scoundrel."

Valentine had no doubt in his mind that she meant him. He thanked whatever gods had prevented Emily from trying to compromise herself from one marriage into another. The countess would have never agreed, and Emily would have been locked away in Scotland for the rest of her life.

Emily's body jerked away from his in shock as she leaned forward and gasped, "Mother I did not—"

"Don't bother to deny it, Emily. I know you have not accepted that he is not suitable for you, despite all I have done to convince you." The countess's anger had cooled just enough that her words were sharp and carrying. "Let me be clear with you now, child. If you do not marry the marquess, your cousin will not supply the dowry your father has set aside for you. Your prospects will be much diminished and you will be fortunate to find a husband with a minor title and enough money to feed you properly. But it will not be Valentine Fenster. Not ever."

Emily's hand left his shoulder at last. "I know that, Mother."

The countess laughed unpleasantly. "You are a romantic, Emily. A fool. Even when hope should be gone, you hold it to your heart. But I tell you now, my fortune may have gone into your cousin's hands, but my reputation is still strong. If you ask anyone to intervene and break your engagement—including Simon, who has been deluded into marriage by Valentine's sister—I will ruin them all, from the cad who tried to elope with you to the youngest of the Fenster sisters."

"I—"

"No, Emily, do not protest. I should have said this long ago." Her voice faded and Valentine realized that she was near the door. But she did not leave without one parting shot. "Star-crossed. Only you could think that when you are two weeks away from marriage to a wealthy marquess. One day you will thank me for this." She closed the door, and the key sounded in the lock.

Emily's trembling grew, and he realized that she was crying. Cautiously he sat up, ignoring the burning of his bloodless arm, to embrace her and bring her against his chest.

She curled into him as if she had done so a thousand times before and he held her tight as she sobbed. It wasn't sensible and he knew it even as he felt the warmth of her body burning against him, but he could imagine her hopelessness. The countess was not a woman to brook opposition. Emily was brave—foolishly so, as she had proved more than once. But she was no match for the countess.

He allowed himself to brush his fingers through her hair, which fell in a loose braid down her back. He had imagined it so, but had never thought to see it. "We'll find a way out for you, I promise."

She burrowed her face in his neck, and whispered, "Never mind me. I got myself into this pickle, I should get myself out. But what about you? She meant it. She will set the dogs to search for you. If she finds you, she will ruin you. We must get you away."

"Your mother can do no harm to me," he lied. He did not want Emily doing anything foolish to protect him.

"I could not bear it if she hurt you—or one of your sisters." She turned her face up to his, and in moving, brought her body even more fully against his. He saw the awareness of their position dawn in her expressive face, and he fought the urge to kiss her. She was close enough. Too close for a woman he could not ever marry.

"This is not wise, Emily." He pushed her away gently, the loss of her warmth more than just physical. He could give her nothing but scandal and shame, he reminded himself in order to drive away the disappointment that had slowly taken hold of him once he realized that Emily did not mean to reveal his presence and force the countess to consent to a marriage between them.

She would have protested, he could see it in her eyes, but he rolled to the side of the bed and stood. The blood raced painfully back into his cramped muscles. With a sigh, he shook off the last of the dizziness from the laudanum.

"Never fear, I will escape with my hide intact." He smiled. "Although I doubted it when I first woke and found myself in your bed. I thought you were setting out to have yourself thoroughly compromised." He could not help a lingering glance upon her slightly clad form. "To be honest, I had adjusted myself to the notion, though it would have been a disaster."

For a moment she only stared at him in surprise. "Compromise you?" Following the line of his gaze, she seemed to realize, at last, how little she wore. At once she pulled the covers up around her neck. "A disaster indeed."

Belatedly, he averted his gaze to preserve the remnants of her modesty. She seemed more horrified at the idea than he might have expected, considering she was the one who had donned her nightclothes and climbed into bed with him. Obviously a night spent next to him snoring away in a laudanum-induced stupor had cured her of any romantic hopes.

"I'm sorry. I was obviously mistaken about your intentions." He suffered a twinge of anger that she no longer considered him a fit husband. He then immediately rejected his nonsensical reaction. He knew he was not suitable husband material for her;

it could only help matters that she should know it as well.

Her voice trembled as she replied. "I don't see why you think I would do something so horrid. Even as desperate as I am, I know that a man can't have two wives." He glanced at her. She was crying once again, quiet tears instead of wrenching sobs. "And I don't think your wife would appreciate your cavalier attitude, either."

It took a moment for her words to make sense. When they did, they struck with the impact of a lightning bolt. His wife? She thought he already had a wife.

"Emily." He saw the flush of shame start up her neck and he realized that if she had not thought him a married man, she might already have suggested they make a run for the border. Perhaps he should not disabuse her of the notion of his marriage.

Her flush had risen to the top of her forehead when she spoke through her tears. "I know it was wrong of me, Valentine. I behaved so badly. I will apologize to your wife. I will explain it all, tell her it was all my fault—"

He could not lie to her. "Emily," he said, hoping he was not making a mistake. Hoping he could be strong enough to keep them apart if she was not. "I am not married."

Emily could not take her eyes from Valentine. *He was not married.* This man who had caught her in his arms, and lain in her bed as her mother and her fiancé tried to force her into an unwanted marriage.

But how was it possible? Her mother had seen the notice— Or had she? It was completely believable that her mother had lied. No doubt she had considered the lie a necessity to cut off Emily's hopes.

All her perceptions shifted as she stood in her familiar room. This man who now stood in her bedroom where she could see him, touch him if she dared, as he stretched and eased his tight muscles, smoothed the wrinkles from his clothing as best he could, ran his fingers through his hair, and watched her with wary eyes. She needed him to confirm the truth once more. "You have no wife?"

He shook his head, but there was a caution in his gaze that made her heart still. Was he lying to her? Was he perhaps on the verge of marriage as she herself was? His next words dispelled that possibility. "Surely you understand that I am not in a position to take a wife? I have barely begun the job of patching up the leaks my father left in the estate."

"But . . . an heiress . . ." It had been his original plan, before he met her, after all.

His eyes darkened with anger—or pain. "I will depend on no woman's money. How can I look across the table every day at a woman who knows I am a purchased husband? No. Marriage can wait."

The fierce burn of her anger toward her mother died suddenly in a new realization. Emily felt at once a great relief and a terrible understanding. Valentine had been free and he had not come after her, not even— She broke the thought. He had, after all, come to warn her that Lord Granbury would not make a good husband.

He had proved his friendship true, even if he no longer loved her. "I wish I could say the same. But it seems marriage is my fate if I cannot think of an escape." She watched his face, and felt hope bloom inside her. There was an answer. Would he think of it? And did she care whether he thought of it as a friend, or as a man who loved her still?

Her heart fell when he merely answered, "You must trust me. I will find a way to get you out of this engagement. I just need a little time to think." Of course, he hadn't thought of the obvious answer. She was a fool to hope that he still cared for her, still loved her enough to consider marrying her.

Horrified, she found herself blurting the thought on her mind. "This is Scotland. We could be married in an hour's time." She clapped her hands over her mouth, appalled at what she had just said.

Valentine appeared equally shocked. But then he smiled. "Joking at a time like this. How like you, Emily. Wouldn't that please your family—breaking your engagement with a runaway marriage to a penniless man with five sisters to marry off."

Unbidden, her mother's warning threats against Valentine and his sisters echoed in her ears. Her cousin would not supply a dowry if she managed to break her engagement to Francis, certainly he would not support an elopement. She could bring Valentine no good, only trouble, disgrace, and ruin. She knew her mother well enough to know that her threats were not made idly. Simon and Miranda were virtually untouchable. But could their protection spread to Valentine and the remaining unmarried sisters? She could not risk it.

"I always try to imagine the most amusing absurdities," she said. "It makes the situation somehow more manageable that way." Usually. She bustled toward him, pretending that her heart had not just broken. "You must be off, now. To be caught here would be a catastrophe."

For a moment, his eyes were focused on her and she had the uncanny sense that he knew how his words had hurt her. But all he said was, "I will contact you as soon as I have heard from Simon." He leaned down and fished the spare set of keys out from under her pillow.

She shuddered, thankful her mother had not ferreted them out. There would have been no explanation for that, as she would not have had sheets out the window if she possessed keys. Her mother would have known that she had indeed successfully climbed out her own window, retrieved the spare ring of keys and locked herself back in.

The countess was a clever woman. She would recognize that was not a sensible action for anyone, especially someone with Emily's reputation. There was no way her mother would have rested until she had had the truth from her. And then her wrath would have had no bounds at all.

Bleakly, she realized that she must not accept help from him. "No. I will do this myself. It is safest for us all."

"First I must show you the letter—"

She held up her hand to halt his words. "You must

leave and leave now, Valentine, before you are discovered."

"But you do not know—"

"I know all I need to know. Somehow I shall convince Francis that I am truly star-crossed and marriage to him will bring only bad luck."

"Emily—"

She slapped her hands down upon her dressing table, making her little bottles teeter and rattle. "I will not risk everyone's happiness just for my own. Even now you risk your life, Valentine. Mother thinks I do not know you were here yesterday, but I do not think she will take any chances. Watch for the dogs as you leave the grounds."

She saw the argument die in his eyes as they both looked toward the brightening window. "I hope to be long gone before she has mustered the gamekeeper and his minions for a search."

Even as he spoke, the sound of a key startled them both. "My maid . . ." Emily whispered.

Quickly Valentine moved toward the window, but her mother had taken the sheets with her when she left. In the moment before the maid bustled in, he dropped to the floor and rolled under the bed. As the maid greeted her cheerily, and put the pot of chocolate for her breakfast down, Emily heard the sound of hounds baying in the distance.

Four

Valentine had never really noticed how much time a woman's toilette took. Six sisters and still it astonished him how Emily's maid flitted from one thing to the next, always with the comment of "Lady Emily, you cannot hurry or you will disgrace your mother."

First, the maid examined one outfit after the other, until, perhaps after twenty minutes, she found the one she thought was right for this day, this weather, this temperature. Emily merely laughed as she endured the torture, saying "Nancy, I think you worry more about how I look than I do."

And then, during the time Emily's hair was dressed—another twenty minutes choosing the proper style and ornamentation—there was discussion as to whether the color went well with my lady's pretty pink cheeks, and wasn't my lady bright-eyed this morning?

You would be pink-cheeked, too, my girl, Valentine thought as he shifted cautiously to relieve the cramp in his leg, if you had a man hidden under your bed.

He could imagine his sisters' amused faces if they ever learned of this.

Finally, the garments chosen, the choice of hair ornament and the very number of curls in front of Emily's ears must at last be complementary to the countess's own choice of dress and hair style. This required several whispered conferrals with the countess's own maid.

It was peculiar torture, lying under the bedstead, catching tantalizing glimpses of Emily's bare ankles and narrow, elegant feet while she was whisked into one garment upon another and donned stockings a scant foot from his nose. He valiantly resisted the temptation to tickle her sole, to remind her that he was there, as she tried on fourteen different pairs of slippers.

At first he had been light-headed with relief to have escaped detection, then titillated at being privy to a lady's private toilette—especially Emily's. But as he watched the variety and richness of the silks, satins, and other fabrics he could not name but could recognize as costly, he sank deeper into despair. The urge to throw decency and honor to the winds and elope with her burned fierce within him.

She still wanted him for her husband. It had been there in her eyes from the first time she'd realized who had caught her as she fell from her makeshift rope. However, it was also clear that she had given no thought to what life would be like with him. No matter how miserable her mother had been to her, Emily had been given every material comfort possible. The economies that Valentine had put in place in order to rebuild his fortune would be a starvation diet for her love of beauty and society.

He would have to be a dullard not to realize that Emily still hoped that he would sweep her away from this miserable existence and into some fairy-tale life with him. It had not taken him long to realize that was a dream he could not encourage. Even if he somehow miraculously convinced Emily's mother and cousin that he was a suitable candidate for her hand, he could never give her the lifestyle that she had been born to enjoy.

Theirs would be a life of struggle and economy, at the very least until little Kate had had a successful season. Thinking of his untamed youngest sister, he knew he'd have to allow extra time to marry her off, and so add a minimum of ten years before all the girls would be settled and off his hands. By then, he could have a daughter of his own to be planning a season for, as well.

By the time the maid had left to empty the basin of wash water and Emily knelt by the bed and peered anxiously at him, he knew that any foolish notion to elope with her must be crushed, no matter how it hurt him—or her.

She whispered hurriedly, as if she did not realize how sound carried, even under the bed. "Mother has commanded me to go down and entertain Francis."

"I know." Trapped, he had heard the maid deliver the message during all the bustle of the morning preparation. *Assure him that all is well with the wedding plans,* had been the exact command. Emily's agreement had sounded more determined than he had expected. He worried that she had concocted another ill-thought-out plan. The only question was whether he could talk her out of it before she left the room. "Emily—"

She rushed on, as if instinctively realizing that he would warn her off. "It is not safe for you to leave yet. The hounds are well-trained and Parker will suffer none without excellent noses in his pack. You do remember Father loved to ride to the hounds . . ." She trailed off as if realizing the absurdity of the conversation.

She paused, and he battled the impulse to ask her to leave with him. When he weighed the dangers of Emily left to her own devices, plotting to thwart the marquess's intention to make her his bride, he could not decide which was more dangerous.

The thought of her being braced by a pack of hunting hounds made up his mind for him. No matter the dangers posed by the marquess, it was much less safe for her outside the castle—at least for now.

He said, knowing it would reassure her, "Tonight should be soon enough for me to leave. Tonight, while the rest of the house sleeps and there is no risk of discovery for you."

"I'm sorry," she whispered. "Sorry for everything. I will bring you something to eat as soon as I can."

Her despair was heartbreaking to him. And he could see no way to ease it, trapped as he was at the moment. But then he did, and chuckled softly. "Please ensure your mother has not had a chance to dose it with laudanum."

She laughed out loud, then muffled the sound with her skirts. He had known she would laugh at his poor joke, despite her own troubles. It was one of the reasons why he loved her—she could laugh even when things seemed bleak, and yet not in a silly or frivolous manner.

And loving her helped him to accept the truth: he had to stop trying to find a way to convince himself that elopement was possible. "I will not abandon you to him, Emily. You will not have to marry a monster, I swear it. Your future will be all that it was meant to be." For the first time, he felt he could make that vow honestly. He would see she married a man better than Lord Granbury. And better able to keep her than Valentine himself would ever be.

"I will not marry him. I know the caliber of man I wish to marry, and he does not approach your worth." She smiled at him, a hint of the old mischief in her eyes, and he realized that he had not yet warned her against trying to break the engagement on her own.

"Emily—" He halted himself. Now, right before she was to go down to see the marquess was not the time to show her the letter. He doubted she could keep the knowledge from showing on her face or in her manner.

She made a face at him. "Don't worry, I won't be so impulsive as to actually tell him so. I might be tempted, though, I promise you, if I did not know that Mother would take out her anger in damage to your sisters' reputations." There was a look in her eye that he remembered all too well.

"I will take care of my sisters and their reputations. You must not let temptation overtake you. Lord Granbury is not a man to cross lightly." How could he quickly convince her of the danger such action would bring? Nothing occurred to him but to show her the letter—and that was unthinkable while he was trapped under this bed, unable to protect her. "It is not wise to let him know you despise him."

She nodded. "I know that. I intend to make him think *he* despises *me*. Much the safer goal when dealing with a man, don't you think?" She smiled, amusement and determination shining in her eyes.

"Emily, leave it to me." He would have spoken some further discouragement, if only he could have gotten the words out before she reached her hand under the bed to grasp his once, tightly.

As if she were comforting a child awakened from a nightmare, she said softly, "I must go see to convincing my fiancé that I am a bride worth abandoning. I have a plan that I am certain will accomplish my goal without bringing danger to your family—or you."

He took hold of her hand and would not let it go when she would have pulled back. "He is dangerous, Emily. Let me handle this." He could see the stubborn twist of her lips and he squeezed her hand once. "Promise me, Emily. Promise me that you will not put yourself—or your reputation—in jeopardy."

"I will not. I promise. Now release my hand before someone comes in and finds me here like this."

Reluctantly he let her go, though instinct told him to tug her under the bed with him and let the world pass them by. Her mother had threatened him in Emily's presence, and all that he knew about Emily suggested she would do whatever was in her power to protect him—which would leave her exposed to danger. He could not allow that.

"It was too good of you to come all this way to reassure my natural worries, my lord." Emily settled her skirts around her as she sat where the marquess had indicated, certain that she would scream if the man came any closer.

Before her mother's untimely missive, he had behaved as nothing less than a gentleman, although she had known from the gleam in his eye and the way he watched her avidly that after the wedding she must not hope for circumspection. There was an animal fervor in him that only social expectation held in check.

And now she intended to convince him that he did not want to marry her. Valentine was right—it was a dangerous game she played. Still, the alternative—marriage to the man—was infinitely worse.

"My dear, I could do no less. You have had a most distressing few years and I could not bear to think of you suffering." He grasped her hands and she was shocked to feel his skin, smooth and cool. He had shed his gloves and she had neglected to don her own in her haste to be out of her bedroom.

"That's very generous of you, my lord." She pulled her hands away with difficulty, and moved as far away as the settee allowed, so that she didn't feel so suffocated by the marquess's presence. "I don't know why these things keep happening to me. I believe there may be some curse upon me and I fear not for myself, but for you."

She smoothed her skirt with nervous movements and the fine fabric beneath her fingers reminded her of the torture she had just undergone. Dressing this morning had been an exercise in tension. Down to her undergarments and Valentine only feet away under the bed. Valentine, *unmarried*. How dare her mother lie to her? And how foolish of her to believe the lie, knowing her mother's manipulative ways.

"It is my job to worry for you, my dear, not yours to worry for me." Granbury reached for her hands again and she stood up as gracefully as she could in her haste. She could not bear his touch today. Not knowing that Valentine, her ally, her protector, waited for her in her room.

"You are too kind, my lord," she murmured absently as she crossed to the window. It gave a good view of the gardens, and two men and four hounds nosing into the rosebushes. She was glad that he had remained safely in her room. Under the bed was surely more comfortable for him than to fall into the clutches of the estate employees.

Granbury came to stand beside her at the window. "It is not kindness to see to the comfort of my bride-to-be. It is duty." She smiled, although her thoughts were uncharitable. Apparently, seeing to her comfort did not include keeping a respectful distance.

"Indeed?" Emily smiled, though she wanted to

stomp his toes and escape his presence. "I regret putting you to the trouble."

"It is duty, indeed, but a most pleasant one. I think you will find after we are married that I see to my duties down to the last detail."

Emily nodded, pretending not to understand the nature of his comments. "That must be a comfort to any wife, I expect." She wondered what Valentine was thinking. Did he consider her brazen to carry out her toilette knowing he was scant feet away? No, he was a sensible man, and no doubt understood there was no alternative.

Granbury moved minutely closer. "Still, I feel there is some distance between us."

Emily sighed, uncomfortable at how near he flirted to the truth. "As I told you, I am concerned for you. I feel that I may, unwittingly, cause you to suffer the same fate as the previous two men who were kind enough to ask me to be their wife."

Her only consolation was that Valentine's view had been severely limited by his position. Otherwise, she'd never have been able to face him again. Unbidden, the feeling of being in his arms, dressed only in her nightgown, flashed in her mind. She could feel the heat seep into her cheeks. How could she have been so shameless?

Suddenly, Granbury was leaning in toward her, his soft fingers biting into her chin, forcing her to look into his eyes. "There is no one else, is there, my dear?"

"Someone else?" Shock made her clumsy. How

could he know? Was the truth there on her face to be read?

"Another swain, some importunate fool who has given you his heart and dazzled you with poetry?"

Emily gathered her wits enough to realize that he did not know about Valentine. He could not. He was simply trying to understand why she no longer wanted to marry him.

"I am not easily swayed by poetry," she said sharply, tugging her chin away from his painful grip. "And I have had dozens of hearts laid at my feet during my seasons, enough to know that means nothing."

He did not back away, and his eyes narrowed. His displeasure was plain. "My heart is yours, my dear. Surely you are not telling me that means nothing to you?"

"I would not have agreed to marry you otherwise," Emily lied. "And that is why I am so very worried about you. No man I have agreed to marry has lived until the wedding day." She bit her lip, wondering if he would laugh at her melodrama.

"Except, of course, the one with whom you ran away."

She did not have to feign her displeasure. "That is an unworthy rumor to repeat, my lord. And it does no credit to the two men of whom I speak who made honorable offers. Neither of them knew that asking me to marry them would lead to their untimely demises." She wondered if she had laid it on a bit thick, but desperation was pushing her.

His reaction was curious and unsettling. A gleam

of satisfied amusement lit his eyes. "I am not an ordinary man. Some have said that I was blessed with the nine lives of a cat when I was born." Obviously, the idea pleased him.

Emily knew she was treading dangerous waters to disagree with him, but she could not help replying sharply, "No one truly has nine lives, my lord, not even a cat. And I have two men who pledged to marry me and never made it to the altar. You can call me superstitious if you please, but the cold facts remain unchanged."

"I would not give up my prize because of a foolish superstition." His voice was chilling. "Nor would I give her up to another man, not without a fight." He smiled again, his voice pleasant and easy. "And I always win, my dear."

Just then, her mother arrived, giving Emily a chance to break his gaze and move away from him. *His prize.* Was that how he saw her? She suppressed a shiver. Where had her wits been when she accepted his proposal? He was a toad. Worse—he was a poisonous toad.

To her great relief, her mother kept them company—ensuring the conversation would remain innocuous—the rest of the afternoon. What Granbury had said preyed on her mind. So much so that she took the opportunity, while her mother was distracted with a matter in the kitchen, to continue her plan to dissuade him once again.

As the tea things were delivered, she debated how to deal with his apparent belief that he was meeting some kind of challenge by continuing on with the plan of marriage. "I must tell you, your words when we spoke earlier have moved me, Lord Granbury."

"Indeed?"

"Yes. Greatly. I agree that you are not an ordinary man, my lord."

"You are a discerning young woman, then."

"But I must tell you that your extraordinary character is my exact concern."

She handed him his tea, two lemon slices. Crafting her own expression carefully, she hoped she looked sufficiently distraught as she poured for herself, cream and one sugar. "For I am no ordinary woman. I must confess that I have brought ill-fortune to every man who sought to marry me." *Including Valentine,* she thought to herself. Why else but for her sake did he now lie under her bed in danger of being torn apart by the hounds, whipped out of Scotland by her mother, or utterly destroyed by the marquess of Granbury?

Infuriatingly, he still did not take her seriously. His voice was pitched as if she were a child when he said, "I will take my chances, slight though they be. You are a prize worth winning despite a little danger, my dear."

Emily wanted to toss her spoon at the dratted man. "I cannot bear the thought that you might be injured on my account. If this . . . this curse is mine to bear, then I must do so alone."

Irritation erased the indulgent smile on his lips. "Emily, I do not wish to discuss this matter again. I am not a superstitious man, and I do not wish for my wife to harbor fanciful imaginings either."

"But—"

"Emily!" Her mother's voice was stern as she entered the room and overheard the direction of the conversation. "Have I not taught you to listen to your husband in all matters?"

"Of course," Emily said politely. "But he is not yet my husband, Mother."

Her mother's lips pressed tight together. "He will be, in less time than you seem to realize." She waved a hand toward the tea tray. "Pour for me, please."

Emily poured without protest. She would simply have to try again. She could not fight against both the marquess and her mother at once. With her teacup poised lightly in her hand, and a false smile set firmly upon her lips, the countess set out to convince the marquess that Emily's worries were just the mark of a high strung young woman who could be easily reined in by the proper husband.

As Emily, gritting her teeth, rose and poured a second cup of tea for her mother, she could not help a quick glance at the doorway. If she ran quickly enough, would she be able to escape? Even as she had the thought, she realized the futility of running away. The dogs had been called out, Granbury would consider it only a new challenge to win, and Valentine would be trapped up in her bedroom without anyone to rescue him.

Five

Valentine lay cramped and uncomfortable as the chambermaids tidied up the mess left from Emily's tumultuous morning toilette. Giggles were clearly audible once or twice as one or the other held up a garment to herself and took a sweeping circle around the room. Though they were for the most part quiet and efficient—a feather duster thrust under the bed had nearly made him sneeze—their low-voiced comments on Emily's situation made him realize that the servants were not as blind to the situation as the countess herself.

"It's a true pity that 'andsome boy couldn't ha' eloped with 'er again," said one with a little sigh.

" 'E'd better not, not unless 'e makes sure ta do it right this time," the other replied, and then spoiled her severity with a giggle.

Valentine cringed at the truth of the comment. Even the servants had no confidence in his ability to protect their mistress. It was no wonder that Emily felt she needed to devise her own plan of action in dealing with the marquess of Granbury. He turned his mind from that worry, there was nothing he could do to prevent her carrying out her plan as long as he was stuck under her bed. Later, however, he would make sure she understood the danger. He would make her promise to let him handle the matter alone, for her own safety's sake.

He could not help but think of Emily as she had been this morning, clad only in her nightgown, looking at him as if she wished he would sweep her away. And he, shameful cad that he was, considering the option eagerly.

Of course, that had been before she realized that he had no wife. Knowing that, might her desperation lead her to agree to a plan which would not be good for her future?

Perhaps he should have let her believe he was indeed married? No. He had never lied to Emily before, he would not start now. It was enough to tell her that he could not marry her and let her believe the reason was that he no longer loved her.

Caught up in his thoughts, it took some time for him to notice that the room had become quiet. The maids had gone. Careful of his limbs, stiff from their cramped positioning, he eased out from under the bed, on the side away from the door. As he stood, enjoying the sunlight that streamed in from the window, he noticed Emily's room as he had not the night before in the dark.

It was her design, he had no doubt—the dark oak of her armoire was lightened by an emerald green scarf that matched the color of her bedclothes, which were complemented by the cream lawn curtains sprigged with tiny flowers.

There was a lightness, an airiness to the room that spoke of Emily, despite the drafty, dank nature of Eddingley Castle itself. Like his sister Miranda, she believed in fairy tales, and the room reflected her belief.

He imagined, briefly, the changes Emily might have wrought at Anderlin by now, if their elopement had not been foiled. It was unproductive to wonder, and painful as well, so he deliberately turned his thoughts to his present predicament. What should he do?

He moved restlessly, unable to come to a decision. Her dressing table, neatened by the maids, held little bottles of all shapes, sizes, and colors. He lifted one, a cobalt blue with a curved and sinuous shape. She must have chosen some of these simply for the shape and color of the bottle. But once chosen, the bottle would have been cherished—which was why there was scarcely room for the silver brush and comb set.

She deserved a man who would cherish her as she cherished her own possessions. Granbury was not that man. But if Valentine were discovered here, Emily might find herself married within the week. He sighed, wanting to pace, but feeling constrained.

The room was a young woman's room and he felt badly out of place, despite living in a household of five sisters for as long as he could remember. He started at every creak of a board, afraid the maids had returned. Emily expected him to remain safely here. But he would not risk the danger to her.

There was nothing he would not give for her. The ache to see her again was as familiar as the feel of his heart beating. He paced the room as best he could, stopping only to touch a discarded ribbon that lay on her dressing table. The jade green was a good color for her. If she were his wife he would dress her in it exclusively—if.

He dropped the ribbon back onto the lacy table covering and paced to stare out of the window. He glanced down into the gardens, remembering how Emily had felt in his arms after she loosed her hold on her makeshift rope. The dogs had moved off, their baying no longer even faintly on the air. Perhaps he should go now, before the gamekeeper brought them back to the kennels and they caught his scent?

Knowing it was the wise thing, he considered and discarded the idea to leave a note of explanation for Emily. There was no telling what curious eyes might find even the most innocuous missive and create trouble for Emily.

Cautiously, he pressed his ear against the door. There was no sound from the hallway. He eased the door open, thankful for once that the countess was a perfectionist who expected hinges to be oiled and squeak-free.

He felt exposed and vulnerable in the hallway as he tried to remember the direction of the hasty run they had made from the kitchens to Emily's room in the dark. He turned down the wrong corridor and corrected himself, turning back just as a door to his left opened, and a maid stepped through the doorway and caught sight of him.

She opened her mouth to scream and for one frozen moment he stood there waiting for the shrill sound, wondering how Emily would pay for his mistake.

He wasn't under her bed. Emily rummaged through her armoire, feeling foolish—it was more than obvious he never would have fit in there. She checked once again under the bed, under the mattress.

He was gone.

She felt unaccountably bereft, considering she had not seen him for three years before yesterday. And considering that he had as much as told her he no longer loved her.

She knew she should not have taken so long trying to convince Granbury that marriage to her would cause him ill-fortune. For all the good her efforts had accomplished, she would have been better served pretending that she herself was dying.

She stopped, considering and then discarding the idea. It was fraught with problems, as her cousin Simon had discovered several years ago when he tried the ploy on his new wife.

For one, both Lord Granbury and her mother would take her from doctor to doctor. For another, she did not think herself capable of languishing for any convincing length of time.

She smiled, remembering how Simon's wife had

confided to her that he had seemed a bit too healthy to her, but she couldn't imagine him lying about such a matter. Neither her mother nor Granbury were as trusting as Miranda, for certain.

And though she wished she had Simon's commanding way about her, Emily was positive that she did not. One must have to be born to oversee a dukedom to ever achieve the required level of self-confidence and assurance.

She looked around the room, as if she might discover that Valentine had been there all along and she had somehow overlooked him in one of the corners. But finally even her ever-hopeful mind had accepted that he was not to be found here.

Had he been discovered by the maids who had tidied the room? She could not believe those two giddy girls would not have made some fuss at the discovery.

She tried to think back. Had she heard anything unusual at all over the sound of Granbury and her mother conversing about polite nothings? A shriek would have been loud, surely loud enough to have disrupted her time downstairs with Francis?

She tossed away the napkin full of sandwiches that she had sneaked upstairs with her. Had he simply gotten too hungry to wait and gone for something to eat?

Or had he come to his senses and abandoned her?

For a moment she felt helpless with despair. The key had turned loudly in the lock as soon as she was safely in her room. She had no doubt that she was locked in as securely as ever. And though the maids had tidied the room they had not replaced her sheets—no doubt upon her mother's instructions.

The key ring! Had the chamber maids found it when they tidied? She struggled to remember what had happened to the ring of keys in the confusion of the morning. Valentine had held them, meaning to return them to their place, no doubt he had still held them when he dove under the bed.

The question was, would he have left them for her, or taken them with him? It didn't help that she wasn't sure whether he had gone willingly, or whether he had been discovered and taken by force. Perhaps if she found the keys, she could sneak downstairs and find out for herself, instead of waiting for the gossip to reach her ears—if it ever did.

With a new sense of hope, she searched under her pillows, under the bed, under the mattress. Unfortunately, the set of keys was nowhere to be found.

Perhaps that was a sign that Valentine has not been discovered by the servants and had made good his escape. Otherwise he would have left the keys safely here . . . if he had been discovered here. He could always have been seen as he made his way down to the kitchen. . . . Not knowing what had happened to him was unbearable.

She buried her face in the pillow that had cushioned Valentine's head just a few hours before. His scent was still there; she had not imagined last night. She had not. She began to sigh once more and stopped herself. This was no time to play the languishing maiden.

Where was he? Had he gone for good, or was he

planning to sneak back in to see her? Half of her hoped that he did, while the more sensible half hoped that he had gotten safely away and was waiting for word from Simon.

Blast the man for not leaving her a note! But even as she had the thought, she knew he never would have left something behind to lead her mother to suspect Emily's own complicity in Valentine's infiltration of the household.

So what was she to do now? Her mother had told her to nap, so that her night's escapade did not put unwanted lines upon her face. . . . As if a few lines would discourage the supremely self-confident Lord Granbury—if she even thought it possible, she would scowl until she was as wrinkled as her mother's favorite pug dog, Daffodil.

But sleep was not possible until she knew where Valentine was. Until she knew if he would be able to help her avoid marriage to the marquis of Granbury. And if she could win back Valentine's heart. Quietly she contemplated her options, which seemed to be shrinking by the minute. How could she convince Granbury that she was not the wife for him? And Valentine that she was?

In an hour or two Nancy would be here to dress her for dinner. Dare she ask the girl if there had been a stranger found either in the house or on the grounds? It was a risk, probably too large a risk. Nancy had always seemed a sensible girl, but she was the countess's servant, not Emily's own, and that was a lesson Emily had learned early on.

How could she question Nancy without revealing

herself—or worse, if he hadn't yet been discovered, Valentine's presence in the household? She was to have a bath and wear a new gown. Perhaps while she bathed, she could toss a question out?

Nancy would be occupied with laying out her gown and petticoats, and might be distracted enough not to think too hard about what Emily was asking.

And if Nancy knew nothing? To bring up the conversation—even obliquely—at dinner would result in more trouble than it was worth. Her mother had made it clear that she was not to broach the issue of her unfortunate past again. And Valentine was most definitely part of that unspeakable past. What punishment her mother would choose to inflict had been left vague enough to make her uneasy.

Obviously, the countess was concerned that Francis would be swayed by her words, enough to call off the engagement, but Emily couldn't understand why. He had been utterly impervious to the suggestion that he might be in danger of succumbing to the curse that dogged her.

He had, perversely, considered it a challenge to be met and mastered. She shuddered. No doubt he thought the same of her.

She simply could not marry him.

Having discovered no solution to her dilemma in the hours of quiet contemplation, Emily gave herself up to the ministrations of her maids as they made her ready for dinner with Francis. She asked a few idle questions about the household, but frustratingly, she learned nothing of whether Valentine had been captured.

Instead, she felt as though she was being readied as a human sacrifice—a sacrifice to the god of the marquess of Granbury, to be specific. Every wrinkle in the gown must be smoothed—the gown had gone out three separate times to the ironing room, with much sighing and *tsking* on the maid's part.

Her hair, of course, must be curled into glossy ringlets that looked more like strawberry blond silk than hair and adorned with feathers that scratched at her scalp. And the jewelry was to be an emerald necklace that came from the marquess' family vaults.

Adding to Emily's feeling of being a sacrificial victim were the glances that Nancy sent her occasionally. The girl seemed almost frightened to look at her directly. Her eyes focused on nothing whenever her gaze neared Emily's face. Her terrified manner unsettled Emily even more, as though Nancy knew that Emily was marching downstairs to her death rather than to dinner.

Once, when in the hectic pace of work the maid dropped one of the pretty bottles on the dressing table and it broke, she burst into tears. "Don't worry, Nancy, it was an accident," Emily said quickly, but the maid still took several minutes to compose herself.

And then, in a fit of nerves she had never displayed before, she gave a wrench to Emily's hair when the countess's maid arrived. Fortunately the countess's maid did not witness this dereliction of duty, as Nancy and Emily returned themselves to more serene countenances in the time it took her to unlock the room and release Emily from her prison—for just the time it took to convince Granbury that she was no longer an unwilling bride.

Though, as she went unhappily down the stairs, Emily secretly wondered if he might actually prefer her unwilling. He seemed to enjoy a challenge more than anyone else she had ever met. And unwittingly, she had set him one.

Dinner itself was difficult. She sat through the courses, touching very little, making polite conversation about the wedding trip she and Francis were scheduled to take to Italy. She found herself miserably wondering if Italy would sound more appealing if she were to go there with Valentine.

Granbury, for his part, smiled at her as if he had not held her chin in his hand and threatened her this very morning. "You will like the country, I am certain, Emily. I have always found it an interesting place to visit—especially Rome, which is, after all, the cradle of civilization."

"I thought that was Greece, my lord," Emily murmured in reply.

"Emily, I have no doubt Lord Granbury's education was much more thorough than yours," her mother scolded her. "Apologize for questioning him at once."

Emily could not bring herself to utter an apology for her statement. Instead she said blandly, "What does it matter? I very much want to see Rome, whether or not it is the cradle of civilization, Mother." *But not with Lord Granbury,* she thought. So that she would not be required to keep the conversation alive, she asked politely about his experiences there in the past.

He answered with enthusiasm, reminding her uncomfortably of her governess, who had enjoyed the lessons she taught much more than her students. Although the woman had known enough to teach Emily that Greece was the cradle of civilization. Tactfully, she kept that fact to herself.

But for the most part it was her mother who kept the conversation going with her own observations of Italy, her land and her people. Apparently her mother found the place dirty and foreign—her worst epithet, meaning not managed at all the way the countess would have done.

There was a new footman, too, who stood much too close when he served her. Toward the end of dinner, when her mother and Granbury were engaged in a lively discussion of whether Italians or Germans were the more barbaric race, the footman came unbidden to her side and offered her a second helping. As she still had most of her first portion on her plate, she waved him away.

In flagrant indifference to her signal, he did not retreat. Instead, a tiny white square fluttered in the corner of her eye and dropped onto her lap.

Puzzled, she gazed down. It was a tightly folded note, she realized. Was it from Valentine? How had the footman gotten it?

With a quick glance at her mother to ensure she had Granbury's complete attention, Emily unfolded the note and read, *"I will come to you tonight. Eat more, you must keep up your strength."*

Surprised, she glanced up and nearly fainted. Valentine stood next to her, rigged up in the livery of a footman.

Six

Valentine found that he had been holding his breath as he watched Emily's face. It was the last test to determine whether his disguise would hold. Her eyes had widened in surprise as she read the note. Then she looked up to meet his gaze.

He had known she would be somewhat shocked, but her face had gone white. For a moment he had been certain that she was about to stand and reveal him by her inadvertent reaction to him. But, after an instant, she looked back down at the note in her hand, crumpled it up into a tiny ball, and dropped it into a puddle of lemon sauce on her plate.

More amazingly, from his perspective standing there on the edge of being exposed, she did it all cleverly under cover of delicately wiping her mouth with her napkin. A quick flick of her fork ensured the paper now looked like no more than a lump of pastry.

It was an awesome act of self-control. He began to understand, at last, what life had been like for her with the countess as mother. She could be impulsive, but she had also learned that there were times when she must control her impulses.

He did not like to think of what unpleasantness must be buried in her childhood. Perhaps it had been sheer desperation, and not love, which had made her so willing to elope with him? His heart rejected the idea immediately.

He knew she had questions to ask, could see them bubbling up inside her, until, suddenly, she turned her face into the placid mask of boredom she had been wearing throughout the tedious dinner. Lifting her wineglass to her lips, she waved him away yet again, as if she still thought him no more than a faceless footman.

A swift rush of pride flooded through him at her grasp of the situation. At the same time he found it necessary to dampen the prickle of irritation he felt at how easily he had become invisible to Emily and her family by donning a footman's uniform. He dismissed his own foolishness with a silent scoff. If it had not been for this faceless disguise, he'd be lucky to still be alive.

He watched the countess from the corner of his eye—a footman never looked his betters in the eye, Nan had whispered to him hurriedly. Soames, the butler, had given him the same advice—along with much more along the same vein—in solemn tones after hiring him. He had obviously been overawed with Valentine's references, which were forged in the name of the Duke of Kerstone.

No doubt his brother-in-law would forgive him for using the title in such a worthy cause. Simon had given him a spare signet ring and sealing wax so that he could handle certain matters in a discreet and timely manner.

Dinner continued for a short time before the countess suggested that she and Emily retire and leave Granbury alone to his cigar. Politely, he declined the need to smoke and insisted on joining the ladies immediately.

The countess nodded her assent, a pleased gleam in her eye. Emily stood, quiet and demure. Valentine marveled that she could look so, when he knew what effort it must take for her to avoid glancing his way.

As they passed from the dining room into the music room, where Emily was obviously expected to put her musical talents on display for Granbury, Valentine felt himself relax. The countess had overlooked him, despite the fact that he had stood next to her, offering her dishes, refilling her wine, taking discarded dishes away.

He warned himself not to get too cocky, but it seemed likely that as long as he behaved in the unexceptional manner of a properly trained footman, he could remain here and keep an eye on Emily—at least until Simon and Miranda arrived to do the job properly.

As he carried his heavy tray into the kitchen, Nan stared at him, wide-eyed with worry. He knew he needed to talk to her quickly—but how to do so privately, as well, in the bustling kitchen?

Before he could decide on how to draw her away, she batted her eyes at him and asked him to help her with a heavy pail of water that needed to be carried to Lady Emily's room.

They had no sooner reached the relative privacy of the back stairs before she turned to him. "Well?"

He smiled at her imperious question. "I avoided discovery, thanks to you."

Nan studied him critically, "The clipping I gave that neat 'air of yours makes it more raggedy, and your 'ands are not too fine for a footman, I suppose. But you still walk too tall, and your step's a bit too cocky."

"Is it?" He tried to match the gait he had seen the other footman use. It would have helped to have some recent experience with such servants, but Anderlin hadn't had a footman in years.

He shrugged away the concern. He'd just have to rely on Nan's tutoring. The maid's allegiance had been a surprise. When she discovered him in the hall outside Emily's room, he had hoped to keep her silent for long enough to escape.

Instead, she had declared herself fully in favor of breaking her mistress' engagement, and had come up with a plan to keep him near Emily so that he could keep an eye on her while they pried away Granbury's hold. He supposed it was the letter proving Granbury's misdeeds which had convinced her of his desire to protect her mistress.

Though he did not yet fully trust her motives, so far she hadn't led him wrong. "Is this walk better?"

"I suppose." As they hurried up the back stairs, Nan whispered nervously, "Did all go well?"

"The countess did not once look at my face." The

girl's forehead was still creased with worry, so he added, "And I only dropped the fish into her lap once."

For a startled moment she stopped on the steps, and then, realizing he was joking, she forced a giggle. " 'Eaven's above, you near gave me a fright."

Valentine smiled in return. "Forgive me for teasing, Nan. I have just spent two hours wondering if every time I approached the table, I would be found out and whipped senseless—or worse. I am a bit giddy with relief that your idea worked so well."

She beamed at the compliment to her ingenuity. "Then Lady Emily did not give you away?"

"No, she did not. I safely delivered my note and she understood matters even more rapidly than we had hoped."

"Good. The only thing to give your disguise away would likely be Lady Emily making moon eyes. It would not go well for 'er if 'er ladyship found out that you were 'ere."

Or for Nan herself. Valentine admired the girl for not saying so aloud. "You're a good girl, Nan, to help Lady Emily. I promise no one in this household will ever know of it from my lips, no matter what happens. And I will see that you are properly rewarded when this business is finished."

They had reached Emily's room as they talked, and he carefully poured half of the bucket of water into Emily's pitcher, and used the rest to fill a large washbowl that Nan indicated to him. He reflected that this masquerade involved doing a great deal of real work. But for Emily, he would do anything.

"It'll be reward enough if you can keep 'er from marryin' that devil." Nan's voice quavered slightly with emotion. "I knew 'e was a bad 'un, but after the letter you read me, I'd rather kill 'im meself than let Lady Emily wed 'im."

If only Emily had read the letter, as well. Apparently she had survived the afternoon without his aid. Her expression had reflected sheer misery as she picked at the tasty dishes he had set before her, but that was only to be expected. Without the knowledge that he had not escaped the household and left her alone to face Granbury, she must have felt that the marriage was inevitable.

She did not realize that Valentine had discovered the man was more than simply unsavory, he was a murderer. No one would expect Emily to honor the engagement once that information became known. He would show her the letter tonight, even though it would be painful for her to learn the details. If. . . . He whispered to Nan, "Is everything set for me to visit her tonight?"

The girl bit her lip and looked uncertainly at him. "It ain't a bit proper, you goin' right to 'er room, you know."

He thought, with guilt, of seeing Emily in her nightgown, holding her against him, never wanting to let her go. "I can promise that I will be a gentleman where Lady Emily is concerned, Nan."

She didn't look eager to accept his word, which made his estimation of her intelligence rise even further.

"I must let her read the letter, so that she will understand the kind of man she is dealing with."

"I could give it to her," Nan offered, reluctance to help sneak him up to Emily's room plain on her features.

For a moment he considered allowing Nan to show Emily the letter. But no. It was the only piece of hard evidence he had, he could not let it out of his own hands. Nor could he bear the thought of Emily reading those cold, horrible details of murder and dishonor without him beside her to ease her shock. "I must keep it with me, Nan. If Kerstone were to arrive tomorrow, he could use it to convince the countess that her plans for Emily are not only unwise, but dangerous."

Stubbornly, the girl crossed her arms and replied. " 'Is grace would take your word—"

If only Simon was the only one he needed to convince, he'd have had to agree with her. "But would the countess take his?"

She gave in with a little frown and a shake of her head. "You've got that right." A little sigh escaped her. "Very well, I'll 'elp you sneak in tonight—but I'm staying, too. I can be a . . . a chaperone."

Valentine readily nodded his assent to that condition. He could not afford to let his emotions get the better of him while he was alone with Emily. Nan would make sure that he kept to his good intentions. "Will you have a chance to warn her? I don't want to startle her."

"I'll warn 'er. If she says she doesn't want your company, then I can't help you." She uncrossed her arms. "An' it'll be past midnight before it's safe for me to come and get you."

They hurried down the stairs, aware that their simple errand had taken them longer than was reasonable. Soames was an exacting man, and already Valentine had seen evidence that the butler kept a close eye on every household matter within his purview.

As he slipped into his hard cot, unnoticed by his fellow footman snoring away on another cot, he felt like a mouse trapped in a house full of lazy cats. It would only take one to notice him, and then—he did not want to think further than that.

"Lord Granbury is exasperating, to say the least." Emily tossed the feather that had been scratching her scalp for the last three hours onto her dressing table. What she really wanted to do was pound on the door until they let her out so that she could find Valentine and scold him for choosing such a dangerous disguise.

Her heart still beat like a hammer when she thought of what could have happened if she had not gotten control of her first reaction to seeing him. She could have blurted out his name, she had been so shocked.

"The marquess does have enough presence for two or three lords, my lady," Nancy agreed dryly.

"Hah! Enough presence for ten men. After all, he told me himself that he was no ordinary man." How had she managed to survive the rest of the dinner?

To pretend she had not paid Valentine any more notice than she might have the usual footman? It had been sheer torture not to look at him, or drag him aside to question him about how he had ended up in a footman's uniform in the countess' dining room.

Nancy stepped around to pick up the feather, wrap it carefully in tissue paper, and put it in its box. She said soothingly, "It's time for bed now, my lady. You needn't see Lord Granbury again tonight. Don't get yourself all worked up. 'Er ladyship will not like it."

"Her ladyship likes very little I do these days. I must have played a dozen songs partway before she found one pleasing enough to let me finish it through. My fingers are aching." Emily was horrified to find tears in her eyes. Surreptitiously, she bent her head and dashed them away.

Crying in front of Nancy would be the final humiliation of her day. And, despite wracking her brain, she could not think of a single way to ask about the newest footman without betraying unusual interest. Locked in her room as she would be, she could not even sneak below stairs to speak to him. It was maddening not to know what he was planning.

Nancy fumbled at her hair, not at all the smooth lady's maid that Emily had come to take for granted. She looked into the mirror and gasped as she saw that the girl was pale and trembling. "Nancy, are you ill?"

"No, Lady Emily. I . . ." the girl's eyes were huge and dark in her face. "I . . . need to ask you if you mind a visitor tonight—"

Emily could not suppress her gasp of outrage.

Nan hurried the next words, "I'll be with you, my lady, I will protect your reputation."

Anger coursed through Emily and she stood and half turned to face the girl. "Do you mean to tell me that Lord Granbury has seen fit to bribe you to admit him to my room tonight?"

"No, my lady." Nancy's tone lowered in shock and her eyebrows wiggled comically in her effort to be subtle and discreet. "It is . . ." she lowered her voice further ". . . a footman, my lady."

Valentine. "I see." Emily sank back onto her seat, her heart suddenly beating fiercely. So he had not abandoned her for a career as a footman. "I see."

And how was it now that Nancy was delivering his messages? She gave the girl an assessing look and Nancy began frantically brushing out her hair. So busy with her thoughts, Emily did not even take time to suggest the girl be more gentle unless she wanted her mistress to be bald in a fortnight. "How did he come to give you this message?"

The girl trembled as she answered. "He was coming out of your room just as I carried in fresh laundry, my lady."

Emily shut her eyes, imagining the scene. "I take it you chose not to raise a hue and cry, then?" The question was, why? Emily hoped the answer was more than that Nan had been swayed by Valentine's smile, as charming as it was.

In the mirror, their eyes met and Nancy blurted out, "Please don't be angry at me, my lady. I don't think he means you any 'arm."

Emily did her best to smile reassuringly. "I am grateful that you did not raise the alarm, Nancy." But she was puzzled, too. It must have shown in her face, because the girl rushed to explain herself.

"I took a breath to scream, my lady, and 'e clapped 'is hand over my mouth and dragged me back into your room so fast I fair thought I was to be kilt."

Emily smiled, thinking of gentle Valentine menacing susceptible Nancy. That meant it was not his engaging smile or his boyish good looks which had caused the maid to trust him. "He did not hurt you?"

"No, my lady, he just asked me to 'ear 'im out—for sake of your safety."

"Obviously you found his story convincing." How much had Valentine confided in the maid?

"I did indeed. I've never really taken to the marquess, begging your pardon for saying so. I always 'oped you'd come to your senses before you married 'im."

She stopped, putting her hands over her mouth as if she'd just uttered the worst blasphemy imaginable. "I'm sorry, my lady. But it seems 'e's not just the kind to make a maid's neck 'airs rise, either. 'E's a bad man and you can't let yourself marry 'im."

Emily could only agree, although she wondered why both Valentine and Nancy found the man even more despicable than she did. "Thank you, Nancy, for your loyalty."

"I don't want to see you come to 'arm, my lady. I think the countess let her grief over your father's death affect her judgment. I'm sure 'is grace, the

Duke of Kerstone, will set things right, soon as he gets 'ere."

Emily raised her brows at the maid, surprised at the extent of Nancy's knowledge. "No doubt my dear cousin will find some way to convince my mother that she will not be lauded for pressing this marriage forward against my wishes."

"If anyone can explain it to 'er right, it will be the duke, I'm certain of it, my lady."

Valentine appeared to have confided quite a bit of the story to the girl. She could only hope it wouldn't be a problem if Nancy had a change of heart. She examined her maid in the mirror as the girl concentrated on brushing out the elaborate curls and braiding her hair for sleep. Could she be trusted?

It had been her former maid who had betrayed their elopement plans to Simon three years ago. The silly girl had been shocked when Emily's parents had sacked her without a reference for letting the plans get as far as they did.

She closed her eyes, remembering. They had been so close . . . an hour more and they would have been safely wed. She no longer blamed Simon, or even the maid for her betrayal. Elopement had not been Valentine's choice. He wanted a real wedding, an honorable match. Instead, through no fault of his own, he had gotten a near scandal.

No, it had been Emily's own fault. She should have stood up to her parent's indignation sooner. If she had done as Valentine begged, and allowed her father time to come to know him, things might have been so much different now.

But she had been in love and impatient with her parents' unromantic concerns with title and wealth. And she had caused Valentine more pain than she had ever meant. She still recalled the way the color had bled from his face when Simon stepped into the carriage and said quietly, "I had thought much better of you, Fenster."

Valentine had been deeply ashamed, true. But it had been love in his eyes when she left the carriage, and when he looked directly into her eyes and promised that he would never breathe a word of the near scandal to anyone.

He had loved her then, she couldn't bring herself to doubt it. His feelings for her had obviously cooled, although it spoke well of him that he had come when Simon had been unable to. He apparently considered her an obligation to be met.

Unfortunately, she hated feeling like someone's obligation. She was not going to be a burden to anyone, least of all to Valentine. She would make that clear to him the moment she saw him tonight. But how?

Perhaps there was a way to deal with that role, without feeling a fool. Valentine might be insulted, but she was willing to chance it, nevertheless. Surely she could put it in such a way that he understood it was to the benefit of both of them?

She must pay him for his help in rescuing her from this intolerable engagement. She would not need to be ashamed to be rescued by a former love, and he would not lose because of all the trouble he had gone through on her account.

She nodded. He would see the sense in it. A business arrangement—nothing more. He would be comfortable with that kind of relationship with her, especially since he did not seem to want more of her any longer.

And she would just have to accept that she had lost his love and trust long ago because of her impetuous behavior. If she wanted his love again, she must win it back . . . somehow.

Seven

Nan was skittish as they crept up the unlit staircase.

He followed her lead, avoiding the loose boards, making no noise, though their progress was less rapid than he would have liked. The risk of being found here was great. But he could think of no other way to ease Emily's mind.

He tensed as they approached Emily's room, both moving quietly. There was silence from behind the door.

Nan did not even trust him to use the keys, instead barring the way to the door with her body, and holding out her hand for the key ring. He relinquished it reluctantly, aware of how much trust he had put in the hands of a mere lady's maid. There was something about Nan, however, which suggested she deserved that trust. Perhaps it was the way she continued to protect Emily, even against him.

He did insist on recapturing possession of the keys, though, as soon as she had the door unlocked. She gave them back with a scowl and scratched lightly on the door to warn Emily of their arrival.

She would have barred him from the room while she checked that Emily had not changed her mind, but he made certain to insert himself in the gap in the doorway before she could push it closed. He did not want to be standing alone in the hallway for any longer than absolutely necessary.

Emily had not yet been to bed. She turned away from the window, outlined by the light of the moon. There was a small lamp burning by her bedside table.

The room felt unbearably intimate, even more so than it had last night. Perhaps it was Nan's presence, or perhaps it was the way Emily stood waiting for him. She was dressed for bed, with only a robe thrown over her nightgown for modesty's sake.

Her eyes were steadily focused upon him and he felt that he was about to learn what it felt like to be an errant husband brought to account by his angry wife. She said accusingly, "When you weren't here, I was afraid the dogs had found you."

He shrugged, acutely aware of Nan's unwavering gaze, daring him not to misbehave. "Actually, I never got outside the house." He smiled. "Probably truly confounded them." Again, he was grateful for the maid's presence, since it prevented him from doing what he most wanted to do—take Emily into his arms and kiss away her anger and her fears.

"No doubt." She was cool. He wondered if she was embarrassed by this morning, by his playing hidden witness to her toilette.

"I am sorry for the way things went this morning. I wish I could have made my escape earlier, and saved you any embarrassment or discomfort." Though the memory of her bare ankles would remain with him forever. He did not think she would forgive him any more easily if he told her so, though.

Flustered by his reference to the morning, she started to say something then halted, apparently changing her words. "Thank you for wishing to cause me less distress than you did." Her voice, if possible, was even colder. Why?

He searched his memory of the previous night—spotty as it was because of his laudanum-induced sleep. Had he done something to offend her? Had his words implied that he had enjoyed more than a view of her shapely feet?

To reassure her, her said, "I would not take advantage of circumstances, Emily, I assure you."

Nan *tsked* and he realized he had forgotten to call her Lady Emily. So much for not taking advantage.

"Take advantage? You spent the night in my bed, the morning underneath it, and then you left without a word, a sign, anything to let me know that you were safe." He saw that she was not angry, but hurt instead.

"I could not—"

"Why didn't you leave me a note? Or some kind of sign, so that I would know you hadn't been taken up like a thief!"

He clenched his hands into fists, warring with his natural instinct to pull her into his arms for comfort. "A note might have—"

"—warned others. Yes," she sighed. "I knew that, but it did not make it any easier, wondering whether you had made for London, or been cornered by the pack of dogs."

He supposed an apology for leaving her uncertain and wondering would not be out of place. "I could not stay here, Emily, it was only a matter of time before I was discovered. I did not want to bring harm to you."

When she did not soften, he said tensely, "I came to help you, not put you in further danger."

She pressed her lips together in exasperation. "Certainly, danger is too much. If I truly do not want to marry Lord Granbury, I may be destitute and without reputation, but that is hardly danger—I might not want the lot of a governess, but surely I am sturdy enough to survive it?"

She was standing there looking so defiant and courageous, he had difficulty disagreeing with her. He thought of the silks, the expensive clothing she wore. Saying nothing, he looked around at her well-appointed room—a prison to be sure, but a luxurious one. Could she survive being a governess? Two dresses, and, if she were lucky and her employer generous, an extra one for special occasions like Sunday service?

"I don't doubt that you could make a success of yourself however you might. But some people have no scruples, and you might not even be left with the ability to be a governess. The situation is not easily explained, but I must tell you that Lord Granbury is much more dissolute than you could ever have realized."

Her eyes dipped away from his, as if she were

ashamed and wished to hide something from him. "He is not a kind man, I agree. But dissolute?"

"Even worse than dissolute, I'm afraid." What was she hiding? Had Granbury already shown his true nature to Emily, even protected as she was in this castle? He had not expected that. Granbury's preferences seemed to be for servant women who were helpless and dependent upon him for their very lives. As a prospective wife, Valentine had assumed Emily would see nothing of the man's worst side.

"I've seen only one sign of behavior that suggests he would be anything but a model husband."

He heard the slight rise of discomfort in her voice. Granbury *had* done something. "And what sign was that?"

She must have heard the menace in his voice, because she could not keep the alarm out of her face when she replied. "Nothing terrible. It just seems that Lord Granbury has a strong streak of jealousy."

"And how did you discover this?"

"When I tried to convince him that I am star-crossed and he should break our engagement or he might not . . . remain healthy, he suspected there was another man. I denied it, of course."

"Did he say who?" Had he seen through Valentine's disguise? No, that was impossible.

"He said he did not care. And then . . . he suggested that he was up to the challenge of winning me, from another if necessary."

A challenge. Yes, that would be how Granbury would perceive it. With Emily as the prize. "I cannot overstate the hazards of the situation you are in. You have to believe with all your heart that this man has no scruples. Jealousy could lead him to do something dangerous."

Emily laughed, as if she were too afraid to believe what he had to say. He couldn't blame her, since she might very well be married to the man soon. How could he convince her?

"Show 'er the letter." Nan spoke and both Valentine and Emily started, having forgotten for a moment that she was in the room.

"What letter?" Emily moved toward him, but then, as if recollecting their circumstances, kept her distance, and asked again. "What letter, Valentine?"

He hoped it would not be the last straw for her self-restraint. He had to pray that she would not read the truth about her intended and run away for certain this time. It was certainly difficult trying to protect her reputation when she was so willing to throw it away.

He took the letter out and, careful to keep a respectful distance, approached just close enough to hold it out to her. "This letter."

She read swiftly, bending over the bedside lamp, and was silent for a moment. Wiping away a tear, she lifted her gaze to his. "This is monstrous!"

"Yes."

"We must expose him."

"First, we need to extract you from your engagement and then we can worry about exposing him. My concern is your well-being, Emily. If we achieve that, I will be satisfied."

"I will not." Her eyes flashed in the lamplight and

she turned to read the letter again. "Monstrous! And to think I considered him a bit on the dandyish side. How could he? How could anyone—"

He thought of the club to which the marquess belonged, a club which encouraged such depravity. "It is not as uncommon as you might think. You have been sheltered—"

"I may have been sheltered, but I also have been taught the rules of moral and ethical conduct. To enslave someone, to put your hands around their necks and squeeze the life out of them because—this behavior is . . . is . . . madness."

She collapsed onto the bed, unable to find a more fitting word for what the marquess of Granbury had, in the past, considered an evening's entertainment.

He could see that she was shaken to the core by the revelations in the letter. But he sensed no urge to flee in her. Instead, it seemed these revelations had kindled a revulsion so strong that she wanted to wipe it out, not escape from it.

For a moment he regretted that he had been unable to protect her from the truth. But, no, she was the one in danger, if Granbury truly thought he loved her. He had freed many of the women he had tormented. Strangulation had been reserved only for those he loved too well to let go.

Thinking of Emily struggling to breathe as the life choked out of her, he supposed it was for the best that she understood exactly why he had been willing to travel to Scotland, and was willing to help her escape marriage.

After all, it would not do for her to think it was

because he still loved her. "I had hoped, when your mother read this, that she would command you to break the engagement. But she would not allow me to show it to her."

"Perhaps I should try—" Emily shook her head and sighed. "She will not read it from my hand. She will think it a ploy." She put her head in her hands for a moment and stood still as a lamplit carving before she sighed and looked up at him. "I dare not even try, or she could take it into her head to destroy it before Simon had a chance to read what it said."

Valentine tended to agree with that assessment. "She refused to take it from me when I offered it to her. Do you think if I showed it to the new earl, your cousin—"

Emily shook her head emphatically. "Harold and mother are not blood relations, yet their temperaments are quite similar. We must pray that Simon arrives soon."

What he was about to say was a dangerous gamble, but she must not decide to run away without at least consulting him. "If he does not, I will take you away, I promise."

She frowned. "Why not—"

"Trust me. I want you safe." He moved nearer, but suddenly Nan was between them, fussing with the lace collar of Emily's robe. He smiled and stepped away. "But if we can salvage your reputation a little longer, then perhaps we needn't toss it away except for cause."

She sniffed, darting an annoyed glance at the

maid. "What is my reputation compared to the lives of those young women?"

"Emily—"

She looked at him as if some of the silver of his suit of armor had tarnished before her eyes. "I want him to pay for what he has done."

So did he, but not at the expense of Emily's well being. "That is for the law."

Nan agreed with him, " 'Tis not for the likes of a lady like you to be putting yourself in danger. Leave it to others to make sure the marquess doesn't get away with his misdeeds, my lady."

She cocked her head sideways, in quintessential Emily challenge. "Do they suspect him?"

What answer could he give her that would convince her she must put her own safety ahead of exposing the marquess' misdeeds? "I believe they do, but that was not my first concern. I've come to help you break your engagement. You must understand that we can see to justice only after that is accomplished."

"I suppose I do." She stared at him as if seeing him clearly for the first time, and a smile tugged reluctantly on her lips. "I nearly choked on my lemon tart when I saw you there. What possessed you to pretend to be a footman?"

He relaxed, glad that she had finally shifted the topic, though he wondered if she had truly reconciled herself to doing nothing about Granbury's crimes. "I'm not pretending."

"What do you mean, you are not pretending? You

are a viscount, you are Valentine Fenster. You cannot be a footman, no matter how pretty you might be."

The compliment was unexpected. So she thought him handsome, did she? "Pretty? Handsome, I will concede, but I have impeccable references, I assure you."

"References, from whom?"

He said nonchalantly, "Soames was impressed with my reference from the household of the duke of Kerstone. He hired me this afternoon, right on the spot."

Emily gaped at him. He had hired himself into a household which wanted his blood? "Are you mad?" Or, more likely, was he simply foolishly bravehearted? And all for a woman who he had once loved, with a young and foolish heart.

The cad dared to laugh at her reaction. "Don't blame me, the idea was Nan's."

Emily turned to her maid. The girl obviously had skills at subterfuge. After all, she had Valentine using her below stairs nickname with friendliness and familiarity in under a day's time. "Nancy, I can only say that I'm sorry you weren't my maid three years ago."

Nancy blushed and bobbed a confused curtsey. "Thank you, my lady."

But Emily needed to know more about Valentine's narrow escape, especially as it seemed to have ended in voluntary servitude. "How can no one have noticed who you were?"

His gaze shifted from hers for a moment, as if he was embarrassed. "Nan found me some suitable clothing for a man looking for work as a footman, and she took a pair of shears to my hair." He smiled, and her heart melted again. Why couldn't he have come here tonight to ask her to run away with him?

Unaware of how her thoughts had turned, Valentine continued, "It seems my haircut was simply too perfect for any servant."

"I see." But she didn't, really. She couldn't recall ever paying close attention to a footman's features, but to be so oblivious when it was someone she knew well was an uncomfortable revelation. "And voilà, you were transformed?"

"Nan assured me that no one looks at servants, and it seems she was right." His voice was quiet, and she sensed his unhappiness.

"Isn't that what you wanted?" It shouldn't make her happy that he was bothered that she had not noticed him at once, but somehow it did.

"Yes." He shrugged. "But it takes getting used to, this business of waiting on people who don't even want to look in your face and remember who you are."

His words stirred up an unpleasant memory. A cold shiver chased down her spine as she remembered the look on her governess' face when the woman finally left her post. She had had a bleak, haunted look as she stared from the carriage.

Emily, eager to begin her first Season, had thought she was just a bitter woman. But now she rethought her conclusion.

Was that what she would be in for if she did end up having to seek work as a governess, or worse, a paid companion to an invalid or a recluse? At the very least, Valentine was fortunate that his servitude would end very soon and he would once again regain his status.

She sighed. "I suppose anonymity is a good thing, though, for you—and for Nancy. Otherwise, you would have been dealt with severely. My mother is not one to make idle threats."

He brushed her concern away as though her mother had threatened to make him eat burnt scones for breakfast. "That is of no consequence, not until we can find a way to break this engagement of yours without raining scandal down upon your head. Whatever payment I might make, it will be worth it."

Her heart ached at the sight of him, so generous and serious. The knowledge that he did not love her any longer had no affect on the longings of her own heart. Which perhaps made her harsher than she might have been otherwise when she said, "I know you had intended not to involve yourself in this personally. I assure you that your added assistance will be well rewarded, when I am safely out of this engagement."

It was his turn to gape. "That is not necessary. I came to your aid as a friend, and in the stead of your cousin Simon."

She did not allow herself to soften, even when she saw the hurt shining so clearly in his eyes. "You risk not only your own life, but the happiness of your sisters, Valentine. And all for a woman to whom you owe no allegiance."

She paused briefly, hoping that he would, somehow, declare that he loved her still. He did not, merely staring mutely at her with no expression at all upon his face. "If you do not allow me to pay you, when this is all behind us, I cannot accept your help."

She thought he would refuse, the way his hand reached out and then stilled. But he did not protest, merely stiffened, and said softly, with a bow, "I understand."

Eight

It was much easier to be a nobleman, even an impoverished one, than to be a footman, Valentine found. His duties kept him in the house for the most part, where he could keep an eye on Emily, but he was not free to speak to her, nor even to look at her without causing attention to be drawn to him.

It was sheer torture to help her on with her wrap, careful to be circumspect. He could not look her in the eye. He could not ask how she was bearing up under the strain of entertaining the marquess. The only comfort was that she was now convinced not to put any more effort into making Granbury believe she was star-crossed.

Star-crossed. He had laughed when she had explained the concept to him. But now he wondered if Emily herself had begun to believe what she was telling Granbury? He hoped not.

Still, despite the fact that the engagement was soon to be broken, she must still spend time in the marquess's company. She must pretend to have become resigned to the engagement. Perhaps, he thought with a twinge of jealousy, she even tried to seem to welcome the marriage itself?

To his great frustration, he was not privy to much of their direct conversation. During the day he was rarely even in the same room as Emily.

Dinners were, to the casual eye, uneventful evenings full of polite conversation about when the guests would begin arriving and what the arrangements were for the wedding trip. There were often—sparked by Emily—long monologues on the marquess' travels and his unique and essentially tedious opinions on the morals and customs of those inhabitants he had come across.

Still, there was no doubt that the days were taking their toll on Emily, no matter how prettily she smiled, or how often she drew the marquess into one-sided conversation. Dark circles had begun to appear under her eyes, and he suspected she was not sleeping well.

He had not dared to ask Nan to sneak him back into Emily's room again, and the tension was becoming unbearable. Though the maid would reassure him that Emily was bearing up under the strain of her pretense, he could see Nan's worry for her mistress. He both admired and found frustrating the maid's loyalty, however, which led her to say little of Emily's true state.

Not that he would have taken Nan's word on the matter. He wanted to hear from Emily's own lips that she could bear this masquerade for at least a little while longer. He wanted to see the truth reflected in her eyes when she answered.

His dreams were haunted by visions of Emily escaping Granbury and Eddingley Castle only to be taken up by brigands on the road. She had managed to slip him one note, but the marquess had paid such close attention to her that they had otherwise remained steadfastly in their roles as mistress and servant, with Nan giving them both highly abbreviated assurances that the other was not in dire need of rescue.

At last, he knew that he must do something. It had been over a week and Simon had still not appeared, nor sent a note to the countess's household to announce his imminent arrival. He and Miranda had, of course, been invited to Emily's wedding ceremony. They were, however, not expected to arrive until the day before the ceremony.

That was cutting the timing too fine for Valentine's comfort. He did not think that Emily's reputation would survive her actually jilting her bridegroom at the altar, with all the guests as witnesses.

After a great deal of thought, Valentine decided to force matters to a head. He would send the countess the damning letter anonymously. Most likely she wouldn't believe it. Still, there was a possibility—as long as she didn't realize the letter was from him—that she would recognize the authenticity and realize, at last, the danger her daughter was in.

He approached the countess's small parlor, the room she preferred for her moments of solitude, and wondered if he was making a mistake. He imagined her there, plotting some new way to move the wedding forward—and hesitated at the door. Just as he began to turn the handle, he stilled. There was someone inside the parlor. Was it a parlor maid?

His hand poised upon the doorknob, he debated whether he should give up before he was discovered, or wait until whoever was inside departed. He leaned his ear against the door.

He heard the countess's voice and froze in confusion. Hadn't he just seen her walk off with the marquess for a stroll around the garden? How could she be inside?

A moment's thought made him realize that the countess's parlor had doors which led out to the garden. Thank goodness he had not been any quicker, or he'd have been in the room when she entered from outside.

He would have backed away then, except there came the sound of a second voice, that of the marquess, which said quite clearly, "Have you heard any more of Fenster?"

The countess answered with a sneer. "No, he seems to have come to his senses and returned to London without contacting Emily."

"Is that confirmed by your acquaintances there?" Apparently Granbury was willing to take no one's gossip as truth without confirmation. *More's the pity,* Valentine reflected.

"I will know shortly, but I expect to find that he has gone home. He has enough troubles with those five sisters of his, he can't possibly want to take on the responsibility for Emily as well."

Granbury demurred silkily. "Unless he thinks her fortune worth a little inconvenience."

"I convinced him well enough that there would be no luck for him in that arena. I maligned poor Harold a bit, but it did the trick. I am glad for Emily's sake—and my own—you do not need a fortune along with a wife. Harold keeps me on such a meager allowance I swear I do not know how I manage. It is a great boon to me that you will allow me to keep her dowry."

The marquess murmured agreement. "The girl need only provide me an heir, my dear, not renew my fortune."

The countess laughed in return, but it ended on a bitter note. "Not all women are capable of giving their husbands a male heir, my lord. Emily will do her duty, I have no doubt of that. But if fate—"

"As I have said before, I do not believe in fate. I will have a son. I will not settle for less."

"Then I wish you well with her."

Valentine felt a chill run up his spine. He had hoped that Emily was wrong about Granbury's attraction to her. That would ensure the danger to Emily was less than to the marquess's other victims. An unhappy life, a husband who was, indeed, monstrous. If she gave him a son, that would be the best—and the worst—that she could expect.

He had not considered one additional outcome. If she did not provide the required heir . . . the marquess had proved his ability to dispose of inconvenient females permanently, and with an utter lack of conscience. What would he do if Emily were to disappoint him with a daughter or two—or fail to conceive at all?

He knew that it was not unusual to marry only to provide an heir, but Granbury did not even deign to hide his own motivations in this marriage.

One thing confused him more now that he had overheard this conversation. What would make the countess agree to wed her daughter to this man for money? Did the marquess hold some secret indiscretion over her head, that she would sacrifice her daughter to a heartless beast so that she would have more pin money?

The countess answered his question with her next words. He was shocked by the bitterness and the anger as she spoke of her own daughter. "Then I hope Emily does not fail you, as she failed her father and I by being born female."

Valentine wanted to burst through the door and take the countess to task. It was only because of the risk to Emily, and to his sisters as well, from the countess's wrath that he stopped himself from coming to Emily's defense.

Perhaps it was his own sister's mistreatment by their father that fueled his anger—as twins, he as the boy and heir had received favored treatment, while Miranda was expected to be faultless and yet trusted to do nothing without guidance. It had rankled her all her life.

The marquess, however, seemed to find nothing objectionable in the countess's attitude. "I shall do my best to see that she bears me a son, rest assured."

Valentine clenched his fists, thinking of Emily as she had been the night he spent in her room, vulnerable and yet brave. He could not allow this marriage. He would not allow it.

The countess's laugh was not pleasant. "I have perfect confidence that you will, my lord."

Valentine backed away from the door, glancing left and right to make certain that he had not been seen spying here at the door. He was cold and numb. Emily's mother would not change her mind. Part of her was actually hoping that Emily would be miserable—that she might not even bear the marquess a son.

He glanced at the papers in his hand. No letter would change that fact. Could even Simon, the faultless Duke of Kerstone, make her see reason? She bore no love for her daughter, her words proved that.

And how could he tell Emily of this? It would break her heart to know that her mother was well aware of the caliber of man her daughter was marrying. He couldn't imagine how painful it would be to know that her own mother was secretly glad of the danger in which her daughter's life would be until she bore the marquess a son and heir.

It was only to be hoped that the countess did not realize the marquess was a murderer as well as an unscrupulous seducer. Surely even she would draw the line at such a man for a son-in-law—for propriety's sake at least.

Emily had been allowed to take a turn in the garden—with an eager footman at her elbow. It was most vexing to feel as if one were boxed and packed in cotton. Despite the years of seclusion at the castle, she had never felt her isolation and imprisonment so oppressively as she did now.

Perhaps, she reflected, it was because the marquess was stalking her like a fox with a hare, or perhaps it was because Valentine was under the same roof, and yet still as far away as he had always been since Simon had halted their elopement attempt. Nan assured her each day and night that he remained unnoticed in his role as footman. But she had little more information on how he fared.

She thought she could have borne the marquess' attentions, wanted or not, if only she had been able to look at Valentine, to find out what he was thinking, what he was planning. At the very least, to tell him what she was planning herself. She had been too afraid to even send messages through Nancy. Though Valentine obviously thought her trustworthy, Emily herself was too aware of how her previous maid had betrayed her.

Perhaps she should be surprised at how unexpectedly difficult it was to forget that Valentine was under the same roof, considering that she had been separated from him for three years. But she had never lost her faith in him and now she knew the depth of her feelings—how fully she trusted him, and how much she wished she could discuss this situation with him.

For one brief moment, she had hoped that Soames would assign Valentine as the footman to accompany her in the gardens, but he had not. She glanced at the face of the young servant who had been chosen to accompany her. Deliberately, she memorized his features.

Soames had called him Ned. She promised herself she would call him by name from now on. And perhaps it was even a blessing that Ned had been chosen rather than Valentine, considering what she planned to do. Valentine had an uncanny knack of knowing when she was about to spring some plan into action. He might have stopped her out of misguided chivalry.

After being locked in her room for so long, the fresh air in her lungs was sweetness itself. She breathed deeply, and wandered the gardens aimlessly, keeping just ahead of Ned so she could pretend that she was actually alone—perhaps even waiting for Valentine to join her for a stroll. A pleasant but useless fantasy.

She was not terribly surprised when her mother and the marquess joined her after only fifteen minutes. If she hadn't had a plan in place, she might have dreaded seeing them. But she not only had a plan, she had a great deal of hope that she would at last convince the marquess that she was unhappily star-crossed—even for a man who had been born with the nine lives of a cat.

A quick glance confirmed that there was a bench nearby. Without warning Ned, she veered from the path and headed for it. With an ostentatious sigh of exhaustion, she sat. It would not do for her mother to insist she walk with Francis. They must be seated for her plan to work.

They approached her deliberately, neither hurrying nor dallying. She felt like a mouse being toyed with by a pair of cats. Nervous tension crept into her fingers and toes, and she pushed it back down. Now was not the time for timidity or cowardice.

Carefully she took the bottle full of bees from her skirt and placed it under the bench. It had taken three days to collect the bees at her window. They had come one by one, lured by the honey she set aside from the morning tea Nancy brought her each day. She had been stung only once, thankfully.

Gently, she eased out the stopper and dropped it to the ground. She knew the marquis was afraid of bees, or so Nancy had been told by a servant of the marquess's. His one unearthed vulnerable spot, despite Nancy's pointed gossip over the last weeks. She supposed she would not know for certain for another few minutes whether the rumors were accurate and it truly was a weakness of his.

Her mother's voice carried clearly, even when they were still far down the path. "Emily, my dear, what a beautiful day. I am gratified to see you enjoying the outdoors. It does not do the constitution good to wall oneself up in one's room too much."

"Yes, Mother." Emily did not waste her breath reminding her mother that she would have happily spent more time in her garden if only the door to her room were not constantly locked, preventing her from doing so. She forced herself to appear unworried as they approached.

Her ears were pricked for any sounds from beneath the bench. Were the bees too loud? Would Granbury be warned ahead of time? She glanced up, but only saw pleased complaisence on his face as he smiled down upon her.

His gaze was more avid than she liked. "Your hair looks like spun gold in the sunlight. Quite delightful. Perhaps I shall have you painted like this, so that I can keep the memory always." Did she imagine that he licked his lips?

"That would be delightful, my lord. I have always wanted my portrait done." Emily tossed her head coyly, to hide the shiver of distaste which traveled up her spine, even as she wondered if either her mother or Francis could hear the rising hum of the bees beneath the bench upon which she sat. Moving deliberately to create a distracting rustle with her skirts, she left half the bench open.

She wondered how uncharacteristic and suspicious Francis might find her invitation for him to sit beside her on the bench. Fortunately, she did not need to extend the offer, he simply took the place as if it were his due.

Her mother beamed down upon them and then, with an unusual lack of subtlety claimed a headache and gestured to her maid to see her back inside the house and prepare a remedy. It was only the thought of what lay under the bench that kept Emily in her seat as Granbury took possession of her hands in his own and said chidingly, "I believe you are avoiding my company, my dear."

"Avoiding your company? But we have been walking each day, we picnicked by the pond only yesterday, I played for you last night after dinner. I cannot see how I deserve such a slanderous accusation, my lord." She kept her voice frosty, and addressed him formally, as any young woman might who was so unjustly accused of neglect.

His eyes seemed to probe deeply into her soul as he stared at her. "You were there in body, perhaps, but I have doubts about mind and heart. Perhaps your thoughts were full of someone else? A young man you used to know? Valentine Fenster, perhaps?"

Emily felt as if she had turned to stone. She must answer, and she must answer in such a way that the marquess gave Valentine no more thought. "We do not say that name in this house, my lord. The man is a bounder."

"Ah, but all young women secretly desire the very men they name bounders, do they not? Do you not?" His smile was not pleasant.

"How dare you!" Emily rose, allowing her indignation to show, hoping to escape this conversation by escaping the garden. Suddenly she did not care if her plan succeeded. Indeed, she was willing to abandon it altogether.

But he still held her hands tightly in his own, so her actions were severely hampered and she ended up looking foolish instead of furious. However, the stir of her skirts had evidently sent the bees into the frenzy she had been waiting for, and suddenly they were everywhere.

Francis screamed as one landed on his cheek, and he released her hands so forcefully that she staggered back, not even reacting to the feel of several bee stings upon her outstretched arms.

For a few seconds, as the bees buzzed and stung,

Emily watched as her formerly controlled and collected fiancé danced and screamed and stomped. He slapped himself so hard she was afraid he might knock himself unconscious, as he threw bees to the ground and then stomped them into paste with his boots.

By the time the hapless Ned had gathered his wits enough to understand what was happening, and come to the besieged marquess' aid, Francis was bright red and breathing hard. She could see that he was very near hysteria.

Not that she could blame him. If she had been ambushed by bees, she would have been hysterical herself. Perhaps she should be regretful for what she had done? His face had welts beginning from the stings, and she could imagine that there would be more rising under the collar of his shirt and upon his hands, where he had swatted at the bees in his panic. But somehow she could not feel sorry for him. He had done much worse to others.

Suddenly, as he struggled to regain his breath, his eyes fixed upon her. Her breath stopped in shock. She had not schooled her features to hide her own lack of surprise at his display. Like quicksilver, his demeanor changed rapidly from panic to fury. Though his breathing was still ragged and his face still choleric he grew completely still and pushed away Ned's frantic hands, which were still swatting at the few remaining bees.

She blushed hot all over with fear as his stare mesmerized her. Did he realize she had done this on purpose? If so, what would he do to her? But the fury disappeared as swiftly as it came and he was suddenly calm.

If she hadn't seen his panic, heard his screams, she would not have believed he had been beyond control a moment before. He smiled as if nothing had happened and said gently. "I'm sorry for losing my composure, my dear. I am not overly fond of bees."

She tried to recapture the moment of fear. "Now do you see? I am truly star-crossed, my lord. No one who comes near me is safe!" Emily struggled to hide her disappointment that he was regaining control so easily. She had hoped he would be distraught enough to take her suggestion of a curse seriously enough to break the engagement.

"Or the garden is so beautiful it calls to the bees, my dear. Do not be superstitious." The man seemed to have pulled himself back from the edge of hysteria without considerable effort.

Emily was speechless. This had not worked at all the way she had envisioned. At the very least she had hoped he would cut short his visit and head back home to recover and perhaps reconsider, so that she could think of how to escape without his watchful eye always upon her.

As he kept his gaze fixed upon her, she forced herself not to fidget. Instead, she said simply, "You are stung."

He drew near and pulled her hands into his again. Lifting her fingers to his face, he brushed the backs of her knuckles against his own growing welts.

It had to have hurt, but there was something like

pleasure in his half-closed eyes. "So are you, my poor little Emily." And he bent to press kisses on each of the welts developing on her outstretched arms.

Nine

Even from a hundred yards away it was clear that Granbury's face was swollen where the bees had stung him. Valentine had to school his face to the traditional footman's impassivity as Ned, the footman who had been out in the garden with Emily, came rushing ahead of the others into the house. His voice was high pitched and on the verge of frantic as he called urgently for Emily's maid and Granbury's man.

But Ned was considerably more discomposed than Granbury himself. The marquess had at least five large welts on his cheeks and chin, and even one on the bridge of his nose. Large, red, rapidly swelling welts, which had to be painful. And yet the man was showing no signs of discomfort.

Indeed, he seemed more concerned for Emily than for himself. Had she been stung more seriously than he had? Valentine watched them both anxiously as Granbury carefully led Emily into the house, showing all solicitous care for her.

It was only Emily's pale face and shaking hands

which told Valentine that she was not feeling comforted by the marquess's attentions. He could not be sure what had happened, but the way that Emily stared at the marquess reminded him of his youngest sister Kate. She had the frightened look of a high-spirited child when she was very afraid she would soon be punished for some transgression or other that had yet to be discovered.

He suppressed an urge to groan when he saw her arms. She had been stung. His instinct was to brush the marquess aside and personally take care of the red welts the bees had left upon her. The sight of that murderer's hands upon Emily tested his composure most thoroughly, and he could feel it failing.

Fortunately, Nan pushed past him and took over Emily's care before he could expose himself—as well as Nan and Emily—to discovery. The maid was as pale as Emily herself, and her hands were shaking where they touched her mistress's injuries.

"My lady, what has happened?" Nan managed to insinuate herself between the marquess and Emily, which brought a frown to the man's face.

He lifted a hand and would have pushed her roughly away, but just at that moment, his own man-servant arrived and began tutting at the sight of his master's face. "Bee balm, and bark poultice. I'll have some made up directly."

The countess, drawn by the disturbance, appeared to be more upset than the marquess. "What has happened to you?"

"Courting your daughter has a bit more sting to it than I expected." Granbury's words were soft and pleasant, but his expression was intense as he fixed his gaze upon Emily.

"What have you done?" The countess turned her fury upon her daughter.

"Nothing, Mother." But Emily's expression was transparent with guilt and Valentine felt himself tense.

"It is nothing I cannot deal with," Granbury said. His expression held a momentary ripple of irritation as he was forced to take his gaze from Emily to address the countess and calm her concerns.

Nan took advantage of the man's interruption to whisk her mistress up the stairs and away from the marquess. Valentine forced himself not to bristle as Granbury, staring intently at Emily's fleeing figure, made as if to follow. There was an expression of focused emotion on his features. Concern? Anger? Dismay?

Struggling against his own impulse to interfere, Valentine didn't relax until, again, Granbury's man stopped his master with a light hand on his arm. The valet, apparently knowing where to find the vulnerable areas of the marquess's pride, said quietly, "My lord, your face will puff like a pastry if we do not treat it immediately."

Valentine felt himself let out a breath he hadn't realized he was holding as the marquess allowed his man to lead him to his own room. He was shocked at how barely his temper was held in check. He had come so close to exposing himself, and leaving Emily open to an unknown retribution from her mother.

Not to mention the trouble she would cause for his sisters.

He stood for a moment, regathering his wits and his patience. Where was his common sense? Perhaps he should leave the household for now. Just turn and walk away while everyone was still in an upset over the latest incident.

For several seconds, he gave the option his most serious consideration. As a footman, no one would stop him. He would not have to return to his true identity until he was well away and no longer in any fear of discovery. And he did no one any service by bringing the countess's wrath down upon their heads because he could not control his own emotions.

He struggled to calm the rapid beating of his heart. If he left, if he tried to find Simon, perhaps he could do more good than he was doing here— unable to talk to Emily, unable to protect her even while he stood a handsbreadth away.

An unwelcome thought came to him. He remembered Emily's near terror as she stood in the hallway, the marquess's hands upon hers. Did that guilty look mean more than she had been caught in some unexpected mischief?

Even as the thought dawned, he hoped it was not true. But he considered Granbury's words carefully. Had this been some benighted scheme of hers? Had she actually *planned* this? If so, he could not dare leave her here alone. There would be no telling what she might choose to do next.

The decision whirled unmade in his mind. Should he go, or should he stay? It was time, he decided, no matter how risky, to see Emily again and find out exactly what was going on with her fiancé and their courtship. He would tell Nan that it must be arranged immediately. Tonight.

He must make it clear to her that the marquess was not a man to challenge on a whim. Perhaps, he thought, remembering how close he had just come to exposing his true identity, they both needed to be reminded of the dangers they courted trying to thwart the marquess of Granbury.

Once he had talked to her, he was certain he would know whether he should leave the castle and find Simon.

The maids fussed over her as if she were still the darling and pampered only child of an earl. Nancy clucked her tongue and wiggled her brows, but she said nothing, too aware of the other ears that might overhear.

Emily waited for her mother to sweep in, demanding to know what had happened. But the countess did not come, which was even more worrying. She knew that her mother was not about to overlook this insult to her favored guest.

She wondered if she could convince her mother that she had not planned it. Bees were not known for their sweet nature, after all. And there was no shortage of bees in a garden. Perhaps her expression had not contained the guilt she felt? Or perhaps her mother had not seen it there, since she had been focused on the marquess and his injuries.

She thought of her mother and shook her head. Probably not. The countess knew her devious qualities just a little too well. Even if she had not actually caused the crisis, her mother would have blamed her anyway. Her favorite accusation had always been that Emily was a scapegrace.

The maids left. She heard the key turned loudly in the lock, an audible reminder to Emily that she was trapped. "I *am* star-crossed," she muttered to herself in frustration. "Why doesn't Lord Granbury see it?"

Did others see it? Perhaps that was the reason Valentine no longer loved her? She had ruined his chances for an heiress bride, after all.

No. He could have found an heiress if he chose. If anything, his guilt would make him the culprit for her misfortune in his own mind.

For a moment in the hallway she had believed he would reveal himself. She hoped no one else had noticed the footman who lost his impassive façade. She had seen it in his eyes then. He loved her. And he had almost given his disguise away.

If Soames had noticed—But she supposed, given poor Ned's completely distraught demeanor, Valentine's slight lapse would not cause a stir.

Would he find a way to see her? She hoped so. They needed to talk. He loved her still. She loved him. It was time to clear the air between them, once and for all. She didn't care that he was only a viscount, or that he had no fortune. He must believe her.

Wondering if Nan would bring Valentine, Emily waited silently in her room, laid out like a Christmas roast. The poultices that Nancy had prepared to soothe her wounds covered her until she felt she would melt with the heat.

Though her mind was working wildly to deduce what consequences her actions would ultimately bring down upon her own head, she was unable to imagine what dire punishment her mother would inflict for this last folly. Would she beat her? Would she starve her? Or would she make her spend even more time with Lord Granbury? Emily had to think she would prefer the beating. It, after all, would be the quickest done and over.

Or maybe, with the wedding nearing, her mother would simply ignore the incident once she was no longer angry. There was no direct proof, at least. Which meant she could protest her innocence, whether she was ultimately believed or not.

Fortunately Nancy had retrieved the container the bees had been trapped in, so that evidence was not there for her mother to use against her.

She had hesitated to trust the servant with the information about the bottle, but she needed to tell someone and Valentine was locked away from her just the same as if he were miles away in London. So she whispered to Nancy and the girl had sneaked out before gathering up the poultices. The bottle was now safely returned to the dressing table.

She looked over at it, sitting among the other bottles so innocently. She shivered, thinking of what the marquess would do if he *knew* she had provoked those bees to attack him.

Still, it was clear that he suspected she had somehow managed to make the bees attack him.

He had pretended to solicitousness for her own bee stings. Yet, there had been no kindness in his gestures. Even the kisses to her welts had been painful and full of subtle menace.

One of the poultices slipped from her arm, and she reached to replace it, but her arm was too heavy to lift. She stared at it in puzzlement, willing it to move and replace the poultice, but, except for a slight wiggling of her fingers, nothing happened.

For a few moments she could not understand why she should be so tired. She had been stung more seriously than this when she was a child and she did not remember feeling this paralyzed. At last, with a buzz of horror in her brain, she realized her mother had managed to drug her.

But how? Letty had not brought up one of those noxious possets . . . Of course, she had been so upset she hadn't thought twice about the tea Nancy had brought up to calm her.

Frantically she tried to move, but nothing happened. Had Nancy known? Was the girl secretly helping the countess? The implications of such a possibility raced through her mind, though her body was relaxed to the point of torpor.

Nancy knew about Valentine.

The maid knew that he was a footman here, she had helped him get the job, had participated in the deception. Would she dare to tell the countess and risk her own dismissal? Was Valentine's identity in danger of being revealed?

Emily tried yet again to rise, but the influence of the laudanum dulled her panic and made her limbs heavy. And soon even worrying seemed too much effort, as she slipped deeper into the twilight of drug-induced sleep.

The marquess was not in his room. Valentine had taken the opportunity to check, as he had every night he had been in the house and Emily had been vulnerable. Where could the man be? Anyone else who had suffered a bee attack would have been soundly sleeping. So where was the marquess? The answer caused a curl of dread in the pit of his stomach.

The household had been subdued since this afternoon's incident. The countess had supped alone, and the kitchen had sent up trays for the marquess and, he presumed, for Emily. The staff had instinctively gone about their duties as if there had been a death in the house and all duties were completed earlier than usual.

Valentine had waited impatiently in his cot for Nan to come and take him to Emily. By now Nan should have scratched at his door, to let him know it was safe. Instead, he found himself prowling the halls, looking for Nan, for the marquess, for a way to get into Emily's room.

There was no help for it, if Nan had been delayed by mishap or deliberate malice. He could no longer wait for her to bring him the keys; he would have to risk checking on Emily himself.

If anyone questioned him, he would simply claim

to have been sent by Soames to investigate a broken window.

If needed, he could break it himself beforehand, just to make certain he would not draw any extra attention to himself. He gave himself a stern warning to be on his guard. It would not do to become complacent simply because his disguise had worked well up to this point.

He would check upstairs just to ease his mind. Surely an ear to Emily's door would reveal whether his worst fears had come to pass, or whether he was letting his frustrated imagination run away with him. Even as he had the thought, a woman began to scream.

The sound, magnified by his growing sense of unease, galvanized him, and he set out at a run. He was all the way to Emily's door before he realized the identity of the person who was screaming—the countess.

She woke to the sound of screams. The sound pierced her ears as well as the drugged fog of her mind. When she opened her eyes she could see very little. A dim light from the doorway, a candle. Her mother. It was her mother screaming.

How odd. She struggled to make sense of what she was seeing and hearing. She had never known her mother to scream before, not even when a mouse had climbed up her skirts at the Denby's ball. She'd gotten a bit red in the face and had lost her train of thought for an instant, but that was all.

Emily tried to rise from the bed, to go to her

mother, but she could not move. At first she thought it was the laudanum, but then she realized that something heavy lay half over her. With a struggle she pushed it off and sat up. She had on her nightgown. When had she changed? Last she remembered she was fully dressed as she had been when she went out into the garden, except that Nancy had removed her boots, of course.

Her mother stopped screaming, thank goodness. Now she was only moaning. Her moan was in the form of Emily's name, said over and over again. The sound echoed in Emily's head until she could not only hear it, but feel it.

There were servants now, behind her mother in the hall. Some were peering over her mother's shoulders, others whispering questions: "What's 'appened?" "Someone kil't?" Emily saw Valentine peering over her mother's shoulder. She saw his stricken face, and then suddenly her mother stopped moaning.

Already a small group of servants crowded around the open doorway, at the countess's back. But Valentine was tall enough to see over them and into the room. Emily in her nightgown. And next to her the marquess, also in his nightwear.

Emily's eyes focused on him, and she looked puzzled and disoriented.

The bewildered, pain-filled look in her eyes was familiar to him from his recent accidental dose of laudanum. She had been drugged.

While she lay insensible, someone had unlocked

her door and allowed the marquess to enter and climb into her bed. And Valentine had not been able to protect her. It was only the awareness that he would not get away with her safely that prevented him from breaking through the knot of servants and carrying Emily out of the room and away from the marquess forever.

"Nancy, Letty, come with me. The rest of you, go to your beds and forget this disgraceful sight." The countess sounded more like herself now that she was no longer screaming. She was full of command and confidence.

He stood rooted to the spot. The door closed, breaking his contact with Emily. Was she hurt? Had Granbury done more than climb into bed with her? If he had, his life was forfeit.

He noticed Soames watching him closely and he began to walk down the stairs with the others. He ignored the buzzing of the servant's ill-informed but imaginative gossip. Each step away from Emily was torture. But what could he do?

Emily needed his help. What could he manage tonight that would not land her in deeper danger? Her mother was no ally. And now he wondered, thinking of Nan in the room with the countess, Emily and the marquess—was the maid true, or would she betray them, in order to save herself?

The door closed on the gaping servants and Emily closed her eyes in relief. But she opened them again at the sound of her mother's harsh sigh.

Nancy's eyes were wide with shock. At first Emily thought the maid was looking at her, and she put her hand to her head expecting to see blood, at the very least. Her hand came away unmarked, even as she realized that she felt no pain. She had been drugged, not knocked unconscious.

But then she realized that Nancy's eyes were focused on the object she had pushed off herself to get up. She turned and saw, to her horror, that Lord Granbury, his face still swollen from the bee stings he had suffered this afternoon, lay beside her. His eyes appeared heavy lidded as if he, too, had just been awoken.

Even as she stared stupidly at him, he opened his eyes fully and sat up. He said soothingly to Emily's mother, "Dear countess, please forgive me for disgracing you like this. I regret that you found us here."

"I am deeply disappointed in you—as well as in my daughter. I did not raise her to behave like this, even so close to her wedding."

"The fault, of course, is all mine. I should never have taken advantage of such a sweet, innocent girl." Emily glared at him, much misliking the emphasis he placed on the word *innocent*, as if perhaps it might be a word that was not descriptive of her any longer.

And then she remembered Valentine's stricken face staring over her mother's shoulder. He must have assumed—Dear God, what *had* he assumed?

Ten

Emily stumbled out of bed, unwilling to believe she had been caught up in this nightmare. She must reach Valentine, now, before . . . Before what? The worst had already happened.

She felt like a fly caught fast in a honey trap. The glances that flew between her mother and Granbury even as she watched were not full of suspicion or disappointment, but collusion and self-satisfaction.

She looked toward the maids, wondering if they were part of the conspiracy or unwitting accomplices. "Mother, I did nothing. You put something in my tea so that I would sleep. I was unconscious, I didn't know. . . ." She babbled on for a bit more before she realized that it would do no good, and managed to sputter to a stop.

Obviously if her mother had drugged her, she had done so in order to see that Granbury could be found here. The only purpose she could imagine for the countess to take such a drastic step would be to hasten the wedding date.

She looked past her mother toward the door, wondering if she could push through the maids and manage to run down the stairs and out the main door before another servant could prevent her.

Maybe Valentine would turn his back on her now, but it didn't change the fact that she couldn't, wouldn't, marry the marquess, no matter what. Outside, away from the castle, she'd be in her nightgown in the dark of night, alone, penniless. Even knowing that, somehow such a fate seemed preferable to being right here, right now.

Emily's heart began a double beat. The gleam of satisfaction in her mother's eye was frightening as the countess said with sharp disdain that Emily knew to be completely false, "I will expect you to correct this situation at once, my lord."

Almost as if he knew that Emily was now focused on the closed, but unlocked bedroom door, the marquess stirred next to her, grasping for one of her hands, keeping her by the side of the bed. "Of course. I will send my man for a special license at once. We can hold the ceremony as soon as he returns."

Emily began to protest, but stopped when Nancy gave a quick shake of her head and a wiggle of her brow. The maid's somewhat panic-stricken look reminded her that she was not the only one in danger of being found out. The better part of valor in this situation was, unfortunately, to play the properly penitent, chastened, and accepting sacrificial victim.

She dropped her head and pretended to be distraught—although it was not a terribly difficult pretense to effect. "I'm so sorry, Mother." The words came out a bit choked because she had to force them out of her unwilling throat, so she followed with a bit of sobbing, which wasn't too hard to muster, considering how dim her future suddenly looked.

What must Valentine think? He must be grateful that he no longer loved her. How much more awful for him if he had wanted to marry her himself, to find her in bed with Francis. Did he think her fickle, or did he suspect the marquess and her mother of subterfuge?

For some reason, she trusted that he would know the truth. That he would still help her, if it were possible at this point to rescue her at all from the fate which seemed to be crushing down upon her with the force of an avalanche.

She managed to pull her hand away from the marquess's sweaty grip, so that she could fumble a handful of nightgown to cover her face.

She was afraid to let her mother know that she still had a shred of hope she might escape this in some other way than becoming the marchioness of Granbury.

What she needed desperately to find out was whether Valentine would finally recognize there was only one solution to rescue her ruined reputation. Marriage. And not to the marquess of Granbury.

If Valentine did, at last, ask her to elope with him, could she do it, knowing that he would not have done so if she were not in dire straits—the alternative being an unwilling marriage to a murderer? Could she do it knowing the cost to his family if she did?

Tears sprang to her eyes and she dashed them

away. For a moment she wished she could disappear, like a wisp of smoke on the breeze. It seemed an easier feat than making her future somehow end up in any way bearable.

He was weary of playing the patient servant, biding his time, protecting Emily's reputation—which now had yet another blot upon it. Fiancé or no, Granbury had no business in her room and the servants would gossip it abroad. There had been too many in that knot for the countess to expect them to keep the news quiet.

Not, of course, that he expected she'd wanted her daughter's disgrace kept quiet. No, this time she wanted the girl married, and as quickly as possible at that.

The effort of lying in his cot, waiting for Ned to fall back to sleep, waiting for the furor to settle down enough for him to go back upstairs, brought sweat out onto his forehead. Seared on his mind was the sight of Emily lying in her bed with the marquess beside her.

Suddenly, all his objections to eloping with Emily were dust in his mouth. He would turn to Simon to protect his sisters if he must, pride be damned.

Emily might never have a lively social life at Anderlin, but she would not be forced to bear the attentions of a monster, either.

The solution seemed so clear to him now, he could only hope that he was not too late. It was fortunate that Granbury had not given thought to the fact that the marriage laws of Scotland were different. Or perhaps he simply wanted an English marriage so no questions could ever be raised. Either way, Valentine calculated that the marquess's man could not return with the special license in less than two days.

Unfortunately, Granbury himself was still here, and still able to create mischief—aided and abetted by the countess, and perhaps by Nan, loyal though he had previously thought her.

At last, the house was still. Afraid to trust Nan any longer, Valentine found the set of keys himself, and hurried silently up the stairs toward Emily's room. No matter what had happened between the marquess and Emily, he was taking her away with him tonight.

He paused, hand upon the doorknob. He did not need the key—the door was unlocked and slightly ajar. He could hear the countess's voice from within and hid himself in the maid's closet just as Nancy emerged from the room.

Deep in despair, Emily watched as her mother shooed out the maids and then departed herself. To her surprise, the countess contented herself with one backward sally. "My lord, I would sigh, but . . . spilt milk and all that. . . ."

Emily stared at the marquess, unable to believe that her mother had left him in her room. At least she had not locked the door. But did that do any good, when Granbury was between Emily and freedom? He did not look like he would let her leave, unlocked door or not.

"Should you not leave as well, my lord? After all, we will not be truly married for a few days yet."

He did not answer her directly. "Did you truly think I would let you play silly games with me, my dear? You are quite resourceful, but you are also very young."

She felt as if he were toying with her, treating her as a cat might do a mouse. It was impossible to forget what kind of man he was, what awful things he had done to young women not that very different from Emily herself. "I don't know what you mean, my lord."

She edged toward her dressing table, hoping to find a bottle sturdy and large enough to serve as a weapon, should she need one.

"Of course you do. Please do not play the innocent with me. No one believes it of you any longer—not after tonight."

So, the marquess had finally shed his pleasant persona. If she thought she had glimpsed malice in the garden, she knew she gazed full upon it now. For a moment, all she wanted to do was curl into a little ball and never uncurl again.

But then she thought about how unfairly she was being treated. She was not chattel. And she was not a milk-and-water miss, no matter how diligently her mother had worked to mold her into one.

Emily glared back, suddenly angry at the way she was being manipulated. "After this little scenario you arranged with my mother's help, you mean?"

Her anger seemed to please him. "Ah, your temper is showing at last. But why over something so trivial? You had doubts, I put them to rest."

"To rest? Do you think I am reassured by the idea that my fiancé is willing to collude with my mother to drug me and pretend—" She stopped. She had no words for what the servants thought had occurred tonight. "I can assure you I am less inclined toward this marriage now than I ever was."

"I'm sorry to hear that, especially now that you must see you have no other choice. Believe me, Emily, I just wanted to ease your maidenly concerns. Your mother warned me that you would be a difficult one to reassure. So we decided this little . . . insurance . . . was the next best way to trust that you wouldn't run away before the vows could be exchanged."

He seemed absolutely impervious to the simple fact that she did not want him for a husband. It was not only frustrating, it was exhausting. "Why do you want a woman who doesn't want to be your wife?"

He smiled as if she were a pupil who had asked a very good question. "I told you before—I like a challenge. And I knew you would offer me an interesting one the moment I heard the gossips picking over your life."

"If you believe the gossips, my lord, you cannot possibly consider me a suitable woman to be your marchioness. Besides," she broke out in frustration, "I don't want to marry you! Why don't you understand?"

His eyes gleamed and he moved toward her. "But

I understand perfectly, my dear. I think the challenge of taming you should add a little spice to my life. I must say it has been unbearably dull for the last few months. Some busybodies like to tell a man how he can treat his servants. But no one dares interfere between a man and his wife."

Some of Emily's internal fire died as she remembered what he had done for entertainment in the past. Common sense dictated that stirring his anger, or his love of a good challenge, was not going to encourage him to leave her room.

Why her mother had allowed him to remain here in the room she did not want to contemplate. Emily had no doubt at all that *she* wanted him out. And, suddenly, she found that she was afraid to tell him so.

Coward, she chided herself, as she said, "I am not Kate and you are no Petrucchio."

"No?" He laughed softly, a sound which set the hairs on the back of her neck aquiver with dread. "You have a temper. Your mother said you were biddable, but I thought I glimpsed some fire under that pretty pose."

"And you are a monster—the kind of man who murders innocent women."

His astonishment was quickly followed by an anger so cold Emily thought she might freeze in his glare. "Someone has been telling tales. Perhaps your mother is right, and this Valentine Fenster has somehow managed to catch your ear. I hope, for your sake, that he has not had the opportunity to catch more than that, though."

Shaking with fear and outrage, Emily wondered if

she would, in the end, be the one to betray Valentine's presence. She tried not to let the marquess see her fear. "You are despicable."

"Yes, well. Knowing what you do, I can see where your reluctance might be a bit hard to overcome. So let me say, my dear, that you will marry me."

"And if I don't?"

"If you don't, I will see that you stand trial for the murder of the two men who did not quite make it to the altar."

That was one answer Emily could not have anticipated and it quite took the wind out of her outrage. She scoffed, "That's absurd."

"You'd be surprised, Emily, what I can accomplish with the right words in a few ears, and a little coin to ease the way."

Could he? Nonsense. "And you'd be surprised by the friends I have who could make sure that you are not believed."

"You are the one who would be surprised, my dear. But perhaps you are right. Perhaps it would be a mistake to charge you with the murders. Wouldn't it be more . . . interesting . . . to accuse Valentine Fenster, the man who tried to steal you from your home and family and now pines away in poverty, wishing he had captured his wealthy heiress?"

His expression was so serene, so certain, that Emily found herself becoming convinced. But no, he was merely playing a game with her mind. "No one would believe—"

"Of course they would. Whichever of you I choose

to accuse, I can assure you, I will also ensure is convicted."

"But why—"

"As I said, I find the idea of taming you a challenge too tantalizing to miss." His eyes warned her a scant instant before he lunged toward her and grasped her arms tightly, binding them to her sides so that the bottle she held was useless as a weapon against him.

She struggled for a moment, and then gave up, hoping to fool him into thinking she would not fight him any longer. But his grip remained strong as he said, "I think perhaps, even though we are anticipating the wedding by a day or two, that it is time for our first lesson in wifely duty. Climb into your bed, Emily."

Frightened by the determined look his eyes, Emily opened her mouth to scream. Though as she did so, she wondered if anyone would answer the scream even if they heard it. After all, the servants now thought she had let the marquess into her bed willingly, thanks to her mother's scheming.

But Granbury's face twisted into a snarl at her defiance, and without warning he lifted her by her arms and flung her onto her bed, forcing the air from her lungs and silencing her scream. He loomed over her, saying quietly, "A wife always obeys her husband instantly."

Before she could struggle any further, she saw a shadow upon the wall. Valentine stood over the marquess, his raised hand grasping a heavy candlestick, which he brought down on the marquess's head.

The marquess of Granbury proved to be an ordinary man after all, as he collapsed like a badly built house of cards, his hands slipping from her arms as he slid to the floor and lay still.

Eleven

He did not spare a glance for the marquess, but instead gathered Emily to him and held her as she buried herself tightly against his chest. After the worst of her sobs had calmed, he looked down at Granbury's sprawled figure. "I should kill him."

In his arms, she tensed and grabbed at his shoulders as if to hold him back. "No—"

"I won't. I'd be no better than he is if I murdered him while he was unconscious."

"He was going to—"

He held his breath as she began to speak, and then, unable to listen to what she might have to say, asked, "Has he hurt you?"

"No. I was only frightened. But Valentine, he threatened me—he threatened you—he said—"

"Never mind what he said. We'll be gone when he wakes." He could feel her trembling against him, but there was little time to waste in comfort. "Come. We are leaving. Get dressed and pack a few things as quickly as you can."

"No." She pulled away from him, shaking her head.

He stared at her, certain that he had misunderstood. "Emily, we must leave at once. If we hurry, we can be wed and in London before anyone can even guess where we've gone."

She stared down at the marquess as he lay insensible upon the carpet. "We can't. He said—"

"It does not matter what he said!"

"You don't understand, Valentine. He threatened . . . he must be mad, there is no other explanation." She looked up at him and his breath stopped at the sheer terror in her eyes. "He said he would see one of us hanged for the murder of those two hapless men who never made it to the altar with me."

"He could never do it, Emily. We can talk about this as we travel. We must leave at once." He pulled at her hand, but she resisted him.

She said again. "We cannot."

It began to dawn on his fevered brain that she had no intention of going with him. It didn't matter that there wasn't time. He needed to find the words to convince her that they must go—and quickly.

It was the threats which seemed to have sapped her will to fight. He took a quick breath and concentrated on the marquess's threat to have one of them hanged for the murder of men who had died naturally, if unexpectedly. The words conjured frightening images, but were idle, surely? "No one would believe him."

She looked up at him, her eyes sad, "Of course they will. They half believe it even now."

"What are you saying?"

"You may think that my mother walled me into this castle to keep me from making a fool of myself, but that was not my father's reason. He heard how people gossiped, and what they said. Attempted elopement, one fiancé dead, the next suffering a foolish accident. It had to be my fault."

"But—one was an old man in poor health, the other a drunkard. How could you be blamed for circumstances beyond your control?"

She sighed, a bitter twist to her lips. "Because it amuses someone to suggest it, and others to gossip about it. If Granbury were truly to do more than spread idle rumors, if he were to try to convince the authorities that I . . . it would not take much for people to believe it."

Unfortunately, he could see the truth in what she said. But gossip was not the same as being charged with a crime. "If we elope, you will already have provided enough gossip for the bored in Society. They would not need to try you for an imaginary crime. No one would hang you."

"Perhaps not. But they would convict me in their minds, just the same. And don't you see? You are vulnerable as well. Everyone knows that you set out for a wealthy heiress bride and tried to elope with me."

"I told no one; we could deny it."

"My mother knows. The servants know. We could not keep the truth a secret. And it could get you hanged, though you had nothing to do with the deaths of my former fiancés."

He could sense that if he did not change her mind immediately, they would lose the chance to escape. "Once we are married, he will have lost—he can do nothing more to us if we are husband and wife."

Emily laughed softly, an unhappy laugh. "I have waited so long to hear you ask me to marry you again. So very long."

He reached out for her, but she evaded his touch. "Valentine, if we marry now, it will be proof to any who doubt the truth of Granbury's outrageous claims. Everyone would be pleased to believe you some murdering scoundrel who would do anything for an heiress and her fortune."

"Emily, we have no choice!"

She smiled sadly and touched his cheek with a trembling hand. "To marry you would be to put the noose around your neck. And that I will not do."

"You are talking nonsense—you're overwrought from tonight's events. But there is no reason we cannot marry. He will not fight when he knows he has already lost."

She looked at him blindly. "You don't understand. He will not allow it. He does not let himself lose. Not ever."

"He does not have the power to keep us apart. Surely he will realize that once all Society knows the deed is done."

"You read that letter. He *does* have the power. He is not a sane man. To him, the game would not be played through until he had separated us forever."

Emily stared at him, conviction in her expression. "He will see one of us hang for killing the hapless men who dared to ask my father for my hand."

"I cannot protect you unless I am your husband. Do you not understand?" He would not let her distract him with her fears, valid though they might be. They had only this night to elope and flee to London. Now that he had attacked the marquess, his presence confirmed, they were both in immediate danger.

"All too well." She said quietly. "You asked me to marry you again. I have dreamed of it for years. And I must say no."

"Emily—"

"Hold me." She leaned into him, and he could feel her trembling like a tree in a gale wind. He wrapped his arms around her and pressed her head into the crook of his neck.

"Emily, I know I've been stubborn about elopement before. You deserve better. But now there is no choice, surely you see that? I know that life will be hard for you, Emily, and I promise to do my best to restore a measure of luxury to your life in a few years, when my fortunes are better."

There were tears in her eyes, he saw, when she raised her head to look into his eyes. "You have no idea how long I've waited for you to say those words to me. And now, sweet as they are, they cannot be true. We cannot marry. You must go."

"I won't let you marry him. You cannot let him destroy you."

She brushed his cheek with her fingertips. "What

else can I do? Let him destroy you and your family?"
A light touch. Gentle. He bent his head to look into
her eyes. She was closer than he had ever dreamed
he would have her again.

And yet so far away. He held her tighter, his breath
painful and ragged with distress. "Of course." It was
foolish to agree, but impossible not to, when she
looked at him with such certainty. He had never seen
Emily so thoroughly beaten before. The marquess
must have shown his true nature, and fully, to have
brought her to this state.

He gripped her chin gently, so that she would not
be able to look away from his gaze. "Emily—has he
hurt you?"

She tried to duck her head, but he did not let her.
She closed her eyes before she said, "Just my arms,
where he flung me down on the bed."

He couldn't determine if she was telling him everything, and he couldn't see her eyes. He urged
gently, "That was now. I mean, before, when he had
you here alone. Before your mother screamed."

"Oh!" Her eyes flew open in horror. "No. I was
drugged. . . . What could he have done with me unconscious beside him?" She shook her head somewhat frantically, as if tossing away unpleasant images.
"No. He must have lain there waiting for Mother.
What else . . . ?" She just looked at him, as if he
might hold the answer to the newest question in her
mind.

"I—" How could he ask the question? How could
he not? He must not treat her any differently. Perhaps it didn't matter what her answer was. "Never

mind." He dismissed the question in her eyes by pulling her toward him again and enfolding her in his arms. "I will not let him hurt you again."

"How—"

And he knew the answer, as soon as she asked the question. "I will ensure that Granbury loses the game, even though he will not know it immediately."

"Lose? How?"

"We will marry tonight—secretly."

"Secretly," she repeated, slowly, as if the word itself made no sense.

He nodded, pleased with the plan which had sprung fully formed into his mind. "That way, he can never marry you legally, for you will be my wife."

Wife. He marveled at how completely his attitude had altered since this morning. But the word felt right. The marriage felt right. "And if we keep the marriage a secret as long as possible, we will not have to expose ourselves to his revenge until I have found a way to make him reveal his true nature in all eyes."

Emily objected. "Granbury has sent his man for a special license. He will be back within days. Will I pretend to marry one man when I am already married to another? The law frowns on such behavior."

"You do not understand. You will be safe in hiding. I will be here, as footman. No one will suspect that we have eloped. And, as my wife, you will be protected even if the marquess does manage to find you."

"Is there no other way?"

He frowned. "Your mother has indicated she will

not protect one hair on your head. We cannot afford to wait even one more day," he said, hating the pragmatism of the statement. "And I can be more bold in my attempts to bring his deeds to light without having to worry about your safety."

"He will follow me."

"Perhaps. But I will not let him harm you." He hoped he was not making an empty promise. For Emily would still be exposed to danger, even if she was no longer going to be able to be forced into a marriage with Granbury. The man was unbalanced, as he had proven. He would take up the challenge of Emily's disappearance with relish.

"I believe that might work," she said slowly. "If we disappear, and do not reappear as a wedded couple, no one can be sure we have eloped." She looked up at him, a half smile on her lips. "After all, Valentine Fenster is supposed to have quit Scotland, and even I would not be assumed to have eloped with a footman." There was worry in her eyes, though, and he could imagine her mind looking for the flaws in his argument, and he decided to remind her of the necessity to hurry.

"Then get dressed, quickly. And we can be gone before morning, safely away before anyone has missed you."

"And I will be your wife, then." She looked up at him, suddenly shy, with a hint of fear.

"Yes. You will be my wife." The responsibility for her happiness—and safety—were now his. He hoped he could live up to the duty.

She moved away to dress and pack, tripped over

Granbury, and made a small sound of distress. "Whatever shall we do about him?" They both stared in consternation at the marquess on the floor.

He did not stir.

They went quietly out to the stables in the darkness. Eloping. Again. Emily remembered the joy she had felt the first time. There was none of that heady rush of blood this time. Valentine had only proposed the elopement in order to save her from Granbury. He still was not convinced they belonged together. But he loved her. And she loved him. She would simply have to do her best to convince him that love was all they needed.

They saddled the horses and led them quietly outside. She thought them nearly safe until a rustling noise from the gardens to their left caught her attention.

"Where are you off to at this hour?"

Emily turned at the sound of the unexpected voice. She suppressed a squeak of surprise with difficulty. Who would be in the gardens at this time of night?

"Nan? Is that you?" Valentine's voice was low and urgent.

"Yes. I'd come to 'elp Lady Emily and I saw the two of you 'eading down the stairs." Nan came toward them in the darkness and Emily saw that she had thrown on a dark cloak which muffled her figure and made her nearly impossible to see. "Where are you going?"

Emily didn't know if she would have answered or not, but Valentine saved her the dilemma by replying quietly, "We're going to get married and don't try to stop us."

"Stop you?" Nan snorted. She swung something from her shoulders and Emily realized that the girl had two dark cloaks on, one of which she was now draping over Emily. "I thought I'd make sure you didn't get caught before you got away. That dress is so light it's like a beacon."

Emily wanted to cry at the kindness of the gesture—and kick herself for not having realized how her long, light yellow gown would stand out against the dark of night. She was speechless, though, until Valentine said quietly, "Thank you, Nan."

"Yes, thank you Nancy," Emily forced herself to say stiffly.

"No need to thank me. I wish you well, my lady." Nan squeezed her once, in a fierce hug that took the breath from Emily's lungs. "I want nothing more than the best for you, for both of you."

Emily was surprised to notice that Valentine's voice held a note of regret as he helped her up onto the waiting horse. "I hope you do, Nan, because you're coming with us."

"What? I—"

Emily gasped when Nan came catapulting up onto the horse behind her. "Valentine, what—"

He reached for her hand in the darkness and pressed it to his lips to silence her before he spoke. "There's no help for it. We must all go. We need a witness, after all." Both women began to protest once more, and his voice came just as quietly, but with more iron. "This way there is no chance that Nan will sound the alarm before we have accomplished our goal."

He mounted his own horse and began to walk it away from the castle, leading Emily's horse at a slow and steady pace behind. He turned back once and said tersely, "Explain what we are about, Emily. Perhaps she will be useful in coming up with a story to tell the staff about why the marquess is passed out in the library, smells like brandy, and has an empty bottle next to the chair in which he is slumped."

Nan gasped. "My lady, you didn't murder 'im, did you?"

Emily gave a mental shiver, thinking how quickly Nan had asked the question. Would she be any slower to jump to such conclusions were Granbury to exact his revenge by accusing her of the murder of her former fiancés? "Of course not, Nancy. Valentine hit him over the head with a candlestick when he attacked me. We put him in the library and spilled a little brandy on him."

"Why would you do that?"

"To make him think he had passed out after drinking too much." The idea had been Emily's, and it had seemed like an excellent one at the time. Her father had been known to spend whole nights in the library with a brandy bottle. Why should the marquess not do so, too, without too much suspicion being aroused?

"What difference does it make what 'e thinks? You two'll be safe in London by then."

"We're not going back to London just yet. The marriage is to be secret for a while, until we expose Granbury for the snake he is." With distance, now, she was beginning to question herself. Valentine had been right when he agreed as a last resort.

"You're going to try to expose 'im?" Nan's voice was shrill with disbelief, but she quickly hushed her tone for the next question. "Are you two completely mad? The man will kill you."

Or see them hanged for a crime that was not even real, Emily thought to herself. "We have no choice, Nancy. We must convince others of the truth of the man, or too many people will suffer."

"And what will the countess say when 'e tells 'er what you've done?" Nancy moaned softly at the thought.

The marquess had been hit hard, his head would be bound to ache. No doubt there'd even be a lump or a bruise. His man would surely notice and question Granbury even if Granbury himself didn't remember events clearly.

"I suspect he will say nothing to anyone. He is a proud man."

" 'E'll want blood, then," Nan whispered. "Yours, I fear, my lady."

Emily sighed. Yes, he would. "We need time to bring him to justice. This should give it to us." We hope.

" 'Ow can I 'elp?"

"Oh, no. Nancy, I wouldn't want to involve you in the danger."

"I'm already involved, my lady. I've been trying to bring that monster to justice for near a year now."

The statement shocked Emily speechless for a moment. And then the questions filled her mind. "Did he . . . did he hurt you, too?"

" 'E killed my sister, and I'll see him 'anged for it, I will." The normally sweetly docile timbre of Nancy's voice was gone, replaced with an implacability which made her statement seem a certainty rather than a hope.

"We can use your help," Valentine said abruptly. "Are you willing to go back into the castle?"

Emily protested. "But that is too dangerous. I forbid it. Nancy will stay with me, where she can be safe."

Nancy shook her head vigorously. "I 'ave to go back to the castle. I'm not the only one who's looking for ways to bring the man down. There are others who must know that you are working in the same cause as we are."

"Other servants?"

"Yes, my lord. We may serve others, but we serve our own needs as well. Granbury has 'urt his last female servant." She touched Emily's shoulder and cleared her throat. "Begging your pardon, my lady, Granbury has 'urt his last female—servant or better."

"Then we're agreed. After I have Emily safely tucked away from his wrath, I'll join you back at the castle and we'll make sure the murders stop here."

"We are not agreed." Emily held back on the reins, stopping her horse.

"Emily, we have no time—"

"If you and Nancy are intending to risk your lives, then I can do no less. I will go back to the castle with you."

"You cannot."

"Why not? We will be married. Granbury cannot make me his wife, so I am safe enough from that threat, at least."

"Have you forgotten that he tried to—"

"I haven't forgotten. You can stay with me at night. During the day I will be a fiancée beyond reproach, and there will be no need for him to show his ugly side."

"I'm not sure 'e needs a reason, my lady. 'E seems to like 'urting pretty things." Nancy's voice was low, and Emily heard her grief for her sister clearly in the husky vibrations.

"I can't agree to these terms, Emily."

"Then I can't agree to marry you." Emily turned her horse around and Valentine let out a hoarse cry and grabbed at the horse's reins.

Twelve

"Emily!" He held on to her reins and leaned in so that she could clearly see the dismay in his face. "This is madness."

"You know as well as I that you are only marrying me so that Granbury cannot! And now you want me to hide like a frightened child while you take care of the man."

"I cannot put you in danger."

"And why not? You will allow Nancy to help—to risk her life. But I cannot? I am tired to death of being treated like a pretty package that must be petted and primped, sold to the highest bidder, or gather dust upon a shelf. I will bring him down myself, if you cannot help."

"I am sorry, I do not mean to treat you—"

"Of course you do . . ." Emily bit off her tirade. It would do no good now to point out to him that he treated her just as brainlessly as her mother had. Did he not think her capable of living a life without luxury? "We have little time, as you have so often reminded me tonight. Do we marry and return? Or do we return unmarried?"

"Emily—"

"That is your choice. Make it." Her voice was cold and betrayed none of the sick shaking fear inside her that he would rather not marry her if he could not then hide her away.

"We marry." He was angry, and his tone was curt.

But Emily's heart was beating faster with relief and she barely heard the choked anger in his voice. She leaned forward, to look into his face. "Promise me."

"What!"

"Promise me. I know you will keep your word if you give it."

"I promise." He ground the words out. "I will allow you to put your own life in danger in a reckless desire to help where none is needed."

She ignored his uncharitable addition to the promise. If it soothed his pride, she could be gracious. "And then we shall—all of us—bring Granbury to justice."

"That we will, I 'ope." Apparently Nancy was none too sure that it would work, either, from the dubious tone of her reply. But she settled to her fate rather easily, as she changed the subject with something approaching cheer. "Then a wedding it is, I suppose. Where are we going?"

Valentine did not reply. Emily realized with a sinking heart that he had no ready answer.

Nancy clucked her tongue. "I know a man who'll do the job. You've coin, 'aven't you? You didn't forget coin, I hope."

Valentine answered, his tone stiff, "I have plenty of coin."

Nancy nodded fiercely against Emily's back. "Good. Won't take long, now, and you'll be wed right and tight. Then we'll see what the marquess 'as to say about that, won't we?"

The ceremony was lit by a single candle. It was enough, however. She did not want to see his face clearly. Did not want to see his doubt. Her own doubts were making her heart knock against her ribs. She closed her eyes and reminded herself she loved him.

For years she had dreamed of this moment, but not once had she dreamed it as it occurred in reality. Cold, dark, furtive. The scrape of their boots, the rustle of rats disturbed before dawn by strangers too impatient or foolish to wed in daylight.

Their vows were whispered, so as not to wake the patrons of the establishment who snored, heads down on the rough tables of the inn. He had a ring. She could not see it in the dark, but she knew, somehow, that it was the same ring he had purchased for their elopement so long ago.

Tears blinded her as he fumbled it onto her finger in the dark. He had kept it—and not locked in a safe to give to another wife, but upon his person. What did that say about his belief that they would one day be together?

Even as she puzzled out the meaning of the ring, he took her hand. "It's done then." He did not even kiss her. Instead, his arm came round her shoulder and he hurried her away, a whisper in her ear—"We have little time before dawn. We must hurry."

Before the break of day, they arrived within sight of the castle. Valentine, who had said nothing as they hurried back, stopped the horses and took the lead of hers, to muffle their return. He looked up into her face.

For one moment, she hoped he would say that he loved her. Instead, he said, "I would rather send you away, Emily. But I will not if you still insist on this foolish need to prove yourself more than an ornament by risking your own life in this enterprise."

"Is my life so much less valuable than yours, then?" she challenged him.

He didn't answer, so she said, "There is no time to waste. Let's go." She didn't know whether she had won a victory or suffered a defeat when he said nothing more, but turned to lead the horses back to her long-hated prison.

Once they reached the castle, Nancy checked to make sure that none of the servants had yet begun their morning chores, and then motioned for them to hurry into the house. Emily gave Valentine's hand a quick squeeze and he went off to his footman's cot, even though they were now husband and wife, at long last. He would spend the nights with her, now, yes, but since it was nearly daybreak, they had decided it would be wiser to prevent any risk of discovery so soon.

Her insides churned tightly and she could barely breathe at the thought that he was her husband as she hurried with Nancy up the back stairs. She and Valentine were married at last.

True, the ceremony had been rough and hasty in the darkened inn, but they were married all the same. And now, if only Nancy could sneak her back into her room undiscovered, and the two of them could convince the marquess that he had been hit on the head by accident—

Her joy at having finally married Valentine was quenched at once, however, by the thought that she and Nancy now must deal with the marquess. They had devised a plan to blame the candlestick blow on Nancy's overeager desire to protect her mistress. Granbury's back had been to Valentine, he should not question their story.

But even if he didn't question it, he was still likely to be angry. She hoped Nancy would not be let go for her part in their hastily laid plans, but she and Valentine both had promised the girl a better job at Anderlin if the marquess demanded that the countess dismiss her.

She could not help a smile, no matter how dire her current predicament. She was now a viscountess and the mistress of Anderlin. It was all she had ever wanted. But would it all disappear in the morning mist?

"Off with your dress, my lady. The 'ouse will be stirring soon," Nancy whispered. Within minutes, she was undressed and in bed.

"I'll set out your clothes for tomorrow and then just sit in the corner quiet-like while you sleep," the maid whispered.

Emily nodded. She and Nancy had decided that it would be easier for the maid to pretend she had been attending to her mistress rather than trying to sneak back into her bed at this dangerous hour of the morning.

It helped that no one had thought to lock her door in the time she was away. Obviously, everyone thought she was well watched over by the marquess. She could only thank the stars that Valentine had been there to help. None of the servants would have come to her aid, if she had managed to scream.

The thought was frightening, and she fought a sick twisting of her stomach as it preyed upon her mind. Had she been a fool to insist on coming back with Valentine and Nancy?

Granbury did not have a motive to hurt either of them, as he considered them mere servants. She, however, seemed to be a special target of his. And it was because of her that he was now nursing a painful bruise on his head.

But, in all honesty, though she was afraid, she also knew that Granbury's desire for her would help them bait the trap that might bring him to justice. She needed only to avoid being alone with him for a few days more and then there would be nothing at all for anyone to fear. She was suddenly very glad that Nancy had decided to stay in the room with her.

Was she really expected to sleep? How? She looked around at her familiar room and tried to imagine it as it had been last night when Francis had been threatening her and she had thought herself on the verge of being murdered—or worse. But all she could think of was Valentine, lying in the bed next to her as her mother lectured her and the marquess stared.

A warm feeling began in the pit of her stomach at the thought of Valentine lying next to her. Miranda and Simon shared a room, a bed. Emily's mother had been scandalized to learn of it. She would never have tolerated not having her own spacious bedchamber, as befitted a countess.

Would Valentine, like Simon, want his wife with him through the night? She hoped so. She could have him in bed beside her every night soon. The thought was both frightening and exhilarating. Thinking of it, she fell asleep before she even realized that she was exhausted.

Nancy shook her awake, saying, "Lady Emily, your mother 'as requested your presence in the parlor." The girl's eyes were wide with fear, and her hands shook so badly that it took forever to get dressed and downstairs. Her mother, unfortunately, was not alone.

"I trust you rested well, my dear," the marquess said. There was no evidence at all to show that he had been knocked unconscious.

Emily looked nervously at her mother as she answered the marquess. "Very well, thank you, after you left, my lord."

Her mother sniffed. "I'm glad to hear it. I was beginning to think your mind had turned to thistledown. I suppose last night has convinced you, now, that you will not be breaking this engagement off."

Emily, confused and yet relieved that her mother

seemed not to know what had happened last night, nodded. Apparently Granbury was, as she had hoped, too proud to admit that he had been bested.

"I've spent the night hours thinking things over, Mother. I am not proud of my behavior." The words burned her throat, but she and Valentine had agreed that she would pretend to have accepted the engagement.

It would be difficult, but she intended to do her utmost to convince both her mother and Francis. "Yes. I am sorry for the trouble I've caused you both. I know you don't like the term star-crossed, Mother, so I will put it out of my head, I promise. And I will be a dutiful bride in two weeks' time."

Granbury said softly, in a voice that made her quake with fear, "I thought we would move the ceremony up. I have sent my man for a special license."

"Oh." Emily frowned, pretending to be taken aback at the news. She turned to her mother and willed herself to be convincing. "But what about all the guests who were to come? What shall we tell them?"

Her mother's smile shriveled to a moue of displeasure. "I suppose I should notify them at once."

"Yes," Emily pretended to agree. "You know how Aunt Emmaline is when her travel plans are interrupted. She does get so unhappy. If you send a message quickly, I'm certain she will not yet have begun to pack." This was patently untrue, as Aunt Emmaline had probably been packed for the last month.

Emily knew her mother would hate to think of having to cancel her daughter's wedding and, worse, having to hear about it in every tedious letter from Aunt Emmaline—who had not only two daughters, but a son and heir for her husband, even though he was only a viscount.

"Francis," her mother said, having taken a remarkably short time to break down, "perhaps it would be best if we keep to the original date, now that Emily has seen the error of her ways and understands the benefits of marriage to you."

The marquess did not look pleased. Emily wondered if he would tell her mother then and there what had transpired last night. It was probably the only thing that could convince the countess to notify all her guests and relatives of the change in wedding plans.

He frowned at Emily, as if he understood that she was maneuvering her mother. "I was looking forward to my wedding trip." His look did not make her feel the same anticipation.

Suppressing a shudder, she said, "We will still make the trip, my lord. And we will not have our friends and family piqued by our thoughtlessness." Thank goodness that she and Valentine had put a stop to any possibility of marriage to this man with their own hasty elopement.

"Of course," her mother prepared to wheedle and Emily crossed her fingers. To her joy, it took only twenty minutes before the marquess, tight-lipped with displeasure, agreed.

At every moment she expected him to expose what had happened last night in order to win a hasty ceremony. He did not. For some reason, he did not want to tell her mother that she had hit him over the head and abandoned him in the library with a bottle of brandy.

Her relief did not last very long, however, as he turned toward her and smiled, saying, "Our walk yesterday was interrupted, Emily. Why don't we walk again today? It is a lovely day."

"Yes, do," the countess echoed.

Emily was trapped. She could see that Granbury did not have a quiet, pleasant walk in mind, but she could not refuse without giving her mother a reason to think that she was still harboring hopes of breaking off the engagement.

To buoy her courage, she reminded herself of what her successful charade would accomplish: the downfall of the marquess and his murderous ways. What she need do was simple enough. The consequences if she did not convince him she had had a change of heart were obvious. Her mother's willingness to keep the wedding plans on course would evaporate, Aunt Emmaline's gloating or no.

She did not know whether to laugh or cry when Valentine was assigned as the footman to accompany them into the garden. She did her best not to show by expression or sound that he was anything more than a footman to her.

It was torture to keep from glancing at him. Torture to smile at Granbury. She had never done anything so difficult in her life as all this pretense. She would be glad when she could be done with pretending and take up her new life as viscountess and mistress of Anderlin.

As they began to walk, with Valentine close upon their heels, Emily said loudly, "I am grateful to you, my lord, for allowing the wedding plans to proceed as originally scheduled. I promise you I do not intend to try to break the engagement any longer." Not now that she was married.

"Then why did you insist that we wait for the scheduled date? Surely if you are eager to be my bride—"

She had the perfect answer for that, though, thanks to watching her mother plan and scheme through three different wedding preparations. "I am a woman. I wish for everything to be perfect on the day I wed."

"And what is more perfection than having the two people there who are marrying? What need is there of cakes and gifts and guests?"

"Friends and family to bless the union, of course. A wedding is a milestone of great importance. Should it truly pass without heralding or celebration?" Emily knew that her words held conviction.

The marquess heard the certainty in her voice, and his eyebrows rose as she continued, "Perhaps I want no gossip. You have convinced me that there are unexpected dangers in skirting scandal."

It was dangerous to remind him of last night, even obliquely. But he was not a stupid man. He must intend to use the incident to gain some hold over her. Perhaps her bold statement would draw him out.

"There are advantages to avoiding scandal, I must admit." Slowly he brought his hand up to rub absently at the place where Valentine must have hit him with the candlestick. "I do not object to your wish to have our wedding without a hint of gossip for hastily altered plans."

"My thoughts exactly, my lord." She thought sadly of how she and Valentine had wed—secretly, quietly, in the dark of night with only Nancy and an unknown man to bind them. How much better to have done so openly, with their friends and family to wish them well.

As if he could read her thoughts, he said softly, "As I recall, you were not so eager for a proper wedding with Valentine Fenster."

Emily pressed her lips together to keep in her exclamation of annoyance. Why had her mother confirmed the rumor for the marquess? Surely it did not make her more marriageable, but less . . . didn't it? "I was a girl then, swept away by a romantic notion. I am older now. I have seen my chance to go to the altar come to nothing twice now."

"I see. So you understand your options are to marry me or be a spinster for the rest of your life."

Emily slowly and deliberately rubbed her neck, imagining the weight of a hangman's rope around it. "I understand that marriage to you means a chance for children, a return to society life, and a break with my mother. As you might guess, I am eager to be my own mistress." She added with heat, "And to have my bedroom door unlocked—" She looked directly at him as she said, "—unless I choose to lock it myself."

"But you would never lock it against me." He sounded quite sure of himself.

"Not after we are properly married." She held her breath. Would he accept her condition? It would be so much easier if she did not have to worry that she would find him at her door in the middle of the night. Valentine would kill him, then. But the consequences of that action might see him hanged. That was what she was fighting to prevent.

"I agree. As long as you do not give me cause to change my mind."

"Of course I will not, my lord." There was no need to argue; the point was settled, even if he was not yet aware of it. Knowing that her words had a meaning the marquess could not guess at, she smiled sincerely and said, "I shall do my best to please my husband in all ways at all times."

Out of the corner of her eye she saw Valentine startle. Fortunately, Granbury was turned away from him and did not see the movement. It was only with the utmost self-control that she managed not to turn her gaze to the footman.

Granbury took her hand and said, "I will hold you to that promise, my dear." His thumb pressed into the soft flesh of her wrist until she wanted to cry out in pain.

Acutely aware of Valentine standing close by, she merely winced and shook her hand free. "I always keep my promises, you can be assured of that."

"Then we should rub along quite well together, after we are married." There was a gleam in his eye that she did not like to see.

Briefly, she regretted not fleeing to London. But then she remembered the poor women he had murdered and knew that she had made the right decision.

Thirteen

He came to her that night, as he had promised. Nancy let him in and then locked them in together— alone. But not before she whispered saucily, "I don't expect to be 'earing from you two until morning."

For a moment Emily was shocked, and then she realized that, as far as Nancy was concerned, they were married and there was nothing wrong with a man and his wife spending the night together without a chaperon.

It was a heady realization.

But Valentine's expression contained concern, not desire. Before she could say anything, he asked curtly, "How badly did he hurt you?"

She blinked and hesitated, not understanding his question at first. And then she remembered he had been in the garden when Granbury grabbed her wrist. She waved her hand in dismissal, and shook her head to reassure him. "Not too—"

Impatiently, he cut her off. "I saw you wince, Emily."

"He startled me, that's all."

He sighed as he put out his palm. "Let me see."

She put her fingers against the warmth of his palm reluctantly. He grasped her hand gently and brought her wrist to the light. Her sleeve slipped away, revealing the purple thumbprint, dark against the pale skin.

His tone was grim. "I should have killed him last night."

All the consequences of such an importunate action rushed through her thoughts—ending at last with the image of Valentine, a noose around his neck. "Don't say that! He is the murderer, not you."

"He marked you." Valentine pulled her into his arms, resting his cheek atop her head. It felt so right to be held by him this way, she wished they could stand so forever. "He deliberately put his mark on you. And I, yet again, could not protect you."

Emily had been so relieved in the garden, when the "footman" had not intervened, that she had not realized how hard it must have been for him to see her hurt and not come to her rescue. To reassure him, she repeated the truth, "You have given me the best protection I could ever have against Granbury."

His arms tightened around her. "The best protection I could offer you would be to see him hanged."

She said solemnly, as she stretched up to kiss him lightly on the chin, "And we will do that. But until then, you offered me the protection of your name." Carried away by a wave of daring, she kissed his chin again and then looked into his eyes, pleased to see that she had sparked an ember of desire to life. "You married me so that he cannot."

Emily's lips moved to his mouth, and Valentine forced himself to step away so that her gesture was just a light brush of warmth. He fought the urge to kiss her properly, so that she would not know how much he wanted her. He had not meant to hold her, to— She was his wife, but when the danger from Granbury was gone would she regret it?

"Why do you pull away?" Her breath was soft on his cheek. "I can see that you want to kiss me. And we are married, now, after all."

He opened his mouth, but in the end made no sound, for he had no answer for her. Yes, they were married. He had put his ring on her finger in the darkness of the ramshackle inn. He had said his vows in a voice kept low and discreet. But there was still a doubt in him.

He had decided that the right thing to do, the noble thing, would be to give her the choice once Granbury was no longer a threat: marriage and a straitened lifestyle, or a return to her family and her familiar luxuries. Without a looming threat, she could make such a decision wisely. And he could be sure that her choice was made with both head and heart, rather than heart alone.

However, he knew himself too well to imagine that he could act as her husband here and then give her such a choice. Once he had taken her to bed he would not ever be able to let her go.

Still, she could sense he wanted her, though she had no idea exactly what it was that he wanted from her but kisses. And he wanted to kiss her very badly indeed. That was the crux of the problem. He wanted more than a kiss. He wanted to make her his in every way. But a secret, dark-shrouded sham of a ceremony did not give him the right to take what he had essentially stolen from her.

There was hurt in her eyes as she filled the silence with a simple question. "Do you wish you had not been forced to marry me?"

He could see quite clearly that she wanted reassurances from him—reassurances to quell her own doubts. And he could not bring himself to hurt her with the truth. So he could only offer cautious hope. "In the end, I hope we are both not sorry for having had to go so far." It would not be a life worth living if Emily were unhappy at Anderlin.

He watched as disappointment turned her mouth downward, but she did not cry, and in a moment her lips tightened into a firm line and she said bravely, "I will not be."

He wanted so much to believe her, but he dared not. "You are not in a position to know how you will feel after your mother stops trying to push you at Granbury, Emily. At the moment, I must seem the answer to your prayers, trapped here as you were, about to be forced into a marriage you did not want."

She smiled as she said, "Don't you think it was fateful that I literally dropped into your arms just as I was about to run away?"

The image made him want to return her smile, but he forced himself to be stern. "I am not one of Miranda's fairy-tale princes come to sweep you off to happily ever after."

She sniffed in annoyance. "I don't need your sister's fairy tales to tell me what you are, Valentine." She smiled at him, a question in her eyes. "Do you think I don't know I love you?"

The question was simple enough, but for a moment he felt as if he couldn't breathe. She loved him. The truth was there in her eyes. "Love can wither away easily enough, Emily."

"Mine has not." Her annoyance was all too obvious in the set of her jaw. "I have loved you since you told Edmund Burke that my feet were too delicate for his dance step and swept me away from him. No fairy-tale prince could have been so bold, but my toes and I will be forever grateful to you for that."

He sighed. Had he ever been so young and feckless? "Be sensible. We haven't seen each other in three years. I tried to elope with you—a young impressionable girl . . . an heiress."

She laughed, as if the scenario he painted were preposterous. "You asked my father, first. We tried all honorable persuasions before we eloped, didn't we?"

He had to fight his own impulses to simply give in to her arguments. "Emily, if you want to be completely honest about our situation, we are no better than strangers."

At that, she looked as if he had struck her squarely in the gut with his fist. For a moment she seemed unable to breathe. And then she said steadily, "Never. You will never be a stranger to me, Valentine."

"Perhaps." There was such conviction in her

voice, he could not but believe what she said. Only the thought of ultimately hurting her kept him from taking her into his arms then and there. So she thought she knew him, and perhaps he would find she did. But what if she did not?

Worse, would he one day find her indifferent to him? Angry that he had not truly prepared her for what it would be like to be the wife of an impoverished viscount?

Oddly enough he had no concern that she would become a jaded society wife alleviating her boredom with a series of meaningless affairs. That was not Emily's way and he did not imagine that even marriage and a difficult life with him would ever drive her to such disloyalty. But could life with him drive her to become a pinch-mouthed society matron?

He looked at her sweet lips, curved upward in a half smile as she watched him deliberate. What kind of life would turn that smile into a permanent frown? The only kind he could offer her? He would never do anything to bring her to that fate. Not if he could help it.

"Do you think of me as a stranger?" Her voice was faint and he could hear her sudden doubts.

He considered dissembling, but she watched him so closely he felt certain she would not accept any answer but the truth. "No, I never could."

"Then why will you not kiss me? Why must you stand apart from me when we are properly wed and there is no law to keep us apart?"

"Darkness and stealth are not the way you should be won." He shook his head. "If we are truly to marry, I want to do it properly—with a courtship, and with you given a fair chance to see what life would be like for you as my viscountess before you must commit to a life with me."

She smiled, as if he had made a jest. "There is no help for that now."

He refused to accept that he had condemned her to an impoverished future without recourse. "I think there might be. Even though we did marry, if a ceremony in the middle of the night by the light of a paltry candle can be called a wedding, we have told no one."

He watched her carefully as he spoke. "Since the marriage is a secret—only Nan knows, and she is loyal to us, I am sure of it—we are not obligated to honor it when we return to London."

"What do you mean?" Emily's expression was both stunned and bruised, as if she had unexpectedly fallen down a flight of stairs.

Hoping to somehow ease her hurt with a logical explanation, he continued, "No one ever need know that we were married, if we are not forced to tell them because your marriage to Granbury cannot be foiled otherwise."

"I see," she said slowly. "You are hoping that we will escape this predicament without actually proclaiming our marriage?"

The expression on her face convinced him that she still held to her romantic notions of love conquering all, including the scarcity of funds. "Exactly," Valentine said, with just a hint of a crease in his brow. He, however, had seen what impoverishment had done to his parents' once affectionate relationship. He would never cause Emily such unhappiness if he could avoid it.

"How?" Emily hoped that he could not see how his careful words devastated her, but feared she had failed when he reached out to touch her. Before his hand reached her face though, he froze. Emily could feel the warmth of his fingers where they nearly touched her cheek.

"I cannot wait for Simon's help any longer. I will provoke Granbury to either leave or expose his guilt."

She turned her head and felt the light brush of his fingertips against her skin as she asked, "What will you do?"

"Blackmail."

"Blackmail?" The thought made her nervous. Blackmailing Granbury would be as dangerous as baiting a wounded bull.

"Seems fitting, considering the man, doesn't it? I will ensure he receives anonymous notes detailing his crimes and threatening to expose them if he does not go abroad immediately and never return to England."

"And if he does not?"

"Then I will find a way to expose him for what he is before the countess's guests." His voice was assured and strong, but she knew he was as aware of the risks he took as she was.

"Very well. But you must remain here with me still, for the nights." And during those hours snatched from fate's hand, she must find a way to change his mind, to convince him to share her bed.

They were meant to be together, and now that they were so close, she was not willing to throw it away because he had some foolish masculine pride about being forced into marriage by circumstance. She didn't need him to court her again, he had won her three years ago—and her heart was still his.

"That doesn't seem wise." She was encouraged by the way his fingers lingered a moment before he snatched his hand away.

"No?" Did he not want to stay with her, or did he not trust himself with her? How could she tell the difference?

"Certainly not. If we were discovered—"

His answer was frustrating in its ambiguity. And then she realized she had the perfect argument to get him to stay, no matter his reasons for being reluctant. "Can you not understand? I am not asking for your company as a blushing bride, but as a woman who fears for her life. He will suspect *me* of sending the notes at first."

He must have sensed the bitterness she tried to hide, because he moved to interrupt her, but she overrode him before he could say a word. "I am asking you to stay with me to protect me should Granbury once again decide he must invade my bedchamber to question me about the blackmail."

Again, he tried to speak. "I—"

Again, she overrode him. She did not want him to offer any argument, good or bad. She was simply determined that he do as she asked. "You can sleep on the floor—perhaps even under the bed, if you wish, since you are so familiar with the area. If he dares to . . ." She could not bring herself to say the words that described what she most feared would happen.

"Of course." As she had suspected, that argument convinced him. His whole attitude changed, and his glance swept the door with a challenging look, as if he'd welcome the marquess to come through it and meet his fate.

It was somewhat comforting to know that she could count on him to protect her from danger. But what would protect her heart from his rejection if she found that he truly did not wish to have her as wife? That she had misread some other, milder emotion in his eye as desire for her?

One question remained—the question which would determine whether she dared try to make Valentine her husband in truth. "And if we do need to declare the marriage? What then? It will be real, as it will have been announced before all your family, as well as all of my mother's guests."

She watched his face avidly as he struggled to compose an answer to her question. At last, resolutely, he said, "Then I will make you a good husband. But it will not happen. I—" he broke off, staring at her.

She did not look at him. She knew why he had stopped speaking. She had begun to remove her robe.

"What are you doing?" His surprise sounded strong, but there was less assurance in the shaky breath he released after his question.

She buried her hands in the folds of her night-gown to hide the fact that they were trembling. "I am going to sleep of course. It would not do to be bleary-eyed tomorrow morning. My mother will ask too many questions." With a turn of the knob, she put out the lamp beside her bed and climbed up into the bed.

A lengthy silence indicated that he was taken aback at her answer for a moment and then he collected himself with a sigh. "Of course."

She moved carefully as she settled herself under the covers, mindful not to upset her collection of dolls covering the other half—the half that Valentine might soon lie upon, if she had her way.

The pale porcelain faces were light, round smudges in the darkness. The girls had been her friends and confidantes—silent, but good listeners—throughout her childhood and since she had been locked away in the castle. "What will he do, girls?" she asked them silently.

As usual, they offered no answer. Oddly enough, however, the weight of them, the light patches of their smooth faces in the dark, seemed disapproving. As if they knew she should be doing something more. But what was she to do if Valentine would not even come near her?

She sighed and settled into the bedcovers, tossing and turning for a bit to find a comfortable spot close to the edge, where she could gaze toward where she imagined he still stood. Would he come to her now, or would he choose the unwelcoming floor over his own wife?

He did not move for several minutes, and then the shadowed darkness shifted a bit, and she heard the creak of his boots as he said again, "Of course."

She held her breath and her heart pounded in her chest as he moved toward the bed. "I think I'll sleep on the floor, but not under the bed."

The threat of tears was so great that she could not reply for fear he would hear how they choked her voice.

After a pause, he sighed. "Things will work out as they should, Emily. If we are truly meant to be together, we will be. Once Granbury is dealt with."

She feigned a sleepy tone, not wanting him to hear her disappointment as she listened to the creak of the floorboards as he settled somewhere in the darkness. Away from her. "As you wish."

Fourteen

Emily glanced quickly out the door. "There is no one in the hallway."

He gave her a brief, hard hug, wishing it could be more. Three days of sleeping on the floor of her room while she was only feet away and obviously willing to be his wife was taking its toll on him.

The tension, waiting for Granbury to acknowledge the blackmail, to corner her with accusations was taking its toll on her, as well. He could see it in her face, hear it in her voice when she lay in her bed at night and talked with him softly until she fell asleep.

She felt small and fragile in his arms and, as he did each morning, he wished he did not have to leave her. If only Granbury could be brought down once and for all—but the plan required all its pieces in place. The three notes he had delivered had provoked no reaction yet. Surely Granbury could not ignore them, not when they were so obviously damning. Any day now he would show his hand.

Still, the waiting and planning tried his patience to the limits. To leave Emily here alone while he continued the pretense of footman felt as if he were leaving a defenseless lamb tied up before a hungry wolf.

He said, more to placate himself than her, "You should be safe enough, but between Nan and I, we will keep an eye on you, just to make certain that Granbury does not decide you should join the others who dared to cross him."

Emily stopped him with a hand upon his arm. "Do you think we can trust Nancy?"

He had been wondering the same thing. The girl had given no sign of disloyalty, but as the days progressed with them no closer to their goal, he found himself questioning everything. "She has not let us down yet."

Which was beyond doubt true. She let him into Emily's room each night, and unlocked the room for him again in the morning. However, it was one thing to expect her to keep a little romantic subterfuge quiet. Blackmail, no matter the reason, was a crime. Granbury's downfall was all Valentine cared about. Nancy might want to save her own neck, and he could not bring himself to blame her if she did.

"I had complete faith in Mary, as well, only to find that she had betrayed us."

He thought of her here, worrying, locked in her room and unable to do anything to help, and knew he must reassure her. He stepped back inside the doorway, closing the door so that they would not be discovered there. "Nan is not a silly young girl like Mary. I doubt the countess could easily sway her to betray us with gold. I cannot imagine her falling under the marquess's influence after what he did to her sister. She has a true understanding of his nature."

"Better than we do, perhaps." Emily then grew silent, thinking of what it must feel like to lose a sister to a murderer and see him prosper as if he had done nothing more than dispatch a lame horse.

Valentine thought of his own sisters. If Granbury had harmed one of them, would he be swayed away from vengeance with gold? He shook his head. "If he killed her sister, I don't think we can doubt her allegiance to the cause of bringing him to justice."

"How can we be certain that she is telling the truth? That Granbury really did kill her sister? After all, you showed her the letter yourself. She could have made that up simply to keep our trust."

True enough. But such thinking was a trap of uncertainty that he was not willing to fall into at this late date. "Is there anything at all that one can be absolutely certain of, Emily?"

He had meant the question casually, to end the conversation, but Emily took it as a challenge. Pressing her entire soft, curved length against him, she put her hands to his cheeks, so that he looked full into her eyes. "You can be absolutely certain of me, Valentine. I will never desert you. I will never betray you. And I will never stop loving you."

Looking into the clear certainty of her expression, he felt humbled by her trust and faith in him. "I can't say I deserve such loyalty, Emily. But I cherish it. And I promise you that I will not let you down." But did his promises mean anything anymore?

Had he not promised Simon that he would never disgrace the family by attempting once again to elope with Emily? And, yet, he had.

Now, he had promised himself that he would not sleep with her, married or not. With her tight against him like this, though, that promise seemed insubstantial. The need to put his arms around her, to kiss the lips that were so very close to his own right now . . .

These last nights had put that promise to the test until he thought he might go mad. Listening to Emily's soft disembodied voice in the velvet darkness of night as they talked of their plans, their future, their past. And—after she had fallen asleep—hearing her even breathing, lying upon the uncomfortable floor wishing he could sweep those dolls aside and—

Emily tapped his chin with her fingertip. "I will see you tonight, then? And perhaps you'll agree to share the bed with me."

Stubbornly, she asked him this each night. He was beginning to suspect she knew exactly how close she was coming to eroding his ability to refuse her. "Emily—" He pulled away from her embrace. "It would not be wise."

She smiled sadly. "I only mean for you to pass a comfortable night in sleep. I understand that I have no hope of anything else from you, for now." She reached up and touched his cheek.

Feeling like a craven coward, he slipped through the door and locked it behind him. He was not his usual cautious self; his head still buzzed with the thought of what promises he might have broken if he had spent one more second with her looking at him as she had.

Thankfully, he made it down to the servants' quarters without notice, due to a small disturbance Nan caused just as he walked into the kitchens and stumbled over a basket of potatoes.

He managed to whisper to her, "Thank you for the distraction. I am clumsy this morning."

She replied, as tartly as she could with her voice barely audible, "The floor is no place for you to get the rest you need to protect your wife. It's no wonder you stumbled. My lady's bed is big enough for the both of you."

It was humiliating to realize that she had come into the room and seen him there, asleep. He had thought he was waking in time to avoid discovery, but apparently he was not. Still, it was none of her business.

He would have answered her just as sharply, as soon as his ears stopped burning, if only he had not noticed the housekeeper's eye upon them. So instead of a scolding, he dropped a saucy kiss upon Nan's cheek and received a resounding slap—she did not soften it in the least—for his trouble.

The housekeeper's smile of malicious glee was thanks enough, and he quickly hurried off to perform his duties in the hopes that neither the housekeeper, nor anyone else in the kitchens, would carry the tale of the friendship between the footman and Emily's maid any further.

It was late afternoon when disaster struck. Several

carriages laden with early wedding guests suddenly appeared. Apparently, there had been no advance warning of the party's arrival, and Soames was nearly apoplectic when he found a footman with a button loose as he lined them up by the door. A straight pin fixed the oversight temporarily, but did not appease Soames at all.

The butler's glower, however, was no match for the housekeeper's. Valentine felt sorry for Nan, who was dragooned into helping to prepare for the guests, even though her duties normally would not have encompassed any needs but Emily's. He was uncomfortable at leaving Emily so vulnerable, until he realized that the marquess had retreated from the chaos into the library—alone.

The staff set a frenzied pace making rooms ready, preparing to unpack the luggage from the coaches as quickly as possible, and seeing to last-minute details of preparing a house for guests. Valentine chanced to be in the front hall when the party made their way into the castle.

Craning his neck to see past the cluster of people in the hallway, he looked to see if he recognized the crests upon the coach. He could not see, but as he tried, a woman's laughter rang in the normally sedate halls of the castle.

He froze at the sound of his sister's distinctive laugh.

They were here! Why had the servants not been told the guests were the duke and duchess of Kerstone? He had been sure that an arriving guest of Simon's stature would be information imparted to those servants who were to uphold the countess's reputation as an impeccable hostess.

A quick glance around told him that he could not escape. Soames's eagle eye would spot him and he would be called back, bringing more attention to him rather than less. Why he was surprised at the turn of events was the true question. Nothing had gone as he planned since the day he received proof of Granbury's true nature.

He had meant to make sure he was nowhere within sight when his sister and her husband arrived. A toothache, a headache, anything that would keep him belowstairs until he had alerted them to his presence—and his disguise. If Miranda saw him here— like this—could he trust that she would not expose him in shock or dismay? She was not the best at hiding her feelings, after all.

There was no place for him to hide. Pleading a headache at this point would arouse Soames's suspicions without doubt. What other option was there? He supposed he could hope that the duke and duchess of Kerstone were as blind to the faces of servants as the countess and Granbury, but he dared not count on it. Miranda was an observant woman, and didn't always keep the strict bounds between employer-servant that most of Society did.

If she saw him, could he trust her to keep her shock to herself? Should he forestall her by going directly up to them and giving her some sign to behave as if she didn't see him? It seemed a strategy with a huge potential to misfire.

Even as he thought it through, struggling to find

the right action to ward off disaster, Soames snapped his fingers. The butler frowned at his delayed reaction to the snap and pointed with a stern finger, indicating that Valentine was to take the bags which were stacked directly next to where his sister and her husband stood being warmly, if insincerely, welcomed by the countess.

Maneuvering so that his back was to the couple even while he wondered just how long it would take his twin to recognize him, disguise or not, he reached for the top valise—one he recognized all too well. He hoped the maid had packed it, not Miranda in her usual last-minute frenzy to add all the items which she had suddenly decided she could not do without.

He had just had the thought that if Miranda had packed her own bag, she had thankfully managed to securely fasten this bulging case—as was not her habit—when the case latch lost its tenuous hold on its burden and popped open.

Clothing and notions packed away at the last minute launched into the air. Naturally, all eyes turned Valentine's way. He saw Miranda's eyes widen just as a fall of silken cloth landed on his head, blinding him to the sudden, furious chaos which took reign as the countess gasped in outrage and Soames barked out a series of orders meant to bring events back to normal as swiftly as possible.

Whipping away his silken blindfold, Valentine saw that, as various and sundry other footmen rushed to retrieve scattered belongings, Simon had Miranda in a tight grip and was whispering fiercely in her ear.

The countess appeared puzzled at her guests' agitation, but not suspicious that it was caused by the footman covered in women's clothing rather than the clothing itself. Valentine turned away and joined the other servants in clearing up the mess. He hoped that would give Simon time to calm Miranda.

Sure that the duke had seen the situation for what it was, he dared relax. Miranda would not do anything overt now—such as call out his true name, or ask the countess why her brother was in her household in a footman's uniform.

It did not take long for order to be restored. Under the strict eye of both the butler and the housekeeper, the stray clothing was gathered, folded, repacked—more neatly than Miranda and her maid had managed the first time. At last, all was secured in a trunk, and the lock was checked four times in an excess of care. No one wanted the incident to be repeated on the trip up to the rooms the duke and duchess were to occupy.

Valentine, hoping to avoid his sister's inevitable questions, lifted the trunk onto his shoulder and moved toward the stairs. He would have to explain this carefully, and it would be better to do so to Simon first. Miranda was simply too quick to leap to conclusions and come up with plans that made things worse instead of better.

His spirits sank, though, when he heard Miranda's clear voice saying that she simply must freshen up before she could enjoy the countess's generous refreshments. He had some hope when he heard Simon's low-voiced reply, but the patter of half boots on the stairs behind him were too clearly Miranda's for him to believe that Simon had dissuaded his wife from finding the answers to the questions that were undoubtedly bubbling up in her mind.

He had scarcely set down the trunk and turned to leave when Miranda called out imperiously, "Help me with this window, please, young man." He loved his sister, but he would much rather have talked to the duke than to Miranda. He knew what her counsel would be and he did not want to tell her that he had already eloped with Emily.

He loved his sister dearly. But she had funny ideas about love and fairy tales that ended with happily ever after. There was no telling what she would do with the news. And most certainly she would tell Simon and then he would know that Valentine had broken the promise he had made the duke three years ago.

Reluctantly, unwillingly, he went to stand next to her and examine the window—which was more than capable of opening smoothly as soon as Miranda's favorite pen was removed from the jamb.

He refrained from pointing this out, however, as his sister was staring at him with an expression that alternated between delighted and appalled. With an unholy light in her eyes, she said softly, "You make an admirable footman. I did not realize that your fortunes were so poor as to drive you to it, though." She seemed so light-hearted he wondered if she and Simon had ever received the letters he had sent them.

She answered that question before he had even

posed it aloud. "I take it the countess did not find your evidence compelling enough to halt the wedding preparations?" she asked quietly.

Valentine could not keep the scorn from his voice. "She knows the worst, and seems pleased by it. She has no love for Emily."

Ever the believer in fairy tales, Miranda sighed with typical sympathy. "Poor Emily."

"It's worse than a bad marriage, Miranda. I think her life might be in danger."

At that, his sister's eyes widened and she lost the half smile that indicated she was thinking of matters of the heart rather than the practical necessity of rescuing Emily. "Where is she?"

"She's been locked in her room."

"How inconvenient." She gazed at him curiously, "How ever did you manage to speak to her? Or have you seen her at all?"

"Yes. Her lady's maid is our ally." Seen and *married* her as well, but now was not the time to disclose that fact—not with the stream of servants still coming and going with final preparations for the room.

"Is that wise, considering . . ." She broke off, but he knew where her doubts were coming from. It was almost a relief to talk to her, though he had been dreading it. Since they were small children he and Miranda had shared an uncanny ability to know what the other thought and felt.

"Nan is not going to turn on us as Emily's former maid did. Her sister was killed by Granbury and she wants him to hang as badly as we do."

The shadow of doubt remained in her eyes. She

was worried about him, he could feel it. Normally, he could expect a lengthy interrogation from her, followed by a dose of her opinion on what he should do. He waited for her to begin, intending to cut her off. Instead of questioning him, however, she simply nodded and said, as she rattled the window, "Where is the letter? Simon will wish to see it for himself."

He reached into the breast pocket of his well-fitted jacket. "Here." He bent so that no one else in the room could see him hand the duchess of Kerstone a packet of paper. "I'm glad you have arrived. Emily needs looking after, and you can help with that duty while Simon and I put Granbury where he can hurt no one ever again."

The glint of humor returned to her eyes as she said with a little laugh, "Certainly we will be willing to help in any way we can—as long as you're not expecting us to dress up as servants, too?"

"Heaven forbid. Could you imagine the duke of Kerstone dressed as a stable hand?"

His sister, unaccountably, blushed. "Probably not in a way that would go unremarked." And then she frowned. "How is it that no one has noticed? The countess surely— Perhaps you should give up the disguise and go back to London, for safety's sake?"

He had no intention of leaving the castle. Not with Emily in reach of Granbury. "I have served the countess turbot, peas and wine. I have accompanied her into the garden and carried her packages. She has given me no more notice than she might a mote of dust. This disguise is safe enough."

"But now that we are here—"

"I must remain a footman in the household, Miranda," he said firmly. "It is the only way I can continue my blackmail of the marquess."

Fifteen

The commotion downstairs was apparent to Emily even locked in her room, as she was—at least until it was time to dine with her mother and Granbury and be tortured with questions and a pretense of being a willing fiancée. She pressed her ear to the door, and, when that was not satisfactory, opened her window and leaned out to listen. Evidently, guests had arrived. She could hear the sound of horses, carriage wheels on gravel, and luggage being unloaded.

Should she dare hope it would be Simon and Miranda, at last? She was torn between wishing it were so, and fearing that they had indeed arrived.

Simon would help them bring down Granbury, but would he approve of their elopement any more than he had done that day at the inn? As for Miranda . . . Miranda would know that she and Valentine belonged together. Miranda had always known.

A spark of hope lodged itself deep within her—if anyone would know what Emily might do to break through the stubborn, prideful refusal Valentine continued to show toward accepting that they were now married forever and ever, Miranda would know. At last there would be someone to ask about what to do when a husband insisted on sleeping on the cold hard floor rather than in the same bed with his wife.

Perhaps, with everything else that was happening, she should not care about such things. But to have him so close and yet so far away was an agony in itself. Like that day in the coach, when they were so near to eloping until Simon caught them. All her hopes, all her dreams, on the verge of reality.

And then Simon had appeared, a dash of cold water that melted away their chance to be happy. It hurt to know that could happen once more. She sighed. There was only one way to get either of the men to accept the inevitability of the marriage. Otherwise, Simon would talk of scandal and family pride—and promises to be honored. Valentine's pride would twist him up inside, until he thought it honorable to deny himself the wife he had—for her sake. If she didn't love him so much, his foolishness would make her scream aloud.

Oh, why couldn't he see it as clearly as she did? If she had to spend one more night beside him without knowing that he had at last accepted that she had married him for better or worse no matter that he was not wealthy, she did not know what she would do. And she was not a fool. The only way to convince the man—or the fastest, at the very least— was to convince him to make love to her, to make her his wife in such a way that not even *he* could question the commitment they had made to each other ever again.

To her surprise, Nancy unlocked her door in the middle of the day and left it ajar behind her. There was a nervous energy emanating from the maid as she put the key back into her pocket without relocking the door. "The duke and duchess of Kerstone 'ave arrived, my lady. And they are asking for you."

So it *was* Simon and Miranda, then. At last her banishment to Scotland was nearing its end. Emily eyed the open door warily. "Am I free now?"

The maid nodded. "There are guests in the 'ouse. The duchess 'as been asking to see you and your mother realized it would be awkward if she had to let 'er into your room with a key."

In a low voice, the maid added, "It should make things easier for a certain 'andsome footman, as well." Nancy flashed a smile and Emily suddenly realized that the girl was pretty in a quiet way. She had heard the rumors that Nancy and the newest footman were acting more friendly than was proper. Until now she had not considered the possibility—

She damped down the sudden jealous flare that rose within her. What a foolish thing to worry over when everything else was going wrong. Valentine *was* handsome. And he loved her. He just hadn't admitted it. He was certainly not paying attention to the maid—not after he had already been burdened with a wife he didn't even want.

Despite her newfound freedom, Emily chose to remain in her room for the time being. Hopes of being released from both her engagement to Granbury and the castle itself had her in a state of agitation she did not wish to have her mother observe. The last thing she needed now was for the countess to become any more suspicious than she already was.

As she had hoped, Miranda came calling soon after the door was unlocked. "My reprobate brother has not rescued you yet, I see," she said with a mock frown which broke into a smile as she swept into Emily's room.

Emily hugged her swiftly and fiercely. "He has tried, but I would not let him."

Miranda looked at her in astonishment. "Is he not good enough to elope with now, Emily?"

It was all she could do not to say that they had indeed eloped already. But that was not information to blurt out without explanation, and her mother's maid was due to arrive to do her hair at any moment. "I can't run away now. We must see that the marquess harms no more women. He needs justice, and I am the lure to draw him to it."

Miranda nodded in understanding, but smiled ruefully as she commented, "Somehow I can't imagine Valentine agreeing to such a thing."

"He did so reluctantly enough."

"I read the letter. I passed it on to Simon, but he has not yet had a moment to himself. Your mother is quite determined that he give his blessing to Granbury, the odious wretch."

"Who? The marquess or Simon?"

Miranda blinked, obviously not able to tell whether Emily meant her words as a joke or an indictment of

Simon. "Does that mean you have not yet forgiven him for halting your elopement?"

Emily relented. Now was not the time to take up old issues, especially not with her cousin's wife. "I know he meant only the best for me, but I wish every day that his horse had not thrown a shoe so near that particular inn on that very day."

Miranda answered pragmatically, "It wouldn't have mattered. Your maid had already alerted your father and you would have been caught."

"Perhaps not. Perhaps we might have got across the border before they—"

Miranda laughed. "And perhaps Snow White wouldn't have eaten the poison apple and needed the prince to kiss her and wake her up? And perhaps Cinderella wouldn't have lost her slipper at the ball . . . ?"

Emily sighed. "Sometimes I wonder if I will ever simply marry and settle to a calm life. I seem to spend my life wishing if only. . . ." Emily had also begun to wonder if the nonsense she had spouted to Granbury was really true. Her life certainly seemed star-crossed at the moment.

"Enough of the past, then. Tell me, is my brother any closer to proposing to you right and proper? Or is the footman's disguise his way of earning your mother's approval in a new and quite distinctive way?"

Emily laughed at the thought of Valentine, in footman's garb, asking for her hand in marriage. "Do you think Mother would favor his suit more?"

"I suppose not." Miranda examined her closely as

she asked her next question. "Has he suggested elopement again?"

Emily blushed, telling only a partial truth. "He does not wish to harm my reputation further."

"My brother can be gallant to a fault at times, I'm afraid." There was a touch of sadness in the duchess's expression. "Don't fear—I will bring him up to snuff before this visit is through. You two belong together. His pride can suffer the blow of not being able to shower you with gold and silks. And I expect you're hardy enough to survive a few less coals on the grate and a more sober attire."

Such a fate sounded heavenly to Emily. "After being locked up in this castle for years, I believe I should welcome rags and a scrub brush if only I could go where I please when I please."

"Then you ought not get married!" Miranda laughed at Emily's shocked reaction to her statement, but became serious again immediately. "Has it been as bad as all that?"

"Worse. Sometimes I feared I would go mad. In my despair, I was even looking forward to marrying the marquess to escape—because my mother had lied to me. She told me Valentine had married."

"I did wonder why you accepted the man."

Emily shrugged, and quoted her mother, "A woman must be married to be a person." She found herself smiling ruefully. "I did try—but two of my prospective grooms did not make it to the altar, and Granbury is—I do not know how to describe him. Even before Valentine showed me the letter, I knew I could not accept him as husband, though he has no more glaring faults at first glance than any other man."

Miranda patted her hand in sympathy. "You have had some unlucky experiences these last few years. However, I am certain my brother will deal with them nicely, now that he has come to your rescue." She patted Emily's hand and whispered conspiratorially, "I am almost glad that Simon and I were out of town."

Emily said with heartfelt honesty, "I am very glad that you were, as well. Your brother would never have come here if he thought the two of you would take care of me." And then they would never have eloped and she would have had no chance of winning him.

Again, she thought of confiding in Miranda, but even as she tried to think of the words to say, Nancy came in to see to getting her ready for afternoon tea. On her heels came Letty to dress her hair. She dared not risk being overheard and having the tale carried to the countess.

As if sensing that there was more to the story than she had yet been told, Miranda gave her another quick squeeze and said meaningfully, "I shall go and change out of my traveling clothes. It will be good to catch up on all your news."

Valentine found himself constantly under the watchful eye of Soames. Interestingly enough, though the chaos in the hallway had not been his fault, he discovered that to those belowstairs it did not matter what caused a disaster, only who was nearest it at the time it happened.

Because that unhappy soul had chanced to be him, he now had the butler, the housekeeper, and several other members of the household staff watching him to make sure he "caused" no more problems.

He reflected that, even if he were truly a footman he would have found the situation unfair and irritating. Since he now imperatively needed to find a way to speak to Simon, it went beyond irritation to frustration and then quickly into desperation as he found himself fetching, lifting, and hefting at the direction of anyone and everyone who needed something done.

It was not until dinner, when he was fortunate to be assigned to the dining room, that he even laid eyes on his sister or her husband again. And there was certainly no opportunity to talk to either of them there with the countess and Granbury present.

Which might have been providence itself. If he had had the opportunity, he would have taken it to scold his sister for the way she shamelessly interrogated Emily. All evening, his sister, under the guise of polite conversation, fired question after question at her.

The first question seemed innocuous enough. "How does it feel to know that you will soon be leaving the castle as a wife at last?" If only Miranda's eyes weren't twinkling, a sure sign of mischief.

Emily, looking more lively than she had at dinner any of the evenings Valentine had been present, answered glibly, "I dream of the moment every night."

"No doubt you do." His sister batted her eyes shamelessly at Simon. "Well I remember those days of waiting for the ceremony, don't you, my love?" Simon's only answer was a noncommittal nod and a raised eyebrow.

"What does your gown look like, Emily?" This said after Granbury, describing a recent horse he had purchased, had taken a breath in mid-sentence. The marquess did not look pleased to have his topic of conversation usurped when Emily, as if she had not noticed his ire, described the gown down to the last details of buttons and lace.

"What do you most want to see on your wedding trip, Emily?"

And so it went. Miranda asking endless, seemingly innocent questions. Emily, with a brave smile, answering the questions in such a way that he had a definite feeling the two women were carrying on a conversation no one but the two of them truly understood the meaning of.

Unfortunately, Granbury also seemed to be of this opinion. Each exchange resulted in a further narrowing of his eyes until he was no longer even pretending to be eating the courses Valentine was setting before him.

More than once he tried to wrest the conversation away from Miranda. Valentine could have told him he was wasting his time, as could Simon, who chose to remain admirably and tolerantly silent.

Still, Granbury made a valiant effort until, after his fourth glass of wine, he abruptly ceased talking altogether and simply glared at his bride-to-be.

That glare reminded Valentine exactly how vulnerable Emily was, even now that Simon and Miranda had arrived at the castle. The marquess already had ample reason to doubt his bride. The blackmail notes had to be causing him unease, at the very least. To make Emily a further target for Granbury's rage was asking for retribution.

Despite the extra attention Valentine was drawing from Soames and the rest of the staff, he could not fail to show up in Emily's room tonight. If Granbury took it in his head to visit her in order to rebuke her for tonight's performance, Valentine would make certain to be there to prevent Emily from being hurt.

He was relieved when Miranda, evidently at last realizing the extent of Granbury's agitation, chose to remove Emily from his presence by the simple expedient of asking her to walk in the night air with her.

"I'd not be comfortable if you ladies went unescorted," Granbury said, rising as if to accompany them.

There was hardly time for Valentine to tense or Emily to formulate an objection before Simon stood and said smoothly, "Let them take a footman, Granbury, I have some questions that I must ask you and that business will only bore the ladies, I am certain."

With the imperious certitude that he would be obeyed, which only a duke could carry off successfully, Simon gestured for Valentine to accompany the ladies.

The countess, seeing Granbury's ire, but not understanding it, did not object. Happily, she did not offer to accompany the ladies into the garden herself, either.

Sixteen

Though he was glad Simon had prevented Granbury from accompanying the women, Valentine was not as certain that he was happy to be the one chosen to escort the pair into the garden. It was a fortunate thing that a footman kept his distance, following a good ten paces behind.

There was a glint of determination in his sister's eye, which did not bode well for his peace of mind tonight. He had no doubt that she had sensed earlier that he was keeping things from her. Which would only make her more determined to learn them. If she didn't pry the truth of the elopement out of him, he was afraid that she would work it out of Emily for certain.

Before they had gotten much away from the castle, he tried to act the part of older brother and ward off her meddling. "Miranda, Granbury is not a man to thwart. You have made him angry with Emily and there is no telling how he might punish her for the way you humiliated him tonight."

Quick to jump to the point, Miranda looked at

Emily sharply. "Has he hurt you already, Emily? You did not say so before or I would have been more careful with my questions. I just could not bear to hear him speak as if he owned everything in sight—including you."

"Your brother is just being cautious—" Emily gasped when Valentine reached for her arm and rolled back her glove to reveal the livid thumbprint Granbury had left on her wrist. His sister drew in a sharp breath.

"With good reason, Emily. Miranda must know the whole truth, or she will get us all into trouble." He rubbed the pad of his thumb over the bruise gently, and dropped her hand when he felt her shiver. It was so easy to forget he shouldn't touch her.

His sister's glare held him. "Why is she still here?" Her gaze turned to Emily. He could see her busy mind working in a way he knew only too well and dreaded. She said briskly, "If the situation is that dire, Emily, you must leave then, there is no way to make certain—"

Emily defended him with more loyalty than sense. "Valentine would not let him hurt me."

"No, he would not, I am certain." His sister's glance was so pointed he looked away, afraid of what she might read in his eyes. "But his disguise limits his ability to be near you—to protect you when you are most vulnerable."

To his horror, Emily rose to his defense once again—with exactly the information he did not want Miranda to know. "I am not a fool. He spends the nights with me, just in case Granbury—"

"On the floor," Valentine interrupted to explain, at his sister's decidedly speculative glance between them. "To guard the door." One glance at Emily's hurt expression made him regret the eagerness of his demurral.

"Oh." If he did not know it impossible, he would have said there was definite disappointment in Miranda's tone. But surely even his irrepressible sister would not believe he should take advantage of Emily's situation to force himself on her before marriage.

Unless Emily had already told her— But no, then she would not be looking so hurt by his denial.

"It matters little to me, considering how matters now stand. I trust you both to do the right thing." Miranda's eyes held a hint of mischief, but she said nothing further on the subject, to his relief.

A tree branch creaked in the wind and they all tensed and glanced uncertainly toward the castle. Aware of his position, Valentine stepped away from the women, not wanting to give any casual onlooker a reason to think the situation odd—a footman standing as equal to two ladies who were distinctly his betters in social rank.

Miranda laughed. "We are all nervous as cats."

Neither he nor Emily could dredge up more than weak smiles in reply.

Miranda searched their faces for a moment. "I have just arrived, but you two have been living like this for weeks." She said softly, "We must find a way to end this matter soon."

Grabbing Emily's hand, she added quickly, "Stay

here a moment, Valentine, and make certain that no one approaches close enough to hear. I need to find out from Emily what the two of you have set in motion—and what Simon and I can do to help."

He objected. "I can tell you all you need to know." It annoyed him that she spoke to him as if he were the footman he was masquerading as. But he doubted she would take note of his objection. He supposed it was because she was now the wife of a duke and some of Simon's imperious manner had naturally rubbed off on his wife. Though in truth he could not remember a time when she did pay attention to him when she had her own idea of what was proper.

Miranda laughed. "Simon would understand if I were to be seen huddling in quiet conversation with a footman, but I think your butler would have your head. Aren't you already in trouble for causing that commotion this afternoon?"

"Soames would not be pleased." Valentine nodded. "But, as for my causing that unfortunate incident, I believe I must put that at your feet. Will you never learn to leave the packing to your servants?"

Miranda clucked her disapproval. "I was only teasing. You are so serious tonight."

"Matters *are* serious."

She looked at him gravely. "Do you think Emily a ninny?"

"I do not!"

"Fine, then keep watch for us as any footman might do, and let her tell me what I need to know so that Simon and I can help and we can all be done with this nonsense."

Still, he hesitated.

She sighed loudly. "Do you want the girl married to Granbury?"

There was no answer to the last question that he wanted to give; who knew what she would do with the knowledge that he had already eloped with Emily? So, unable to argue with her logic, and all too aware of how his every movement had been scrutinized about the household today, Valentine agreed.

He stood obediently nearby, as any good footman might. He watched the castle carefully. Thankfully, there was no sign of anyone the marquess might have sent to spy on them. Nevertheless, it galled him that the two women huddled just out of range of his hearing. And it worried him when he heard several instances of feminine laughter coming from their vicinity. He would have given anything to hear what they were saying.

Although he could not hear what they discussed, when they returned to him and led the way back in to the castle, he had the uncomfortable feeling that he had been more than a passing topic of conversation between them. Both women regarded him with much too much amusement for him to doubt it.

He hoped Emily had not told Miranda about the elopement. He had no doubt that his sister would tell her husband at the first opportunity. They were an exceptionally close couple, despite their rocky beginning. He would rather tell the duke himself, man to man.

What Simon would say in reply to the confession was another matter entirely. Despite anything the duke might have to say, Valentine was not sorry for his actions. If Simon felt the need to call him out for a dawn interview, then so be it. He had done what he needed to do to protect Emily and he refused to apologize for it, despite the fact that he had broken a promise.

Still, it made him uncomfortable not knowing if Emily had told Miranda. The two of them would no doubt have put a romantic glow to the tale. But such matters were not for either of the women to deal with. The promise, as well as the breach, was between men, and should be handled between them.

Having settled matters in his own mind, Valentine gave himself to the pleasure of following them at the proper servile distance. Two feet behind them, he was able to admire how Emily's slim figure moved with grace and elegance. Every so often she would twist herself lithely and look back to give him a quick smile. He, playing the proper footman, did not return the gesture, no matter the temptation.

The glint of the pearls at her neck sobered his thoughts, however. He allowed himself to wonder if he and Emily would ever have a marriage as close as his sister and the duke's. How could she be content if he could not give her any of the things she had always had for the asking since she was a child?

Dinner had been so much more pleasant with Simon and Miranda to take up the conversational duties, that Emily almost felt regret when her mother ordered her off to bed. Almost.

Tonight, for the first time, she had real hope that Valentine would join her in her bed. The entire time she climbed the stairs, and all the while that Nancy brushed out her hair and helped her into her night-dress, she thought about what she had told Miranda.

And what Miranda had told her.

Swearing that she would say nothing to Simon about the elopement for a few days more, Miranda had dictated three steps to ensure that Valentine did not sleep on the floor tonight. The steps themselves were simple enough, in the telling. It was the doing that had Emily worried.

The first step—not one of Miranda's three, but necessary to put those into practice—was to remove the dolls from the other side of her bed. She piled them carefully on the floor in the corner of the room, so that the delicate porcelain of their hands and faces would not be stepped on in the dark and accidentally broken.

She fancied that the dolls, with their little, bright-eyed faces, were smiling their encouragement at her plans. Wish me well, girls, she bade them silently.

"Good for you, my lady," Nancy said with a bob of her head as she stood by with a brush in her hand. "More room in the bed's a good start."

She felt herself color again. So Nancy herself was aware of the situation between the newlyweds? She had a miserable feeling that the maid, though she might never say so, would not have needed to be told how to encourage Valentine into her bed. "I hope it matters to him," she answered softly as she stared at the bed, which seemed huge and empty without all the pretty dolls arranged in rows down the left half.

"I've a feeling it will, my lady," Nancy said with a smile. "You've a look of determination about you tonight. That always counts in the game between men and women, it does."

Emily could not hide her own doubts, but she said forcefully, "In that case, then, the battle is won." As she had hoped, Nancy simply laughed and finished with her duties more quickly than usual.

"Would you like me to stay until 'e comes?" The maid's offer was sincere, but her eyes were doubtful. "It might be later than the past nights, Soames 'as got it in for 'im today."

"I heard," Emily acknowledged. "But you needn't stay, Nancy. I will be fine. You've all worked hard today to prepare for our guests. You need to rest. And I know he will come just as soon as he is able."

Dutifully following Miranda's advice, after Nancy had tucked her into bed, Emily removed her practical and warm nightgown. Nervously, she folded it neatly and placed it on the dressing table chair and then quickly bolted back under the covers, amazed at how different the sheets felt to her bare skin. They were cold to the touch, but warmed quickly with the heat of her body.

Without the dolls to fill half the bed, she felt more alone than she had since she was a child. She looked to the newly open space on the bed and imagined Valentine there, smiling at her.

She warmed at the thought of his smile, the first thing she had noticed about him so many years ago.

Would he be frowning when he realized what she meant for them to do tonight?

After a moment's thought, she got up and quickly retrieved the folded nightgown, placing it under her pillow. That way, if Valentine was displeased with her nudity, she would be able to cover up quickly.

The other two steps, unfortunately, required Valentine's presence to perform. He had warned her, even before Nancy's caution, that he would most likely be late in coming to her because he was being closely watched. She smiled, remembering the way he and Miranda had described the incident that had him the temporary pariah of the household.

Still, it was growing late. Soon he would be here. And then it would be time. Tonight, before she could lose her nerve, she would put Miranda's advice into practice. Would it work?

She could feel a blush heat her cheeks, thinking of what Miranda had told her to do. Could she even bring herself to—of course she could, she must . . . and Miranda had said it would be quite a pleasant thing, after all.

For a moment she wondered if she would be better off simply to wait for Valentine to realize they were meant to be together. But what was the use of being a bride if her groom was going to neglect her?

Miranda had been quite certain that this was one way in which a woman could always be convinced that she would get—and keep—a man's attention. And all she needed was to distract him for just long enough to make certain that he would not suddenly think of duty and honor and break off the sweet kisses he gave her.

She felt her courage wane as she lay waiting. Perhaps she should wait. . . . No. But perhaps she should stop thinking about what might happen when he finally arrived . . . if only that were possible.

In a concession to her own cowardice, she pulled her nightgown from beneath her pillow and drew it on again. It was not terribly seductive, even she could tell that. So she compromised by unbuttoning the neck and bodice. And then she realized she had forgotten one of the most crucial elements to her plan.

She crawled out of the bed once more and retrieved her water pitcher from the dressing table. Clutching it to her chest, she put out the lamp, leaving the room in darkness. All there was to do now, until Valentine arrived, was to wait—and to imagine the best and worst this night might bring.

Her heart raced at the thought of touching him as Miranda had suggested—his shoulders, sleek and warm, his belly, following the line of fine, curly hair which ran down into his trousers. The thought of such things made her restless.

Would he be convinced, at last, to make love to her? Or would he be angry? Or, worse, horrified at her boldness? He was so determined to act as if they were not married. To court her properly. An intolerable thought occurred to her—what if he found it no hardship to keep from making love to her? Miranda had laughed when she suggested it. But he did not touch her. And when she touched him, he backed away as quickly as possible.

For a moment, she doubted that Miranda was right. What good would touching him do, when he was adamant that they must keep apart? But a little thought changed her mind again. Perhaps, since thinking about touching him brought her breath short, as it was even now, her touch might bring him to the same point?

Of course. She smiled, realizing at last what he had been hiding from her. All along he had been avoiding her touch, avoiding touching her, because of how it affected him. Her touch did bring him pleasure—and that was why he was so careful to avoid it.

She tightened her hold on the pitcher of water. As Miranda had suggested, she would ensure that both his shirt and trousers came off tonight—there would be nothing to protect him from her . . . or from himself.

Seventeen

Something was different tonight, Valentine noticed it the moment he came through the door. For a second he felt as if he were taking his very life in his hands to enter the room. He paused to listen, but heard nothing untoward.

It was dark without a lamp lit, but even so, the figure in the bed, and the scent of Emily, drew him like a moth to a flame and he felt his tenuous grasp on his emotions begin to slip. But what was it that was so different about the room? About tonight?

At first he thought that it was simply the lateness of the hour and the fact that Emily herself was silent and presumably asleep. Always before she had waited up to greet him.

He damped his disappointment. She was asleep and he would not get to spend a few precious moments in conversation with her. He tried to convince himself that this was also a relief. He did not have to answer her question once again about why he would not share her bed with her.

And then he saw that something else was different.

The dim light straining into the room from the hallway showed him what had changed. There were no dolls on her bed. The empty space yawned like a chasm, calling to him to dive into it headlong and never look back.

He shut the door, plunging the room back into darkness, so that the sight of the empty half of the bed was no longer visible. If only he could forget that he had seen it. Thank heavens he had been delayed long enough for her to fall asleep before he arrived.

As was his habit, he removed his boots and stockings and placed them by the door, in case he needed to depart in a hurry at some point during the night. He took a tentative step in the darkness, and heard her move in the bed.

He stopped, wondering if she were awake, or simply restless. He would have called softly to reassure her that it was only him, but before he could, he heard the sloshing sound of water in a jug and icy fingers of water drenched him.

He gasped in shock. "Emily—it is me."

"Valentine?" Her voice sounded different. Had she been half asleep? Perhaps he'd woken her.

"Yes. I'm here." Already he was beginning to shiver.

"I'm sorry, I thought you must be Francis." She didn't sound sorry, though, she sounded pleased.

He did not think much of her weapon of choice. "And you believed you might stop him with a pitcher of water?"

"It was all I had, and you were not here. Besides,

if you had not called out, I would have used the pitcher to clout your head."

In the dark, she'd have been more likely to either miss him altogether or clout his shoulder. Still, he forebore to mention it. She had been alone and worried. "I'm sorry you were frightened. I was delayed."

"I know. I've been waiting for you. Did I get you very wet?"

"Not very," he lied.

He heard her moving in the dark, the sound of her leaving the bed, and the next thing he knew her hands were at his jacket, pulling at the sleeves. "You are soaked through!"

"Leave it, I'll take care of it." He shrugged away from her.

She moved toward him again. "Nonsense. I am your wife after all—besides, I am the one who threw the water on you, you poor thing."

It was agony having her hands pulling at his clothes, her warm body pressed against him. He gritted his teeth and said, "Emily—you don't know what you're doing."

"I'm going to undress you of course," she said with a low laugh. "I know exactly what I'm doing."

Undress him. She intended to undress him? What would have put such a thought in— Miranda had put the thought in her head, of course. He knew it at once. His Emily would never be so forward on her own. He tried to pat her hands away, step back from her, but he found himself against the wall. "I don't—"

Her fingers were quickly working the buttons of

his shirt, her knuckles teasing his senses with little butterfly movements down his breastbone. "Of course you do, you're soaking wet. Do you want to catch your death sleeping in soggy clothing?"

He could feel the nervous vibrations of her movements and realized that she was trembling. There was no breath in his throat to issue another protest.

Shaking or not, her hands made quick work of the buttons on his shirt, and he gave in to the inevitable, shrugging out of the jacket, and unfastening his trousers and allowing them to drop to the floor in a sodden heap. Standing there, not knowing where to go from there, he grasped her hands to still them.

She made a small sound of protest, but did not pull away. He could feel the warmth of her bed-warmed body against his stomach and thighs, radiating through the inch or less which separated their bodies. He left his shirt—which had fortunately been spared the worst of the water by his jacket—on, half unbuttoned as she had managed. He could feel that the trembling in her fingers had transmitted itself to her whole body now.

"Are you cold?" he asked with concern, lifting her up and placing her safely in the bed, tucking the covers up around her.

She sat up and he moved away just enough that she couldn't brush against him. He could hear her movements, but in the dark he wasn't certain what she was doing until a fall of cloth slid down his legs and landed on his bare feet. Her nightgown. She had taken off her nightgown. A buzz began in his ears.

"Come to bed, Valentine." And then her fingers found his in the darkness and their hands clasped tightly. Gently, tentatively, she touched his chest with her other hand, exploring, still shaking—with cold or desire he could not tell and was afraid to know.

The bed was trembling now from the violence of her reaction, he could feel it where his thighs pressed against the mattress. Like a waterfall, his good intentions cascaded away and he slipped under the covers next to her and gathered her up in his arms. "You are cold," he said, as if to fool his conscience into believing that was why he had crawled into her bed. But if she was, he could not tell it from the warmth of her bare skin where it touched his own.

She shook her head and burrowed her face into his shoulder. Her arms clutched convulsively around his waist, under his shirt so that they were skin against skin, and he felt as if he were burning wherever she pressed against him as she whispered, "I didn't think you would come to me. I don't know whether I am more frightened or astonished."

He kissed the top of her head, her ears, and whispered softly, "There is no need to be afraid of me, Emily." He hoped he was telling her the truth. "I will not hurt you. I will just hold you if you like. There is no need to do more." A lie, of course, as his body was even now reminding him.

How long had he dreamed of this moment? Just holding her would not quench the desire those dreams had built. But she did not have to know that.

Except that, somehow, she did. Even as he held

her trembling body safely in his arms, her hands reached up to cup the back of his head and pulled his mouth down to meet hers. There was no uncertainty in her kiss, or in her words. "I love you Valentine." His last defenses crumbled in the desire to show her that he returned her love in no uncertain terms.

Emily thought for one agonizing moment that he would pull his mouth away from her much-too-needy kiss, or her declaration of love. Or worse, that he would tell her she had been mistaken in thinking that he had married her for any other reason than to protect her from Granbury's designs.

But as their lips met, he seemed to melt toward her. The change in him was so sudden that it took her a few moments to notice that she was no longer the one in charge of matters any more.

His hands were no longer simply holding her protectively—instead, they skimmed over her back, followed the curve of her hip, brushed against her face, as if searching for something. He broke his lips away from hers with a wordless sound, but only to allow his mouth to settle warmly below her ear, then brush down her neck to her shoulder. She found she couldn't breathe at all. He was not going to reject her.

Somewhere in the back of her mind was the thought that no proper young lady should feel the way she did. She dismissed it easily. There was no doubt that here in his arms was where she belonged, and she meant to enjoy every moment to the fullest.

When his lips touched her breast she found herself shamelessly urging him onward.

Even as he explored her body, she began to explore his in return, encouraged by his soft groans and the intense kisses he visited upon her mouth. The scent of him filled her nostrils as she buried her face in his chest and ran her fingers up and down his back as if she were playing a harpsichord, its music filling her blood instead of her ears.

He pressed the full length of his body against hers and, when she held his hips and pressed him nearer, he groaned into her ear, "Emily, you go too fast—"

But she did not want to hear his objections. She had waited three years for a wedding night with him, she would not be denied it now when she was moments away from being joined with him forever. She arched against him, and when he brushed against her with another groan, she felt as if she had left her own body to hover above, watching, approving, as he moved into her with a cry of pleasure that she found herself matching.

For a moment there was no thought except to answer the increasingly urgent needs of her body, no goal except release, and then it came, in waves that washed warm pleasure over her. When she was back inside her own skin at last, she felt the tears on her cheeks and heard her own breathing ragged in her ears, mingling with the sweet sound of his.

She brought her arms around him as he lay upon her, struggling to catch his breath. She had won him tonight. She would never let him go again.

"What have we done, Emily?" he asked after his breathing had calmed. He eased his weight from her and moved beside her, his arms still encircling her, making her feel as safe as if Granbury didn't exist. He nuzzled at her cheeks, still wet with tears. "My God, what have we done?"

"Nothing to be ashamed of Valentine." Emily was certain of this. She turned herself until her head rested in the crook of his shoulder. Just before she fell asleep in his arms she said sleepily, "I wish we had done this in the first place three years ago. Then I would have allowed no one to keep us apart—not even you."

He didn't sleep. Her words echoed in his ears. Indeed, they were etched deep in his heart as he lay feeling her breathe evenly beside him. Never in his dreams had she come to him so willingly. He had thought to treat her gently, like fragile porcelain the first time. Instead, she had shown him the depths of his foolishness—the depths of her love.

They would have to face up to the gossip their elopement would cause. Perhaps, just to save her some of the more vicious comments, they could pretend to have eloped after Granbury was exposed and her engagement ended. But they would not sleep apart again, no matter how scandalous their discovery might be.

He turned his head to kiss her sweet neck and she murmured sleepily and moved against him without fear. The gift of her passion awed him, and renewed his desire to see her safely away from here.

It was fortunate that he had realized how far he was willing to go for Emily before he fell asleep with her warm in his arms.

The knock on the door was light, there was no time for him to hide, no time to even pull the covers completely over them before the door itself opened to admit Miranda, who grinned cheekily at the sight of him in Emily's bed, and behind her, eyes slanted in disapproval, Simon.

Valentine sat up in the bed, sheltering Emily from their view. He knew he should be ashamed, but after the night he had passed with Emily, he could not be. "Kerstone. Miranda. Your timing is a bit awkward, I'm afraid."

"It couldn't be helped. I'm sorry." His sister's expression did not hold one ounce of regret. He knew her well enough to know that this was her way of making Simon come to grips with the truth of their relationship. But did she know they had eloped? Did Simon?

The duke's expression was every bit as furious as he had expected it would be. "I trust you have what you wanted now, Fenster," he said coldly. "You'll have to marry her. Even the countess cannot argue with that decision now." The duke felt betrayed.

Valentine wished he could be more ashamed that he had broken his promise. He opened his mouth to tell him of the elopement, wondering if the news would absolve him of breaking his oath to the duke, or be an even deeper betrayal.

From beneath the covers, Emily protested. "No! You cannot tell Mother—"

Simon raised his brow at the objection. "She must know. She is your mother, after all."

Emily peeked her head above the covers to plead, "Not yet Simon. Not until we have taken care of Granbury."

"I cannot just ignore this insult to you, Emily—"

Emily stiffened in indignation next to him. Valentine knew he could not stop her, so he braced instead for what she would say. "There is no insult for me to sleep next to my husband, is there, Simon?"

"Husband?" The duke's outraged expression wilted. "You have married? When?" He was not looking at Emily as he asked the question, but directly into Valentine's eyes.

Valentine again tried to answer, man to man, as he would have preferred to deal with this matter.

Emily's indignation was so great, however, that she did not allow him time to speak. "We were married almost a week ago, cousin. You owe him an apology."

The duke's brows shot up. "Perhaps he owes me satisfaction. He gave me his word, after all."

Emily continued, ignoring the chilly reaction to her claim. "You would not dare. Valentine is an honorable man, he would never dream of dishonoring me with an illicit liaison." She rested her head on his shoulder as if to demonstrate what she meant. "He was nothing but a proper gentleman until after we were married."

To his surprise, he caught a swift, telling glance pass between Simon and his wife.

Emily had caught it too, for she laughed softly, "Do I spy a spot of color high upon my proper cousin's cheek? Perhaps you should take a lesson from Valentine, then."

Startled, he, too wondered— But, no. It was unthinkable that Simon and Miranda had . . . had they?

The duke said nothing. Miranda merely took his hand in hers and smiled at them both in satisfaction. "I'm relieved to see my advice worked, Emily." She glanced sternly toward Valentine. "You'll find it makes the marriage much stronger when you share the same bed."

She frowned, as if at long last realizing exactly how improper her impromptu visit was. Turning to her husband, nearly pulling him through the doorway as she spoke, she said, "Why don't we return in a quarter hour, after you have had time to dress and make yourselves comfortable?"

"Tomorrow morning might be more sensible," Valentine grumbled.

His sister stopped at the doorway to throw a quick glance his way. "Don't be so cross that we have spoiled your secret. We have good news for you—we have thought of a way to increase the pressure you have been putting on the marquess. If it works, we shall draw him out in no time."

Still not sanguine about the news of his cousin's elopement, Simon added, "And then we can discuss exactly how to mitigate the damage this irregular marriage—and its abysmal timing—will cause to Emily and to your family."

Knowing he was all too right, Valentine merely nodded his head in agreement as the pair finally left him alone with Emily.

In the sudden pressing silence of the room, Valentine handed Emily her nightgown. Simon's words had struck him hard. Not only had he married her secretly, he had married her while she was technically still engaged to Granbury. That was more than scandal. It was disgrace.

"Come and dress quickly, Emily, so that we can hear what they have to say," he urged her.

"I will." Her voice was faint, however, and not nearly as sure as her words would suggest.

Although he was almost numb from the confrontation with the duke, it amused him to see how nervously she stayed tucked under the covers. After the willing way she had given herself to him so completely, he would not have expected her to be afraid to show a bit of skin to her own husband.

He smiled at her. "I'll turn my back." She blushed deeply, but as soon as he turned around, he heard her clothes rustling at a hasty pace. Tenderness shot through him and he swore that he would not let her be hurt by Society, not when he knew how pure and faithful her love had been for him, despite all the obstacles in their path.

He dressed in his still damp footman's uniform, mulling over the lack of fury in what he had expected to be a complete renunciation of his honor. So that was the extent of the duke's ire? After he had broken his solemn promise? Or would there be more, later, once Granbury was no longer a threat? Would he suggest—or worse, demand—that they divorce?

Eighteen

There was no hint of the answer to his question when, a quarter hour later, his sister and her husband returned to Emily's room. Valentine dared not ask in front of either of the women. He and Simon must settle this matter privately. But neither of the women were likely to let them were they to suspect.

Miranda, apparently quite content for a change to allow Valentine and Emily their privacy in this new phase of their relationship, began with a sharp question that had nothing to do with their marriage. "As I said, we have a plan that will force the timetable to accelerate. Do you think Nan will help us?"

Hesitantly, Valentine nodded. "She has been quite willing to do what was needed, so far. She has good reason to see Granbury hang."

"Good," Simon said, as if that answer was all that was needed to see the man hang in fact.

"Why do you ask?" Emily spoke up, puzzlement plain on her features.

In a matter of moments, Simon and Miranda had laid out their plan. Instead of Valentine leaving the anonymous blackmail notes in Granbury's room, as he had been doing, Nan would leave the newest demand—insisting upon a meeting with him by the castle's pond.

"What good will that do?" Emily interrupted.

Simon raised a finger to silence her questions and continued to explain. "We will arrange for Granbury to see her, but not be able to confront her."

Miranda added, "He will have to do something, then. Once he thinks he knows who is blackmailing him, he will act, I am sure of it."

"No doubt he will," Valentine agreed. "But it is the very nature of his actions that worries me most. I don't like asking Nancy to put herself in such danger if we can help it."

"I don't think we can help it." Miranda sighed. "I have thought about it and Nan is the most logical person."

"Why can't we arrange to have him discover me delivering the note instead?"

"Think about it brother—and forget your honor while you do. Finding Nan, and not being able to confront her right then will force his hand." Miranda leaned forward. "We know what kind of man he is, Valentine. What do you expect he will do if he thinks it is Nan who is blackmailing him?"

"He will think he can deal with her threat himself. But would he feel any differently if he were to discover that a footman was leaving the notes?"

"What?" Her expression was momentarily confused. "I had forgotten your disguise. Perhaps it might work— No. It will not. Even though you are dressed as a footman, you are a man, and a well-built one at that. He would likely be warier of a man, even a servant."

Simon added, with a frown, "Worse, he might take a second look and realize that you are not a mere footman."

Valentine acknowledged what they said, but he felt strongly that Nan should not take such a risk if he could do it instead. "As to my being a male servant, I can tell you that a footman does not command a great deal of respect." He glanced at Emily, and added with a smile, "except among the maidservants belowstairs, of course."

"I suppose that has made the masquerade bearable for you," Emily answered. Her smile held not one jot of jealousy. If he didn't know better, he would have sworn that she exhibited definite signs of a young woman well pleased with herself in regards to her husband.

So she had not feigned her pleasure for his sake, then. It was a heady thought, but also terrifying. For the first time he fully realized that she was not going to be the most docile wife he might have wished for.

"Bearable or not, it *is* just a masquerade," Simon said dryly. "And to risk unmasking you before we are ready is foolishness." He added, "We will minimize any danger to Nan, of course. It is good that she knows the risks better than any of us, seeing that her sister was one of Granbury's victims."

Quickly he went on to outline the plans he and Miranda had come up with after reading the letter Valentine had given them and realizing that there was little time to waste. There was shelter enough for both Valentine and Simon to hide in the shrubbery near the pond and offer Nan protection against Granbury.

"What is Nan's excuse supposed to be for asking to meet with him?" Emily asked. "The blackmail notes have only threatened to expose him if he does not break the engagement and leave. Why is that to change?"

"The new note can ask for money." Miranda said.

"He will not pay—" Valentine began.

Miranda interrupted him. "No, he will not. The point is not that he will or will not pay—not even that he will or will not leave because of the blackmail notes. The idea is to provoke him to attack Nan for her audacity in blackmailing him in the first place."

Emily frowned. "We cannot ask Nan to put herself in such danger without reward. What good will it do to have Simon catch the marquess attempting to murder a maid? He could just deny it."

"Suggest that the duke of Kerstone would tell a lie?" Miranda sounded amused at the very possibility.

"Hush, Miranda, the question is a good one," Simon said with a frown that Valentine felt certain was threatening to turn into a smile. "That is the dangerous side of the venture, Emily. We must make him show his hand just enough to make it clear his intention is to kill the maid. And there must be enough evidence for everyone to believe it."

Emily protested, "But we cannot let her be hurt—"

"No. No. We will not." Valentine saw the way Simon's brow furrowed.

He grasped Emily's hand and waited until she looked directly at him to say, "I swear, I will not let her be hurt." It was a tricky plan, borne primarily of desperation and daring rather than common sense and careful thought. But the outcome was worth the risk. If they caught Granbury in the act, as it were, he would not be able to escape justice.

"You promise?"

"Yes. The plan is risky, but we will let him go rather than risk her life. I promise you that."

After discussing the fine details until dawn began to make itself known, the four were as satisfied as they could be with the time they had remaining. It was a dangerous plan, but what was not, when Granbury was involved?

Valentine stood, a signal that Simon and Miranda should leave. "I will speak to Nan this morning."

"No," Emily objected.

"But I will see her belowstairs—"

"I will see her here," Emily pointed out with irrefutable logic. "I will have ample private time, with no threat of being overheard by the other servants."

"Especially since you, my dear brother, are still being watched by that eagle-eyed butler due to your transgression with my luggage yesterday." Miranda laughed, and laughed harder when he scowled at her reminder.

He kissed Emily swiftly, and set her aside without listening to her protest as he followed the others out of the room. He was being watched more carefully.

It would not do to be discovered in a clandestine meeting with "his betters."

He wondered if he would be released from the extra attention today. Surely some other servant would cause the scrutiny to turn their way? He could hope so, at the very least.

As he crept down the stairs to resume his role as a humble footman, he could not help an optimistic thought. At long last they might be able to end the charade—the endless charades, as it were.

Nancy swallowed nervously, the brush in her hand catching jerkily in Emily's hair despite her obvious efforts to keep her movements smooth. "They'll be right there? If I make so much as a peep—"

"Valentine has promised he will not let the marquess hurt you, Nancy," Emily soothed, wishing she could think of some other way to make this work without putting Nancy at risk. "And I give you my solemn vow, as well."

When the maid still looked doubtful, she added, "The duke of Kerstone has told me that he pledges to see you through this without a scratch."

"Did 'e now?"

"Yes." Emily nodded, wincing in regret when the brush caught and pulled at her hair again. "He is very grateful for your help in this matter."

Apparently the word of a duke was good enough for Nan because she nodded her head smartly. "I guess the risk is worth it to avenge my little Nellie. She didn't deserve what 'e did to her, she didn't."

The maid worked the brush silently for a while. Then she said softly, "Maybe she was a bit spirited, and not as good a girl as she should 'ave been, but she'd 'ave settled down in a year or two, given a chance."

Another silence. Emily was just about to suggest that Nancy stop brushing when the maid whispered, " 'Im doing what 'e did took 'er chance to settle away from 'er, didn't it?"

"Yes, Nancy, it did." Her voice was sharper than she had intended, not out of a lack of sympathy, but simply because of the painful brushing.

The maid put the brush down with a sharp rap, and met Emily's eyes in the mirror. "I'll do it. Tell the duke I'll do it. For Nellie. But you've got to promise me something."

"Anything," Emily agreed, realizing the courage it took for Nancy to put her life in danger like this.

"If something 'appens to me—"

Emily shook her head. "Nothing will happen to you, I promise you, we—"

Nancy tutted. "Promises don't mean nothing when you face the devil, my lady. Just you remember that should you find yourself at the altar with 'im at the end of the week for some reason."

The thought made Emily shudder and the maid patted her shoulder and said sympathetically, "Be glad you've got a 'usband already and can't be made 'is wife against your will." She added solemnly, "If I don't see the end of this, make sure that devil 'angs for my murder."

"We don't intend for it to come to that," Emily

said unhappily. Nancy was right and there was no sensible way to deny it. If Granbury were the devil it seemed he was, none of them would be safe until he'd been brought to justice—maybe not even until he'd been hanged, cut down, and buried.

The maid said softly, "Just promise me you'll see him 'anged come what may. I'll die to see my sister's death avenged, but I don't want to get myself planted for nothing. That cowardly murderer has to get all the comeuppance 'e deserves."

For the first time, Emily realized the full import of what they were trying to do. "He will, Nancy, he will." There was a certain lack of conviction in her voice.

Three weeks ago, all she had been concerned with was breaking an engagement. Now she was trying to unveil a murderer, avenge the death of her maid's sister, and bring a man to a justice that would surely see him dead.

Hearing the doubt, the maid put her hand on Emily's shoulder. Her fingers bit down against bone in her agitation, but Emily did not protest at the pain. "Promise me, my lady!"

Nancy's eyes were wide and focused directly on Emily. "I need to 'ear it from your lips. Everyone says the duke of Kerstone would never lie. That 'is 'onor is so great 'e'd die 'imself before 'e'd break 'is word."

"Everyone says so," Emily agreed. "And I believe he lives up to what people say about him, unlike most heroes."

Nancy nodded. "But I don't know 'im. I 'aven't

served 'im for three years day in and day out. I know you will keep your word if you give it. You and that young man of yours are two of the finest people I've ever met."

Emily spoke slowly, to keep any quaver out of her voice. "I promise you, Nancy, that Granbury will soon be brought to justice. And I promise you that you will not suffer for your part in helping bring him to that justice."

Nancy said resolutely, "I can stand that. Just so's I know 'e ends up at the end of a rope."

Emily stood up and, for the first time in her life, embraced her maid. "It is enough that you have lost your sister; none of us will allow you to lose your own life as well. But if anything were to happen to you, we would not let him escape punishment."

"Thank you, my lady." Nancy quickly hugged her in return and then stepped away, putting the proper distance between them again.

Emily felt the promise she had just made like a weight on her heart. She only hoped that she would not have cause to need to keep it.

And she wouldn't—if Valentine and Simon would do their part to keep the courageous maid safe from Granbury's wrath.

"What must I do, then, my lady?"

Emily handed her the note that Valentine had written. "This is the blackmail note you are to deliver." The missive itself was an innocuous-looking square of stiff cream stock. It was the words that were written upon it that put them all at risk. The note trembled in Nancy's hand.

"You must be seen, but not caught."

"What if 'e knows I didn't leave the others?"

Emily sighed. "Simon and Valentine have thought of everything; the handwriting matches those of the other notes Valentine left in the marquess's room." They had taken great care so as not to rouse the man's suspicions that he had two blackmailers—or, as clever as he seemed to be, that a trap was being baited for him.

A keen awareness of the dangerous mission they embarked upon with this one step made her voice sharp as she said, "You must follow my directions *exactly* Nancy. All our futures, perhaps our very lives, depend upon it."

The tension was pulled tight inside him as he crouched in the maids' closet, waiting to intercept Granbury before he could confront Nan for leaving the note. Simon, Emily, and Miranda all lurked nearby as well. They were not leaving any possibility for this part of the plan to fail.

Exactly as scheduled, Nan appeared, looking nervously right and left. She had the note in her hand, visible to anyone who would be observing her. Valentine wanted to applaud her ingenuity. They did not want to make it difficult for Granbury to jump to the conclusion that Nan was the blackmailer.

The marquess had made one aspect easier for them. His schedule was precise to the degree of obsession. Exactly at two o'clock in the afternoon he returned to his room to change his clothing.

His valet, as precise as his master, had the clothing already chosen and set out, so he returned to the room scant minutes before his master was due to arrive. By two-thirty, the pair were ready to depart the room.

Valentine's routine had been to deliver the notes just before the valet arrived. In order to make certain that the note would be found only by the marquess, he had tucked it into a pocket of the change of clothing.

Unfortunately, that would not work if they wanted Nan to be discovered. So they had devised a slightly different method to deliver the note this time.

The hapless valet had suffered a tumble down the servant's stairs not twenty minutes ago. Though he was not seriously injured, his knee had managed to become painfully twisted—enough to throw his entire schedule, as well as that of the belowstairs staff, completely off.

While the cook was running for ice and a maid was seeing to the cut on his forehead with rubbing alcohol and a sticking plaster, two footmen had been required to remain available to help the incapacitated man up to his room when he was pronounced as fit as household remedies could make him.

Valentine had ensured that he was the footman assigned to deliver the message to the marquess that his man had met with an accident. It was crucial to their timing that Granbury not receive the message too soon. But it had required skill and speed on Valentine's part for him to get past Soames's harried gaze, up the servant's stairs and into the maids' closet without Granbury catching sight of him. There would be no acceptable excuse for not delivering the note immediately if he met the marquess.

He drew a breath, afraid to let it out. There was the sound of a step on the landing. And now Granbury was there, at the top of the stairs. Valentine signaled to Nan that it was time for her to enter the room and slip the note into the pocket of the clothing already arranged in the dressing room.

As Granbury approached the room, just as they had timed, Nan came out. Her start of guilt was superb, but Valentine suspected that it had less to do with her talent for acting and more to do with her terror for what they were about.

"What are you doing here, girl?" Granbury, at first, was not suspicious. He did, after all, assume his man was in the room to prevent the girl from doing mischief.

"N-nothing," Nan stammered, trying to veer around him and make for the stairs.

But Granbury glanced at his doorway and began to wonder what business a maid would have in his room at this hour. "I'll have a better answer than that from you, my girl, or we'll go down to see the countess right now."

Valentine used the distraction to move from the closet and walk swiftly down the hallway to interrupt. "My lord, I have urgent news."

Granbury turned with a frown, and Nan, flashing Valentine a relieved smile, slipped past him before he could stop her. "What is it?"

"Your man has been injured. I have been sent to

serve for you." The thought of dressing Granbury was infuriating, but Valentine was not willing to risk exposing their plan, no matter how much he wished he could avoid this part of it.

The marquess grated out questions. "Injured? How?"

Valentine plastered on a benignly serious expression, as befitted a footman delivering bad news. "A fall down the stairs."

"Clumsy oaf," Granbury swore. "How badly has he been hurt?"

"His knee is twisted and he has a cut upon his forehead that is not too serious. But he cannot walk and he has been taken to his room for the time being. I am to help you dress."

Granbury studied him with such intensity that Valentine began to worry his nondescript disguise had finally been penetrated. Then the marquess turned away impatiently. "I need no help with my clothing. I shall manage for myself."

"Very well, my lord," Valentine said deferentially. Inside, however, he was jubilant. Their plan had worked so perfectly that they had not even had to reveal that Simon, Miranda, and Emily lurked nearby. And he had not been required to help the marquess in and out of his clothes, thank goodness. The fates must be smiling upon their plan. He reflected soberly as he turned back down the stairs, that they needed every advantage they could find when dealing with the marquess.

Now that Granbury had seen Nan coming out of his room, all they needed to do was keep the maid surrounded by people. Unable to talk to her, he would be forced to keep the rendezvous by the pond with his blackmailer. It sounded much simpler than it would be, he knew.

Still, he could not help but feel a surge of hope. Their first move in the game had gone as planned. Soon, they might have Granbury caught in the deceitful web he had been spinning for so many years.

Nineteen

Valentine found that the accident the marquess's valet had suffered had ended the extra alert observation he had been under by the butler and the housekeeper. That honor was now being enjoyed by a young kitchen maid who had been blamed for leaving soap on the stairs and causing the valet's accident.

As a result, he was much earlier than he had been the previous evening when he came to Emily's room. She smiled, a bit shyly—he saw she had decided to wear her nightgown. Good. It would give him great pleasure to remove it.

Joining her in the bed felt natural. He looked forward, suddenly, to a time when he would consider it as commonplace as his favorite slippers, or the chair in the study that he favored. So natural that he gave them no thought, just enjoyed them.

She smiled and teased, "No protests this time?"

"None," he answered, reaching for her. He enjoyed her look of anticipation as he moved slowly to kiss her. Her lips were warm and sweet, just as he had dreamed all day.

"You forgot to turn out the lamp," she said nervously, pulling back.

He smiled and distracted her as she moved to turn out the lamp herself. "Where is Nan?"

Emily's answering expression was so full of guilt that for a moment he had a horrible notion that the maid was hiding under the bed to be safe from Granbury. But then she said, "Nan assured me she is safe enough in her room with the other maids. Do you think she is right?"

He began unbuttoning the little pearl nubbins at the neck of her nightgown. "I expect so. The servants' quarters are tightly packed and the walls thin enough to converse through."

Emily glanced at the lamp again. "I told her I shall not call her during the night. If she hears the bell, she is to ignore it. That way Granbury cannot trick her into coming abovestairs without my knowing."

"Wise plan." He smiled, bending over to kiss the soft skin he was slowly exposing. "I am quite sure we will not need her tonight." When she looked over at the lamp one more time, he murmured against her skin, "I want to see you tonight, Emily. I want to see all of you."

Emily did not look at all abashed at his boldness. Instead, she blinked, and then a smile of anticipation lit her face. "My thoughts exactly, husband."

A touch of guilt made him sit up for a moment. Taking her face in his hands gently and looking into her eyes, he reminded her, "We shall still have to have a courtship, Emily, despite the fact that we are married. Despite the fact that we share this bed."

"Must we?"

He nodded. "When all this is over, you will go to live with Simon and Miranda and we will behave as if we were not married."

She ran her hand along his rib cage, to his hip. "Only in public. In my bed, we will always be married."

He sighed. "Emily, it is only so that tongues will not wag . . . more than they will once Granbury's secret is revealed."

Her reply was mischievous. "I don't like that plan at all, but I suppose it would do no good to argue with both you and Simon. I will not have a long courtship, I hope?"

"Two months, I think," he answered. It seemed a lifetime, but it would—

"And what if there is a child?" she teased, drawing her hand slowly from his hip down his belly.

He knew the proper answer would be to tell her that he would ensure there would not be a child until after they were publicly married. But her lips were working warm on his shoulder and he knew himself better than to make a promise he had no hopes of keeping.

"The dress is beautiful, Emily. I only wish your father could be here to see you. He would be proud."

"Yes, Mother." Emily scowled when her mother's back was turned. She longed to step down from the stool upon which she stood, tear the gown from her back and announce to her mother that she would never have the chance to be married in this dress.

Pragmatically, she knew that if she told her mother she was already married—and no longer a virgin at that—her mother would ruin all the plans they had made. But the temptation was great, especially after a day of being pinned and tugged and having her corset strings tightened until she could no longer breathe.

"One week, my dear. One week and you shall be marchioness of Granbury."

"Why does that please you so, Mother?" she asked somewhat incautiously. She did not want to make her mother suspicious. She did, however, truly wish to understand what drove her mother to worry more about the title of the man her daughter married than the character of the man himself.

The countess stopped assessing the merits and drawbacks of her attire momentarily to train her gaze upon her daughter. The countess liked to emphasize important dictums. "Position is everything, Emily. Everything. And no one knows that better than I do." The bitterness in her mother's voice was plain.

"Surely a marchioness is no better than a countess, except perhaps in the order in which one enters a room in the most formal of occasions?"

"Silly child. You will learn." Her mother had a faraway look in her eye. "Did you know that I had a chance to be a duchess once, and I threw it away because of some foolish pride?"

"What?"

"Your cousin Simon's father might have married me, instead of Simon's mother." Emily stared at this revelation as her mother continued. "But as he already had an heir—Simon's older brother, Peter, who died before you were born—I turned him down. I did not like the thought that a son of mine would be no better than second, inheriting no title and no position."

The countess laughed, with a sourness that came from a deep well Emily had not realized dwelled within her own mother. "Of course, considering Peter's death and Simon's inheritance of the title, I would now be the dowager duchess of Kerstone. And my son would—" She sighed. "If I had a son, that is. Perhaps I would have failed the duke just as I failed your father."

"I don't believe father ever considered that you had failed him by not giving him a son," Emily lied. She had heard the bitter arguments between her parents. Each blamed the other for their lack of a son and heir.

As their only child, a valueless daughter, she had served as a sign of failure for them both. She had learned to bear it, but it was not any easier to hear it even now, after her father was dead and buried and her cousin possessed the title of earl.

"You will not fail your husband, I hope." Her mother's eyes were small and shone bright with what Emily suddenly realized was hope. The ugly truth burst in on her: the countess held hungrily onto the hope that she would fail Granbury and produce no heir—or at the least, no male heir, as her mother had not managed for her father.

"My husband will not mind a houseful of daughters, I am sure," she replied tartly, to hide how shaken she was at this sign of her mother's true feelings for her. Would he? She thought of Valentine, and the way he cherished his sisters. No. He would not fault her if she did not give him a son.

The countess's mouth turned thin with scorn. "You are mad if you think Lord Granbury will forgive you for leaving him without an heir. Assuring the continuance of his marquesate is crucial to him, I assure you."

Her mother's spiteful words reminded Emily that she was still supposed to be marrying Granbury in a week's time. She was glad to know that the plan they had set in motion yesterday was at last ready to be finished tonight, by the pond. Her parents' bitterness had colored her life for as long as she could remember. It would be a blessed relief to be done with it at last.

Of course, that all depended on the success of their venture. She could only hope that they would all survive the night and she would be free of Granbury, of her mother, of everything but the need to be a good wife to Valentine and a worthy chatelaine of Anderlin.

Just as she was thinking how to divert her mother from her unpleasant conversational topic, she heard a light step and a rustle of skirts that came from neither herself nor the countess. "You are a beautiful bride," Miranda said as she entered the room.

Emily smiled at her, glad that now her mother would confine their conversation to matters of dress, flowers, guests, and food for the guests who were beginning to arrive and fill the house with voices and laughter.

Emily tried to pay attention to the conversation, but she was much too aware of Nancy and her misery. The maid watched from the corner, a nervous look in her eyes as she glanced at the door every few minutes. She was rightly worried that the marquess would find her and tell the countess about the blackmail attempt—or worse, attempt to quiet her with his previously successful method of murder.

Although they wanted the marquess to do just that, they did not want him to do it before they had planned. Unfortunately, that meant that Nancy must suffer looking over her shoulder. She could not be left alone—and even when she was in company, she was still nervous. Especially the countess's company. If Granbury told her that he had seen Nancy deliver— It did not bear thinking about.

Emily felt guilty that the maid must live with the fear that Granbury could accost her at any point before tonight's scheduled rendezvous. She doubted he would come into the fitting room, which was why she had insisted that Nancy accompany her, but the girl was miserable all the same.

Miranda apparently noticed the same thing, for she asked quietly, "Emily, I have decided to drive into town for a few ribbons and things. Would you mind if I take your maid with me? Mine is feeling under the weather and I need someone to hold the goods and help me select what I need."

Although the last thing Emily wanted was to be left alone again with her mother, she valued Nancy's peace of mind over her own comfort. After all, she had been dealing with her mother all her life. She could handle one more day.

"Please do." Emily nodded at Nancy, who smiled faintly at the reprieve. "You may accompany the duchess, Nancy. Do exactly for her what you would do for me, or I shall be very displeased." The autocratic command was made more for her mother's sake than Nancy's. She was certain the girl would do as Miranda bade, in the time when the two of them were not plotting some new eventuality for tonight's plan.

At last, when the fitting was through, and Emily had heard the last of the plans her mother had made to create a memorable wedding for her daughter—and, more importantly, to create a favorable impression upon her guests—Emily was free to seek out Simon.

He was reading in the library when she came upon him and looked up when she entered the room. "Emily. Miranda tells me that you have completed the fittings for your gown. She says that you look well in it. It is a pity you will never have a chance to wear it."

"It is no pity, it is fitting that I not marry in such a gown," Emily said forcefully.

He put his book aside and raised one eyebrow. "Exactly why is it fitting?"

"Well, since no one in my family—including you, Cousin—see fit to respect the man I have chosen to give my love and fidelity, I can't imagine that I should marry in a beautiful gown. No, I more picture myself in sackcloth and ashes."

A smile quirked at his lips for a moment, but he answered her solemnly enough. "I do indeed respect Valentine, Emily. But he has allowed his feelings to overcome his sense in this matter."

"If you had not interfered three years ago—"

"If I had not interfered in your elopement, I would never have married Miranda. Did she tell you that?"

"I don't believe it—the two of you are as well matched as Valentine and I. You would have realized it sooner or later when our families joined."

He shook his head and held up his hand to silence her protest. "I have heard enough recriminations from Miranda these last three years, my dear, I need no more from you. Do you have any idea of the gossip you would have had to live down?"

"Would it have been more gossip than I have had to endure because two men proposed to me and died before we could be married?"

He laughed softly. "I always thought you a meek and proper little thing, but I see Valentine knew you better."

"Indeed he does know me better. And I pray he only learns to love whatever he might not know about me in the lifetime we will spend together— with or without your blessing."

He looked surprised. "Oh, you have my blessing,

Emily, do not doubt it." His expression became grave. "But I do not know what good it will do you when it becomes common knowledge that you eloped virtually on the eve of your wedding to another man. I can only hope that Granbury's crimes will overshadow your own behavior as a jilt."

"I love—"

"I do not doubt it. Nor do I doubt that he loves you. I knew that long ago."

That admission surprised the breath out of her.

He smiled. "Sometimes I wish I had not seen you, Emily, for your sake. But I did—and found Miranda in the bargain—and wishing it away will not change that."

"Still—"

"Still, we must try to keep the scandal to a minimum, don't you agree? For your children's sake."

She nodded, hearing the sadness in his voice. Though they did not speak of it, she knew that both Simon and Miranda were unhappy over their failure to produce a child three years into their marriage. "I can agree that a lack of scandal will certainly make my children's lives easier."

"Good. Then please do your best to keep your secret for a little longer—until we have Granbury securely caught, and until we can plan a proper courtship and wedding for you and your impetuous husband."

"And why would we need a courtship and wedding when we can simply say that we eloped without saying that we did so while I was still engaged?"

"Respectability, my dear. Respectability. What if some busybody chanced to find out the truth?"

"I do not care a fig for respectability."

"You will when you have children." He looked at her sternly. "Which may be sooner than can be politely explained, judging by the scene we found last night."

Emily blushed. She would have argued, but just then Granbury's voice echoed from down the hallway and within a moment he had entered the room.

"Here you are, my dear. I have been looking for you," the marquess said with a little chuckle. He nodded at Simon. "Kerstone."

While in another circumstance the duke might have left the two alone, in this case he merely picked up his book and began reading again. He did not deign to notice Granbury's unhappy glances, or his broad hints that Simon might be comfortable elsewhere.

After the third of these hints, Simon placed his book back down. Emily panicked, thinking that he intended to desert her. Instead, Simon did his best to entertain the marquess with stories of his trip abroad.

The distraction was fortunate, because Emily was not in any mind to discuss travel or trivial matters with Granbury. Her head was churning with the thought of how any child of hers might be teased or shunned because of anything she herself had done to heap scandal and disgrace upon her own head.

For the first time, she understood why Valentine cared so very much that her reputation be spotless.

It was one thing to consider withstanding the gossips for yourself. For another, especially an innocent child that one has brought into the world, it was a much less pleasant prospect.

Twenty

Valentine didn't dare rub his neck, or stretch his shoulders, despite the tension that played along his muscles. He had been on alert all day waiting for Granbury to make a move. The marquess had not shown any signs of his intentions. But none of them doubted that he meant Nan no good.

Between Emily's fitting and Miranda's outing, they had managed to keep the maid safely out of Granbury's path. Tonight, within hours, all should be finished. All that was left, thankfully, was to wait for the marquess to appear at the pond. Not that crouching in the shrubbery was his favorite pastime, but if it meant ending this once and for all, he would crouch here motionless all night without complaint.

The air was heavy with an impending storm, the breeze brisk enough to make it hard to hear Simon's voice. The duke had chosen to crouch in another clump of bushes to the left of the one in which Valentine hid. Communication should not be necessary, though, he comforted himself. They had discussed the plan, and alternatives should the marquess not act as expected. There should be no further need to speak until events were in full motion.

He surveyed the area around the pond, moving his head slowly and carefully from right to left and back again. Nan sat upon a fallen log, dressed in white so that she would not get swallowed quite so easily by the falling darkness. Nothing else moved except the reeds and branches brushed by the wind.

Though he could not see Nan in detail from where he sat, he knew that she was still shaking in fear, just as she had been when he and Simon had walked her out to the pond and settled her on the log. Her bravery amazed him. Despite her trembling as they walked from the castle, her eyes were fierce and her jaw set.

He had offered to take her place—covering himself in a cloak to disguise that he was not a woman. She had refused without a second thought. Just now, though, he wished he were the one perched on the log. The branches which hid him also poked and scratched at his skin. And he wouldn't have to worry about the risk to Nan if he were the one out there.

They had convinced her—and themselves—that nothing could go wrong as long as she stayed in the open. There on the log they could see her, and would see Granbury approaching before he reached her. There they could hear the conversation between the maid and the marquess—if only the wind would die down just a bit.

Even as his mind worked the potential scenarios, he kept a close eye on the area. From nowhere, it seemed to him, Granbury walked into the open. The prickle of the bushes against his cheeks suddenly faded as he watched the marquess stride confidently toward the maid.

She sat oblivious to his approach, watching the path that led directly from the castle, rather than the path leading from the stables. Granbury must have chosen a different path on purpose, hoping for the element of surprise. Well, he had gotten it—at least where the maid was concerned.

It was still light enough for the marquess's figure to be clearly seen. He had no weapon in his hand. There was not any menace in the set of his shoulders. Would he speak to her first, or go straight for murder? They had guessed, based on his history, that he would want to torture Nan a little. Make her know her ultimate helplessness.

Valentine felt a bit of that powerlessness himself as he watched Granbury approaching Nan from behind, while she had her gaze glued in another direction. *Turn around girl*, Valentine willed her silently. But she did not.

He tensed, prepared to rush the marquess should their hypothesis be proven wrong. It was all too possible that Granbury might confound them and simply attempt murder without first talking to the maid.

The marquess stopped several feet away from Nan. His voice was calm and quiet, almost inaudible upon the breeze that carried it to Valentine's ears. "Does your mistress truly think I will allow her to blackmail me?"

Nan started and turned to face him, putting the fallen tree between them, as if it might offer her some protection. "Lady Emily has nothing to do with this. It was my idea." Good. She might be nervous and caught off guard, but she had remembered the story the five of them had cobbled together.

Granbury scoffed. "Those notes were not penned by an illiterate servant."

Nan straightened her shoulders, shedding the deferent pose of servant. "I am not illiterate. I 'ave been well trained as a lady's maid and my penmanship is unexceptionable."

"You are still a servant, penmanship or not." Granbury's eyes flashed with ire. Apparently the maid's lack of servility irked him more than her attempt to blackmail him. "I do not doubt that you are doing the work of your mistress. She has made it plain enough that she would prefer to break the engagement."

"Lady Emily 'as her own reasons for wanting you gone." Nan's voice rose. "And I 'ave mine."

"And what could a maid care about enough to risk committing a serious crime to obtain?"

She taunted him, as they had asked her to do. "Maybe I just don't like that others like me can be taken advantage of by you. Maybe I want to see you pay for your crimes." The taunts might have been contrived to cause the marquess to lose control of his temper, but there was truth in them, too. Valentine could hear the maid's honest hatred.

Granbury seemed to hear the sincerity as well. "Are you so certain that I have committed any crimes, girl?" He shook his finger at her in admonishment. "I assure you my peers find me a most

congenial companion." Frustratingly, he had gotten
control of his initial irritation.

"I 'ave the letter . . ." Valentine tensed as Nan
broke off nervously. After a stammered recovery, she
continued, "And don't be thinking I 'ave it 'ere, on
my person. I'm not so foolish as that! It's safe and
sound where you'll never find it."

The marquess's laugh was quiet, but Valentine felt
a shiver of evil pass through him as the sound came
to him. "You should have taken the letter more seriously, young woman. I am not afraid of a simple
maid. I eat them for breakfast."

Nan's voice was steady when she answered. "I
think I took it seriously enough. After all, you'll not
be wanting anyone to 'ear about this—especially not
your bride. She might just change 'er mind again
and bolt."

Granbury remained unrattled, as far as his demeanor showed. "She's past any chance to change
her mind, girl. Don't you remember? She and I have
enjoyed the benefits of marriage a little in advance
of our wedding date."

Nan scoffed at that, which made the marquess
frown. "She didn't even know you were there."

He shrugged, and resumed his calm expression.
"What is true matters less than what is believed."

Nan's voice was low and rich with venom. "Maybe
not any longer. Once I tell—"

He laughed again. "Believe me, girl, I could let
you spread your rumors without a worry. No one
would believe such lies about me."

"I can prove what I say with the letter." Nan

sounded a bit desperate, as if Granbury's very calmness was rattling her.

"Proof?" He shook his head, his voice sounding low and mournful. "Nonsense. I am an upstanding member of the House of Lords—I belong to all the right clubs." He chuckled. "And not one of my peers has ever seen me with blood on my hands."

Nan raised her hand and pointed to his face. Her arm trembled visibly, even from Valentine's distance and the shadow of the growing gloom. "It shows in your eyes. Every evil deed you've done is there in your eyes."

"Ah, but who wants to see something so unpleasant? No one that counts, I assure you."

Nan argued, "All I need to do is make people look. Then they'll see it for themselves."

"Haven't you learned yet that it is difficult to make people see the things they would rather not? And I assure you, accusing me, a peer—the marquess of Granbury—can't you see that no one will *want* to know?"

"That may be." There was a bleak sound to her voice. "But I 'ave to believe all your kind gets what's coming to 'em." Nan spoke softly, but her voice carried. "I'll see you 'ang for your crimes, my lord."

"That could never happen. Not even if you manage to return to the castle alive and well." The threat was so smoothly voiced it sounded like a commonplace remark.

The maid's voice was shaking, but from anger, not fear. "I'll see you 'ang if it's from my grave."

The marquess shook his head sadly. "Too bad you

won't have a chance to prove your theory to me. But I have no intention of allowing you to live to find out if I get what you think is coming to me." Slowly, he edged toward her, as if he thought she would turn and run if he moved too quickly.

Nan said doggedly, "I'll tell 'em. All of 'em—the countess, the duke, my lady."

"I'm afraid I have no intention of allowing you back into the castle." The marquess paused a moment, as if considering her fate. "No. The good people who served with you, your poor mistress, will all be distressed to discover that you have thrown yourself into the pond tonight."

Nan crossed her arms in front of herself and moved back a pace, at last noticing how close he had come. "I will not."

"No doubt you found yourself abandoned by a lover. Perhaps you thought you were carrying a child?" The marquess spoke in a voice that robbed Nan of the will to move. Soft. Soothing. Deadly. "Life can be hard for an unmarried woman who bears a child she never wanted. Yes. I like that rumor. That is the one I choose for you, my girl."

Nan shook her head and said faintly, "No one will believe it."

"Enough will. All those folks you thought were your friends. And your mistress. Innocent as she is, I will take great pleasure in describing the agony you must have found yourself in, poor girl, to think the only answer lay at the bottom of a pond."

His voice vibrated through the night air and Valentine prepared to leave his cover. "Can't you see the tears that news will bring to her eyes? I will enjoy caressing them away, all in your memory . . . what is your name, anyway?"

Valentine was shocked to hear the steel in Nan's reply. "Nancy McGarrity, my lord. Perhaps you recognize it? You did meet my sister once. Nellie McGarrity she was, before you killed her."

Nan had not backed away, seeming oblivious to the marquess's slow approach. She was no longer trembling. The marquess had piqued her anger. Unfortunately, that made her careless of the danger she was in. "And that's what I'll tell them—my lady Emily and your wedding guests. You killed my sister."

Granbury stopped in his tracks for a second. He seemed lost in thought. "Yes. You'll tell them about your sister. I can't say as I remember her specifically." Then he nodded and said quietly, as if commenting on the weather, "But I'm sure I can describe her— blonde, delicate, without many scruples or morals to hamper her ambition to have the best in life?"

Nan hissed in anger. At the same time, she took a step toward the marquess, her hands outstretched as if to push him.

"I see my memory is accurate enough." The heavy dusk did not hide their figures well enough to prevent Valentine from seeing what happened next. The marquess caught Nan effortlessly, turning her away from him and lifting her off her feet so that her kicks landed uselessly in the air. Her arms were pinned to her sides. In a moment she gave up her struggle, recognizing that it would do her no good.

The trap sprang into place as Valentine abandoned his hiding place and stood, heart beating wildly at the sudden arrival of the moment of truth. He met Simon's eyes and the two men, as one, began to run toward the marquess.

Emily had barely stopped herself from letting out a scream when Granbury grabbed the maid, immobilizing her so quickly that there was no chance for the girl to escape. Thankfully, she had not made a sound that might reveal her presence.

Not only would a revealing sound surprise Granbury, but no doubt Valentine and Simon would be furious with her for putting herself in danger. They would not understand that she had promised Nancy as well. How could she keep that promise if she were hiding in the castle like a coward when the trap was sprung on Granbury?

She held her breath and watched from her perch high up in a nearby tree as Nancy's terrified eyes searched wildly for help. The marquess, as calmly as he sipped his after-dinner port, reached one hand to her throat even as his other arm bound her helplessly to him. With a little smile of pleasure, he began to squeeze the maid's throat very slowly.

Nancy began to struggle again, but it did no good. Her face darkened as she fought to breathe. Emily held her own breath as she watched.

Valentine and Simon had risen from their hiding places and begun to run with almost no hesitation. Did they intend to overpower the marquess while he held Nancy captive? And if so, would Nancy be hurt in the inevitable struggle? Emily scoffed at her own foolish thought. No doubt the maid preferred a broken arm to death by strangulation.

Nancy's revelation, her fury, had spurred the marquess to make his move more quickly than any of them had expected. Emily could not bring herself to fault the maid for allowing her grief and anger to blind her to her own danger for a moment. The truth was that the marquess knew all too well how to take advantage of the maid's lapse in attention. Emily prayed that Valentine would know what to do to rescue the girl.

Granbury caught sight of the men running toward him and left off his strangulation to pull out a cord from his pocket and whip it around Nancy's neck. As the men approached he called out, "Halt now, or I'll tighten this until there's no hope for her."

Valentine and Simon stopped paces from the pair. Emily strained to see them. Their eyes seemed to be focused on Granbury. Occasionally, however, their glances strayed toward Nancy, whose face was rapidly turning a rich plum shade as she tugged at the slowly tightening cord fastened around her neck.

Simon's voice was thick with fury. "It's done, Granbury, for God's sake. Release the girl and come with us."

Emily held her breath. Her cousin had infused every ounce of regal command into his words. Would it be enough to convince Granbury to surrender? To release Nancy?

"Never underestimate me, my dear Kerstone. I have no intention of coming with you. And if you want the girl alive—" his eyes were alight with evil as he added, "—although I can assure you that dead would make her much more interesting—you will walk away now."

"We know your secrets, you will have nowhere to hide. The truth will come out." Valentine looked ready to spring. Emily's heart skipped a beat with fear for him.

"The truth that you are no simple footman, you mean?"

Valentine, evidently having learned his lesson from Nancy's lapse, did not rise to the bait. "The truth that you are a murderer. Worse, that you have trapped and tortured those women who were helpless to escape you."

"I merely treated them as they deserved." For a second, Granbury's composed expression slipped. Emily gasped at the darkness she saw there in his features. "They should not have wanted to escape. They did not appreciate their fortune in being adored by me—by a man whose station was far above their common one."

"No one deserves to die in such a manner," Valentine replied angrily. Emily could see how it frustrated him not to be able to just rush forward to free Nancy.

The marquess, still as calm as he might be in a casual conversation, despite the maid struggling in his grasp, added, "I don't suppose you really care about the maids, though. No. You are most concerned my method of wooing wouldn't do for your little Emily, now, aren't you Fenster?"

Valentine started, obviously surprised that Granbury knew his name. He did not reply to the taunt.

Granbury laughed. "Do you think I don't know you covet her? She is a wild thing under that sweet frosting her mother has layered her with, isn't she? I will look forward to teaching her what it is to be a wife."

Emily felt the first drops of the threatened rain as she waited for Valentine to at last lose his own composure. But all he said, with great force, was, "You'll never get the chance." To her surprise, she noticed that Simon was moving closer to the marquess as Valentine held the madman's attention. None of the three seemed aware of the gathering rain.

"*Never* poses such a challenge, does it not?" The marquess set Nancy's feet back on the ground, but held her close with the threat of the noose around her neck. "I do love a challenge." He turned toward Simon's stealthily approaching form, jerking the cord at Nancy's neck to drag the girl backward toward the path that led to the stables.

Emily could not stand by silently any longer. There had to be something she could do to make sure she kept her promise to Nancy. Slowly, carefully, she began to climb down from her safe perch, just as the storm let loose.

Twenty-one

Impotent with fury, Valentine stood in the rain and darkness and watched as Granbury retreated. The man was disappearing into the gloom, taking their hopes of exposing him further away with every step. Taking away his hope of keeping his promise to the maid. He could not bear it if Nan was hurt because he had allowed the marquess to goad him into carelessness.

He would not let Granbury harm the maid. He had promised. He followed, determined this was one promise he would not break.

Carefully, moving as slowly as possible so as not to alarm the marquess, he angled himself to catch the maid's terrified glance. Though she was frightened, he could tell she was alert for any possibility of rescue or escape.

She watched him mutely, and her silent plea begged him to help her win her freedom. She had managed to get her fingers in the noose around her neck, but that would do little good if Granbury gave even one sharp twist. The cord would no doubt strangle her, but not before it cut through her neck and she bled to death.

They had all known the risks, but somehow, facing them, deciding what to do, was more difficult than Valentine had imagined. Nan's life was in danger no matter what he did next. He considered one solution after another, discarding them almost as fast as they occurred to him.

There was one which might work—or might get her killed. Could she possibly bring the marquess down if she tangled her legs in his? And could he save her, if she did? There was no other choice. How could he convey the idea to her?

As if she'd read his mind, the maid blinked at him twice, then swung her legs violently first forward and then backward. She managed to hook one struggling foot beneath Granbury's heel. The marquess stumbled.

It was enough distraction for Valentine to surge forward and grab for the terrified maid. However, although Granbury loosened his hold on Nan to save himself from the fall, he did not release her—or his hold on the noose around her neck.

"Step back, Fenster." The marquess tugged gently at the cord in his hand and Nan whimpered.

Valentine, fury in every ounce of his being, stepped back. There was nothing else he could do if he wished to keep the maid's neck from being severed. Damn. He had been so close, the wool of her cloak had been in his hand!

Like a dash of icy water even colder than the rain pouring down, he heard Emily's voice from behind him. "Let her go, my lord, please. She is a loyal servant, nothing more."

Granbury started at the sound of Emily's voice. His eyes swung to her and he took an involuntary step in her direction, dragging Nan along.

"No." Valentine stepped between them without conscious thought. Where had Emily come from? Why had she— He pushed back the questions that threatened to distract him. In the tone of a husband who intended to be obeyed, he ordered, "You must go back to the castle at once."

"I can't," she said softly, putting her hand on his arm gently, as if to soothe him.

She pushed a drenched curl of hair away from her cheek and stood her ground. He looked into her eyes and saw a sense of certainty that filled him with foreboding. "Emily, this is not the time—"

She stepped past him, ignoring his words. Her eyes were focused on Granbury, with an occasional glance at Nan. "Would you not prefer to have me as your hostage, my lord?"

Granbury's eyes lit with delight as he glanced between Emily and Valentine. "So you prefer a marquess to a viscount, do you?"

Valentine found the urge to strangle him was hard to subdue.

Emily answered quite calmly, "Of course not."

Valentine smiled. He had no doubt her composure was hard won, but there was no sign of the battle in her voice.

The marquess blinked and frowned. "Then—"

"I want you to release Nancy," Emily said patiently,

as if talking to a recalcitrant child. "I realize you cannot do so safely unless you have another hostage."

At last, Granbury's composure cracked wide. "You would give up your freedom for the safety of this—this maid?"

Valentine, realizing at last what she intended to do, gripped her arm. "Emily—"

She broke his grip and moved forward without hesitation. "Of course I would."

Nan whimpered, "My lady, no—"

Emily looked at the maid, whose face glistened with rain—and probably with tears, as well—and was swollen from near-strangulation. "I keep my promises, Nancy."

Before Valentine could stop them, Granbury had released the maid, pushing her into the two men who had set out to trap and capture him.

It was impossible to say whether Emily stepped into the marquess's embrace willingly, or was captured. In the end it did not matter. He had her.

She stood still, staring at Valentine. Her eyes were pleading with his, but he did not know for what. She was now in Granbury's grip. The noose lay loose around her neck and she did not choke or gasp. But the threat was enough to keep him from acting.

Granbury's grin was wide. "So, Fenster. The better man wins, inevitably."

There was nothing to answer the taunt. Emily's life was in his hands. Valentine closed his fists against his desire to batter the man with them. Emily's gaze begged him to keep his rage in hand. But all he could do was wonder what she had been thinking to offer herself up like a sacrificial lamb.

The marquess evidently preferred to see his victims lose control. He did not stop his goading remarks, even as he began to back down the path toward the stables once again. "Don't worry about her welfare, Fenster. I shall treat her decently—as long as she behaves herself."

Desperation was building in him and he fought not to let it show in his voice or his manner. "You can go nowhere, Granbury," he called. "We know what you have done. You will not escape justice this time."

"You sound as naive as that maid of Emily's. Justice is in the eye of the beholder."

"Justice for you is to be tried for your crimes in front of all who used to respect and revere you," he snapped. "And I am the man to see that happen."

Granbury wiped rain from his face. "This is Scotland, Fenster. Remember that. A man can be married in an hour. Barbaric custom. But quite useful to me."

Emily's eyes met the marquess's in horrified understanding, and then comprehension dawned and the blaze of fear in her gaze extinguished. She was already married.

Granbury's threat was impotent, little did he know it. All Valentine could do was thank God he had not fought her on the matter one day longer. If—

For a moment, he was tempted to reveal the truth to the marquess. As if she knew his desire, Emily shook her head almost imperceptibly. He knew she was right. Still, he fought the urge to proclaim her as his once and for all. He was tired of the secrecy.

"What hope do you have, married or not?" Simon asked, his voice steeped in reason. The question seemed simple, but Valentine noticed how the duke stepped forward slowly as he asked, moving ever closer to the pair.

"Would you ruin your cousin's life—the family honor itself—by accusing her husband of murder?" The marquess's smile was once again self-assured as he mocked Simon. "I think not, your grace."

Taking another step closer, Simon asked, "But what about Fenster? He's already tried to elope with her once."

"He cannot marry her once I have made her my wife. Even such a devoted lover cannot argue that truth."

"I could take her away to Europe. She could divorce you." Valentine made his threat by instinct. Granbury was growing much too cocky. He needed to be made to doubt himself somehow.

Simon sighed. "See? He may be my wife's brother, but he has no sense of propriety at all. What makes you so certain he will keep the secret, whether the scandal hurts Emily or not?"

The marquess looked him in the eye and Valentine felt as if his soul was being scoured for clues. But then, with a flick of his gaze, the marquess turned his attention back to Simon. "He loves her enough to play the part of servant. He will say nothing once he has lost her."

"Perhaps, once he knows all is lost, he will want revenge?" Simon suggested reasonably.

Granbury's laughter was pitying. "No, he will pine for her, like the impotent, inferior lover he has always been."

Valentine fought his rage, which made him want to throw the truth in the sneering marquess's face. He had not only married Emily, he had bedded her. And she had not found him inferior in any way.

But he did not. Granbury thought once he and Emily married, he would be safe. If he knew he could not marry her because she already possessed a husband, there was no telling what he might do to Emily in his rage.

Simon had come close enough to touch Emily's sleeve before Granbury noticed and pulled her off her feet, tightening the cord around her neck. Emily's gasp of fright stopped the duke.

"Don't follow us, or I will find it necessary to mar her pretty neck as I did that insolent maid's earlier. None of us want that, I'm certain."

The men stood still, forced to watch as Emily and the marquess disappeared into the darkness, down the wooded path toward the stables.

"Are you just going to stand there like two lumps?" Nan recalled the men's attention to the situation at hand with her caustic comment. They turned to stare at her, but her face was invisible inside the hood of her cloak, with rain dripping steadily down.

"No. We must follow them." Valentine would have

followed the path the marquess had taken, but Nan stopped him with a hand on his arm.

"There's a shorter path—the one the servants take sometimes." Over her shoulder, as she led the way, she said, "It's a mite less well cleared, but we'll get to the stables before they do, if we 'urry."

Emily could feel the cord around her neck. It was not tight enough to restrict her breathing, as it had been for Nancy. But all that would take would be a quick twist of Granbury's fingers. She needed to escape. But how?

Their passage down the rain-slick path was slow and steady as he pulled her backward. But suddenly he forced her to a stop and held his finger to his lips for silence. She heard nothing but the patter of the rain on the leaves above. He uttered a sigh of satisfaction. Evidently nothing but raindrops was what he wanted to hear.

"We'll go faster if I don't have to drag you," he muttered, releasing her, but not his hold on the cord around her throat. He grabbed her arm and began to pull her up the path. She tried to resist, but he would not slow his pace and twice she nearly slipped on the leaves underfoot. Common sense warned her that to fall would mean strangulation or worse, so she went only as slowly as she could do safely.

Too soon they reached the stables. The stable men watched without curiosity as Granbury led her into the stable yard and called for a horse to be saddled.

Despite the weather, despite the darkness, they complied without question.

Where this evening she would wish for them to be shorthanded and slow, instead they worked quickly. In too few minutes a deferent servant, who didn't even look her in the eye and see her plea for help, led out the marquess's horse.

She noticed that he had ordered only one horse saddled. She dared to hope that meant— "Are you letting me go free?"

"No." His answer was short and brusque. Even as he spoke, his gaze followed the shadows of the path.

Emily hoped he had simply overlooked her need for a mount in his haste. "Then where is my horse?"

Unfortunately, he had not. "You will ride with me." He tugged playfully at the cord. "I will not risk letting you out of my sight this time until we are married."

Damn! Emily studied the marquess's horse. If only it had been a more sedate mount that would be easily overtaken by one of the better beasts in her mother's stable. But the animal was magnificent and would no doubt hold them both and still manage to outpace most horses without difficulty.

She was beginning to believe that she was going to be forced to commit bigamy when she caught sight of a flicker of movement in the shadows within the stable entrance. There. It came again.

She watched closely, turning her back to the marquess so he would not see where she had focused her attention. With renewed hope in her heart, she saw Valentine take advantage of Granbury's inattention to step out and catch her eye. He put his finger to his lips.

She nodded, not even allowing herself a smile, in case the marquess might notice and wonder at it. In one blink of her eye, Valentine had disappeared. For a despairing moment, she wondered if hopelessness had made her dream that he was there.

"Up you go, my dear," Granbury said in her ear as he lifted her into the saddle. He mounted quickly behind her. The horse registered its protest of a double burden with sudden skittishness.

Granbury had no trouble controlling the animal, however. "Ho!" he murmured, pulling tight on the reins. The horse gentled at once, to Emily's great disappointment.

"Your mother's stables are not as fine as they once used to be, I'm afraid," he complained in her ear. "Zeus does not balk unless he has been poorly cared for."

"Perhaps the feed was not up to his usual standards," Emily replied with a touch of irony. "Or the stall was colder than he is used to."

Granbury laughed. With his body pressed tight against her back, the vibration was most unpleasant. She hoped Valentine did not intend to wait much longer to rescue her. And then she realized what was holding him back.

She reached up to her neck and pulled at the cord. "If Zeus throws me, this will break my neck more surely than the fall itself."

Granbury's cold damp fingers traced her neck a little above where the cord lay. "A little insurance is always wise when one possesses a valuable investment that is not yet secure," he answered.

"I—"

"When we are married, Emily," he chided her. "I will not remove it a moment sooner." The cord grew tighter as he spoke. "Do not question me again."

She nodded, feeling the cord pull against her throat as she did so. "I won't," she answered meekly. To her relief, the cord grew loose as a necklace. Apparently the marquess appreciated her humility and obedience enough to reward it.

Hopefully, Valentine and Simon had seen the exchange and understood that the cord would not be taken off in the stable yard. She prayed they would not use that as an excuse to allow the marquess to ride away from the castle unhampered.

As Granbury turned the horse away from the stables, the animal shied again. This time, it pawed its hoofs into the air and Emily was afraid of being unseated. Instinctively, she tried to slip the loose cord over her head while Granbury busied himself getting control over the horse.

Just as a groom grabbed the reins and forced the horse to stand still, Emily found herself free. Granbury had providentially loosed his grip on the cord while he fought for control.

Without further consideration, she dove from the horse. For a moment she thought herself free. Then, with a rip of silk, the marquess's hands grasped at her skirts and she was caught, dangling at the side of the still skittish mount.

But not for long. Strong hands grabbed her

around the waist and pulled her away from the horse, even as it once again reared. She embraced Valentine, feeling the tears of relief fill her eyes so that she could not see his face as more than a blur in the darkness.

He pulled her away from Zeus and she saw that Simon held the reins. They had him! The plan had worked after all.

But even as she turned to kiss Valentine full on the mouth in celebration, Granbury slashed away the reins with a sharp knife he pulled from his boot. Before anyone could react, he had wrapped his hands in the horse's mane and spurred the frantic stallion toward freedom.

Twenty-two

Valentine swore as the mud from Zeus's hooves splattered against him like blows. His arms tightened around Emily and he drew her face into his chest to protect her from the brief but thorough assault.

He exchanged a glance with Simon. Should they saddle their horses and follow? In the dark and the rain it would be difficult. . . . But even as he had the thought, he knew that they could not move quickly enough to catch Granbury.

Still, they had to try. To leave at large a monster who valued life so little— It was unthinkable.

"I shall see that the horses are readied." He had released Emily and turned to do so even as he spoke, but Simon stopped him with a gesture.

In a voice that captured the low moment they all felt, he asked, "What use would it be to bring him back here now?"

Wasn't the answer clear enough? The question surprised Valentine. Even Emily turned in puzzlement to glance at her cousin. He said, "We can do as we planned, and tell everyone what we saw."

"We could." His brother-in-law frowned. "No doubt he would claim he had come upon the two of us trying to kill Nan—or perhaps his twisted sense of humor would make him claim he had foiled an elopement between you and Emily. And it would be our word against his."

True. The marquess did seem to have the gift of turning things to his own favor. "We must do something," Valentine said.

Simon nodded, his glance going quickly to Emily and then back to Valentine. "But must we do something that forces the man back here, where not only Emily, but Nancy as well, face danger from him?"

The question made sense. Now that the marquess had left the castle, there was less urgency to unmask his crimes. But they still must look for justice. "You do intend to pursue him, then?"

Simon nodded. "Yes. I will notify a discreet and very competent man in my employ to track his whereabouts."

"Is that safe?" Emily, her voice still shaky from her brush with death, faced her cousin. "What if he decides to return?"

Simon rubbed the rain from his eyes wearily. "I would not return, if I had—" He broke off and sighed. "But then, I am not mad. We shall have to remain on guard until we find where he has run to. The man seems to have no conscience—a dangerous advantage for an enemy."

"So we shall simply give up?" Emily's outrage was obvious. Valentine would have soothed her by taking her into his arms, but it occurred to him that he was still dressed as a footman and the other servants would no doubt notice and question the familiarity between their mistress and a servant.

He said gently. "No, we will not give up. We shall have to come up with a better plan."

"Now that he knows we are aware of his crimes? He will not be so foolish as to let us trap him again."

"True," Simon replied. "But Emily, there are those men who make their living doing tasks such as uncovering murderers and bringing them to justice. I will hire one of them—one I know will handle this matter well."

"So he escapes justice yet again." Emily nodded, her dissatisfaction clearly visible. "At least he is gone from here and Nancy is safe."

"No one is safe until Granbury is brought to justice," Simon answered sharply. There were lines of worry etched around his eyes that gave Valentine pause. Their vigilance would have to double. Granbury was not a man to dismiss—even if he was not nearby.

"Let us return to the castle and let Miranda know what has happened." He glanced around the stable yard, and then looked sternly at Emily. "I can only say it is a miracle that she had more sense than you showed, and remained in the castle as instructed."

Nan, who had been standing silently beside them, did not let that pass. "Lady Emily saved my life, your grace. She may 'ave no sense, but she 'as more courage than anyone I know."

The maid turned her back to the duke, put her

arm around Emily and began to lead her back to the house. "Come, my lady, I will fix you a bath."

Emily laughed softly. "And I will have someone tend that cut on your neck where the cord bit deep."

"I think they've recovered from their ordeal faster than I have," Simon observed dryly.

Valentine agreed, following them all back to the castle. His mind churned with possibilities, but none that satisfied him. He wished that Simon was wrong about the futility of pursuing Granbury. No doubt they would both feel better if they were able to ride hard in the dark, rather than return to the castle and decide what to do now that Granbury had fled.

Thankfully, Simon would have to deal with Miranda and all her questions.

"I am star-crossed, there is no doubt," Emily lamented to Miranda as they all huddled in clandestine comfort in her room. Nancy had provided them with a pot of chocolate for the women and a bottle of port for the men. "How could things go so wrong?"

"How could you have offered yourself in exchange for the maid?" Miranda asked. "I am in awe of your courage."

Emily shrugged. "He wanted to marry me, I didn't think he was as likely to kill me as he was to kill Nancy."

"That was a risky gamble," Simon ground out.

Emily shook her head. "No. I was right. He didn't give a fig for her life. It's a wonder that she wasn't killed. You should have seen her, Miranda, with that rope around her throat. Her face turned purple!"

Valentine tightened his arms around her. "You could have been killed. I have not seen anything so foolish since I saw you climb out your window and hang dozens of feet above the ground on bedsheets you had tied together. I do believe I wish I had let you run away as you intended back then."

Simon cleared his throat. "I wondered how you two met up with each other this time, given the countess's security."

"It was fate, of course." Emily sighed. "I cannot believe all our plans came to naught."

Miranda sipped at her chocolate. "He thought more quickly on his feet than we expected, I suppose. But we can take heart that he is on the run. I expect Simon is right and he will turn up in London, as if nothing had happened."

For a moment Emily hoped that was true, that her part in this nightmare was over and done. But then a horrible thought struck her. "How can he?"

"Those in London would know nothing—"

"No." Emily shook her head frantically. "They may know nothing yet, but the gossip would spread as quickly as a plague. What explanation would he give for not showing up at his own wedding—for running to London without saying a word to Mother—to me?"

Valentine replied bitterly, "He seems well able to find excuses for murder, I doubt jilting you would be hard for him to explain."

But Emily didn't agree. "No. That is not the sort

of thing other gentlemen would forgive, you know. He would be burning his bridges. And I don't think he likes to do that."

"Do you suspect he will return for you, then?" Miranda asked in disbelief. "Surely he does not think we will let him marry you? Not now."

"Why not? Mother knows nothing. After all, he was planning to elope with me. He seemed to think neither Simon nor Valentine would be willing to ruin my reputation by exposing him as a murderer." Emily scoffed, "But that is ridiculous. Neither of them would let justice turn on my reputation!"

The two men said nothing at all to that statement. Miranda did not agree at once. Instead, she said thoughtfully, "Simon would see justice done quietly, I am certain. But he would not accuse the marquess in public—not when it would reflect upon you. As for my brother, don't forget that he gave up all hope of marrying you just because your reputation might be besmirched by a runaway marriage—a marriage against your parents' express wishes."

Emily huddled deeper in Valentine's embrace. He had loved her beyond common sense. And no doubt still did. The thought was almost frightening. Granbury had disappeared. But that did not mean he had traveled far. Which left them in quite a dilemma.

The marquess knew they had found out his secrets and were determined to reveal them. Worse, he knew where they were and they had no idea where he had gone. He could be lurking a mile away, or he could have fled to the Continent.

He could, as unbelievable as it seemed, be prepared to go through with the wedding that the countess was still planning. The thought was suffocating. Would this tangle never be cleared away?

"I had anticipated that we would be able to explain to Mother—and to all the guests—just why the wedding has been canceled," Emily said softly. "I thought Granbury's guilt would ease any questions on my star-crossed life. Now what shall we do? Pretend that we know nothing? Smile and simply ignore the fact that the man I am to marry has vanished and the wedding is set to be held in less than a week?"

"Your mother shall have to be told, there is no choice," Simon said firmly, anticipating her objection before she could even state it.

Emily sniffed. He thought he knew everything, but he had not considered the most important thing to the countess—status. "Without Granbury to confirm the matter, Mother will refuse to believe that he will not return. To do otherwise would be to accept scandal and she will *not* do that."

He said imperturbably, "Then we shall have to give her reason to accept that we tell the truth." His finger pointed to her neck. "The bruise around your neck and the cut around Nan's should be convincing evidence."

For one moment, Emily dared believe him. But then she knew better. "She will explain it away. She won't believe even you, Simon, no matter how perfect you are. Not until she has to, of course. If Granbury does not show up for the ceremony she won't be able to postpone the scandal any longer. But I doubt she will accept it a moment earlier."

Miranda took her hand and grasped it with a strength borne of determination. "Then we shall have to tell her that the wedding is off permanently—whether or not Granbury shows his face here again."

Emily frowned. "So we simply reveal that Valentine and I have eloped and that the marriage will not take place?"

Simon made a sound of disagreement, but Valentine cut him off with a sharp gesture. "We cannot do that. The scandal will be so great that your reputation would be destroyed, no matter how dull and respectable the rest of our lives might be."

"So then we go on, as if we do not know that Granbury has fled?" She could not help a little bitterness that leaked into her tone. "Will you sneak into my room each night, still? Will you masquerade as a footman in the day?"

He pulled back as if she had struck him. "A jilted bride is less scandal than one who elopes with another man and then announces it a week before the wedding without good cause."

She was becoming furious with the lengths they would go just to protect her reputation. "And what if he does not jilt me?"

Valentine said harshly, "What do you mean? He is gone. To come back would be madness."

Miranda said softly, "We do not know that he will not show up in time for the ceremony." She took Simon's hand and looked into his eyes.

"I had hoped you would protect her from scandal, Fenster, not subject her to the worst kind of gossip," Simon exploded in anger.

Emily was stunned to speechlessness by the unfairness of the accusation. Valentine, however, tensed and withdrew his arms from around her. "I had hoped the same, your grace. I could not have foreseen . . ."

"No, you couldn't have, Valentine," Miranda agreed, sending her husband a severe look. "None of us anticipated that he would do something so bold. Although perhaps we should have, considering how boldly he has been abusing and murdering servant women these past two decades."

"No one could have guessed," Emily agreed shakily. "We are fortunate that he did not add Nancy to the list of women he has murdered. Perhaps when we discover where he has fled we shall find out the answers we need. At the very least, that should tell us what he intends to do."

In the end, it was the countess who came up with the excuse for Granbury's absence in response to increasingly curious queries from her guests. "Urgent business in London. He will be back by the wedding day for certain."

She said it with a confident smile that made Emily wonder if she had talked to Granbury. But her mother disabused her of that notion as soon as they were out of earshot of any curious guests. "Where has he gone? Have you insulted him too greatly this time?" Her hands tightened like corset laces around Emily's forearms.

"No, Mother. I have not insulted him at all." She managed to convey enough sincerity to convince her mother. How could calling a murderer what he was be considered an insult, after all? "I would like to know where he is as much as you." *More*. But she did not want to overstate her case to the countess. Her mother, after all, was not a stupid woman.

"Has Simon's man located him yet?" she asked Valentine that night, while he held her warm against him. He had continued his ruse of footman so that he could remain in the castle without attracting attention—not one of the guests would understand why a man suspected of eloping with the bride would be allowed at the wedding—but he spent his days scouring the area surrounding the castle for any sign that Granbury might be close enough to cause them danger.

"Not yet." He sighed. "I believe Nan is at the end of her rope. I thought she would faint dead away this evening when I entered the room a bit too quietly while she wasn't looking."

Emily agreed. "I dread having her brush my hair anymore. She is so easily upset that she has had to cut several snarls out of my hair."

Emily ran her fingers lazily along the curve of his ribs. "I never thought I would say this, but I'm glad the wedding is day after tomorrow. Finally, it will all be over for certain—will he show, or won't he? At least, it will be over for us. I suppose Nan will worry until he is caught, won't she?"

"Perhaps I should take her to Anderlin? My sisters would keep her busy." His amusement was obvious in the curve of his mouth. She stretched up to kiss him lightly.

"Perhaps. But she would be exposed to Granbury's wrath while she travels, so perhaps not. She shall have to bear her nervousness a bit longer, just as you and I must." She shifted impatiently. "We all know the time is ticking away. What can he be thinking? Surely he must understand that even if he did return on the day of the wedding that I would not go to the altar, even if he dragged me there himself."

"I don't expect he is thinking anything that will do any of us good." Valentine's voice was filled with impotent fury and she wanted to ease him, as any good wife would.

"I'm certain of that," Emily said with a shudder. Then she ran her finger lightly down his ribs until she felt his breathing quicken. "But do we have to discuss him all night?"

Twenty-three

One of the guests, a cousin Emily could not remember having met before—probably because that branch of the family did not come equipped with a title—raised the alarm early one morning. The breakfast room was full when he came running in, waving a dirty scrap of cloth and nearly hysterical with shock. "The marquess has been most foully murdered!"

Simon, as was his wont, took charge. He leaped up from his place at the table and strode over to the panting relation. "Come, man, do not upset the ladies like this."

"Forgive me, your grace," the man said, abashed. His voice grew quiet. But not so quiet that Emily did not hear every word he said. "I fear the marquess has been waylaid and murdered on his return from London."

"Are you certain?"

"Quite. Here is his bloody neckcloth—and his torn jacket, bloodstained as well."

As ever, Simon asked the most important question first. "Did you see a body?"

The man swallowed and his throat worked. "No, your grace."

Simon raised his brow imperiously. "Perhaps he is even now being tended within the castle walls—"

The man protested, holding up the shredded cloth. "No man could have survived such a vicious attack. No, I suspect his body lies in the loch."

Emily wondered if Granbury had finally met his just end at the hands of someone who knew what kind of man he was. But somewhere deep inside she was afraid it was another game the man was playing with her—with them all.

That his bloody belongings had been found near the loch made the situation difficult to determine. If he had been thrown in, he might never be found. The depths of the loch were greater than anyone had ever plumbed and it rarely gave up its secrets.

"We shall begin a search," Simon said, motioning to Soames. "Men, we have a duty to do for our hostess." There was a hubbub at that, but the men eagerly rose. Their questions threatened to deafen everyone.

"We need to send men into the loch," someone shouted.

"But we'll never find the body, the depths are too great."

"Who could have done it?"

The murmur rose to a rumble as that question was discussed. Emily herself began to wonder if— But no. Valentine would not have done something like that without telling her. And if he hadn't told her, she would still know. She would see it in his eyes.

Simon restored order by shouting in his most authoritative voice, "Let us not disturb the ladies, gentlemen. I will explain matters once we are all out of doors."

Emily watched as they filed out. She was not surprised when Valentine, abandoning his footman duties, followed in their wake despite Soames's initial objection. When the duke stepped in to request all the footmen participate, though, the butler quickly changed his tune.

Miranda, a triangle of toast dangling unnoticed from her fingers, whispered, "He has begun his game now."

"Do you think so, too?"

"Yes, indeed." Miranda nodded, and then gave a tiny shiver. "I wonder if we are up to playing well enough to win this time."

Emily frowned at the worry in the question. "Of course we are. Valentine will see that we win. I trust him completely."

Miranda paused thoughtfully for a moment and then sighed. "You are right. I suppose it is just knowing what Granbury has done in the past—and how closely he came to murdering poor Nan."

"Nancy!" Emily wondered if the maid had yet heard the rumors that would soon be circulating belowstairs, if they were not already.

Miranda stood, dropping her toast back onto her plate. "We must tell her of this latest development, Emily. The poor girl will be beside herself with fear knowing how close he must be to plant evidence of his own murder."

As they hurried into the hall to look for the maid, they were stopped by the people milling about in confusion as the men Simon had commandeered donned their boots and hunting jackets.

The countess looked furious. At first Emily believed it was because someone had dared murder one of her guests—the fiancé of her daughter at that. But then she waved a letter in the air. "I have no doubts the marquess has been murdered. I know who has done the deed."

As she was standing at the top of the stairs, all eyes turned to her while silence rapidly fell in the entrance hall.

"How can you know—" Simon began, but the countess cut him off sharply.

"I have received information that will shed light on this heinous crime." She studied the crowd, scrutinizing every face. Several people shifted their feet guiltily at the accusation in her bulldog features, but her gaze passed over their faces and settled on one in particular.

"I see the information was accurate." She pointed out the footman who had been serving in her household for weeks without notice. "Valentine Fenster has passed himself off as a servant in my very household."

Those standing around the suddenly no longer anonymous footman shrank back as if he were now revealed to be carrying the plague.

Emily made a wordless cry and would have run to

him, if Simon had not put his hand on her shoulder to prevent her from joining her husband.

Valentine met the countess's gaze steadily. "I have only done what I needed to protect Emily."

The countess's eyes narrowed. "Lady Emily to you."

He bowed at the waist. "Lady Emily, then, if you wish it, my lady."

Emily had never been so proud of him as she was at that moment. Where another man might have cringed in humiliation, he stood tall. It warmed her heart to see that he was not ashamed of doing what he needed for the woman he loved. For her.

The countess leaned over the banister, her gaze for Valentine and no other. "Tell my guests, Fenster. Did you, or did you not approach me less than a month ago in an attempt to encourage me to break the engagement of my daughter to the marquess of Granbury?"

"I did."

"And you were hired—through your own deceit—that same day?"

His lips tightened. "The next day."

The countess's expression of dismay was pretense. Emily had often seen her mother question a young matron in just such a way when she had an ugly secret to spring. She knew the question her mother would ask before she did so. "And where did you spend the night before you presumed upon my household's good nature?"

"Under a bed." His lips turned up in the smile she loved so much as he looked directly at her mother. "And I must compliment you on your staff's excellent housekeeping, my lady. There was practically no dust at all to disturb my rest."

Several of the onlookers laughed at the compliment to the countess's attention to detail in her household. The countess was not pleased at how skillfully he'd evaded the true answer to her question. But she did not pursue the matter.

Emily barely had time to be relieved that those present would not learn that Valentine had spent the night in her bed, when her mother turned her attention back to the guests in general. "I suggest that we have here a prime candidate for the murderer of my daughter's intended groom."

There was a low murmur of surprise. Emily waited for someone to object, but everyone watched her mother expectantly for her next pronouncement.

The countess, enjoying her captive audience, went on. "He is a man who, when he could not convince me to break the engagement dishonorably, lied and misrepresented himself as a *servant* to worm his way into my daughter's heart and turn her against me."

Melodramatically, she placed her hand on her heart. "I fear he has succeeded in both his tasks—to turn my daughter from her mother's wise teaching, and to break the engagement—by murdering the marquess of Granbury!"

"I did not murder the marquess, my lady," Valentine replied firmly, "if he was indeed murdered at all." Emily could see the truth in his expression and found that she wanted to weep in relief.

"If!" The countess shook with outrage. "How can you doubt it?"

"I can doubt it because I know what kind of man the marquess is. As you would, my lady, if you had read the letter I brought to you." Valentine stood proud, despite the dark looks that he was being thrown by the crowd. Emily couldn't stand to see him unjustly accused any longer.

She shook off Simon's warning hand and hurried to stand beside her husband. If he was not ashamed, she would not be. She ignored his unhappy look as she turned to face her mother. "Valentine has protected me as you would not, Mother." She turned to him and grasped his hand in her own.

"Emily—" he began warningly, but she ignored him.

"Mother, be careful of who you accuse of murder. It is my husband you say committed this crime—Valentine and I are married." She had hoped the first time she gave that news to her mother, she would feel satisfaction and triumph. But in the silence of the marble hallway, the words seemed thin and childishly spiteful.

That statement at least had the effect of bringing a genuine expression of shock to the countess's features. "Impossible!"

"It is true, I'm afraid." Valentine sighed. "We eloped over a week ago. I assure you, my lady, that the elopement was a necessary precaution to protect Emily from the marquess."

Emily's mother was not swayed by his heroic deed.

"Cad! Why would my daughter need protection from the man who asked for her hand honorably?"

Again, Emily felt the need to defend him against her mother's unjust accusations. "He would have preferred to marry me openly and honestly, Mother, you know that. But since you refused to welcome his suit, we were forced to this. I told you I would not marry Lord Granbury and you refused to listen."

The countess's fury was truly awesome to view. "This is how you repay all that I have done for you? Ungrateful child. I told you he would not make a good husband, but you would not listen. Let us see how you like being married to a murderer!"

"Valentine is not—"

"Well, someone has killed the marquess. I believe it is clear the man with the most motive must certainly be the one who masqueraded as a footman in the household. The man who deceived me under my own roof with my own daughter. The man who has so few scruples that he dared to elope with a woman who was a week away from becoming a bride to another man."

Emily could see that the crowd of guests agreed with her mother—slowly they were moving back, leaving Valentine and Emily in a large empty circle of floor. She looked to her cousins, her friends, trying to meet eyes which would not meet hers. "But he did not do it."

The countess replied scornfully, "So you say. But can we trust you to know this man?"

"Of course I know him!" Emily protested. "He is

gentle and kind and—and he would do anything to protect me."

"Anything? Even kill your rightful fiancé so that there would be no impediment to revealing your elopement?"

"No!"

The countess's eyes blazed with anger. "You have proven yourself weak-willed enough to have eloped with him—not just once, girl!" Her gaze bored into Emily, and she fed off the scandalized gasp that came from the gathered crowd.

"I love him!"

With a smile of triumph, the countess snapped, "Love! Twice now you have let him talk you out of behaving with common sense, decency, and the good morals that your father and I taught you."

The countess lifted a lace handkerchief to her trembling lips. "I am only grateful that my poor dear husband is not here to see how you have betrayed your family."

Though her mother dabbed at her eyes with the lace as well, Emily was all too certain they were dry. Her mother had at last gotten the revenge she had always wished for on the child who had dared to be born a daughter instead of a son. And Emily had helped her convict Valentine in the court of popular opinion. She could see what she had done at last.

Now that it was too late.

Valentine saw the realization sink in. Emily's expressive face reflected her despair without muting it. But what her face showed him was nothing to his own agony. He had done this to her. Despite his intentions, despite his promises, he had just destroyed the woman he loved.

Ignoring the eyes upon them, he embraced her tightly. "I'm sorry, Emily, so very sorry," he whispered. "You should have had so much better than what I have given you."

"I know you didn't kill the marquess. I don't even believe he is truly dead. I will convince—"

"No." He did not want her to put herself in any more danger. "If I am accused—"

"I will not let them—"

He kissed her gently to silence her fierce defense. "You must go with Simon and Miranda, you and Nan. They will keep you safe, if Granbury is still alive." And if Valentine ended up hanging for the crime in the end. He thought of his sisters. Thank God he knew that Simon would care for them as if they were his own.

She hissed, "He is. No doubt he is somewhere laughing at the trouble he has caused us."

"Take him upstairs and lock him in!" the countess ordered. Two of his fellow footmen looked at him apologetically as they approached. He did not fight them. What good would it do? Everyone was already sure of what had happened.

He could feel the condemnation like a leaden cloak around him as they led him away. Emily's sobs of dismay tore at him, but he did not look back. He had failed her. He had ruined her. And now she had to live with the distinct possibility of being the widow of a convicted—if innocent—murderer.

Twenty-four

He thought he had failed her. She had seen that clearly in his eyes as he was led away to be confined upstairs. But in truth it was she who had failed him. If she had said nothing of the elopement, her mother would not have— But it was much too late for recriminations.

If only the men who sat contentedly discussing the latest scandal would listen to her.

"They will hang him, you know. A peer cannot commit such a bloody crime upon another peer without expecting the most severe punishment possible."

"But they cannot, Harold." Emily looked at the man who had inherited her father's title, the newly made earl. The earnest look on his face told her that he thought his words offered some comfort but she could not understand how he could possibly think so.

"What choice have they?" he asked. "We must send a strong message that this sort of thing is frowned upon. Who else will set the example for the lower classes?"

She repeated the same words she had been saying for some time. "He is innocent."

The doubt on his face was unmistakable, but he patted her hand and said kindly, "Then someone will prove it, I am sure, my dear."

"How? Everyone believes him guilty!" It was true enough. Except for Simon, Miranda, Nancy, and Emily herself, everyone seemed quite content to believe that Valentine had murdered the marquess of Granbury.

The purported motives ran from a fairly honorable duel called by the marquess when he discovered the elopement, all the way to a desperate, murderous bid on Valentine's part to get his rival out of the way.

All versions agreed that after the murder he had then tidily disposed of the man's body in the waters of the loch. The fact that his tidiness had not extended to those bloody items which now condemned him bothered no one at all.

Her cousin thought about her question seriously for some time. And then he answered solemnly, "I cannot say how you might prove him innocent, my dear. I suppose it has been done before, but not often."

Portentously, he added, "It is a hard task I know, my dear. But you must do it soon. Matters as serious as this are dealt with swiftly. It would not do to have the common man believe his betters are afraid to do their duty when a criminal appears among their own ranks."

Emily threw her hands up in exasperation. "Of course not. And the criminal himself need not even be guilty for the appeasement of the masses, need he?"

Harold beamed at her, as if he were a teacher whose pupil had just mastered a particularly difficult lesson. "That is the way of the law, my lady. A man must stand up for the crime he appears to have committed, unless another culprit can be found."

She muttered, as her cousin moved away, obviously satisfied that his duty was well done, "Granbury was right—people do refuse to see what they find unpleasant or unacceptable."

There was no other answer that she could see but to solve the crime herself. "I will find the culprit, then. I will find the true murderer." Or would she find Granbury himself, alive and well?

She knew she could expect help from Miranda, Valentine's own twin. But would Simon help? Or had he, like all the other titled ninnies staying at the castle, decided that since Valentine's motive was the clearest that perhaps he *had* committed the crime?

She decided to approach Miranda and see if Simon had been honest with her about his belief in Valentine's innocence. She could not bear to talk to him if he did not believe her husband innocent. But as she looked for Miranda, she found Valentine's sister waving at her in an urgent signal.

Miranda's expression was grave as she led the way into a private parlor and Emily felt her heart catch. "What is the matter?"

Her voice low, so as to avoid being overheard, Miranda murmured, "Nan is missing."

"What?" What else could go wrong? Valentine accused of murder. Nancy missing. "Are you certain?"

"I've looked everywhere."

"Do you suppose—"

"What else is there to suppose?" Miranda was pale and there were tears standing in her eyes. "Granbury has her. We can only hope he has not already finished the job he tried to do by the pond that day."

Emily tried to find something reassuring about the situation. The best she could think of to offer Miranda some consolation was, "His preference in the past has been a more lingering death for the servants he killed."

Was it better to hope that Nancy had been swiftly and mercifully strangled, or that the terrified maid waited imprisoned somewhere, with time to wonder what her fate would be? With time to suffer.

Feeling as if everyone in the castle was her enemy made Emily cautious. She whispered, "Have you told Simon?"

"Yes. He has gone in to speak to Valentine—" Miranda grimaced in dismay. "My brother is well guarded. Your mother must think he is capable of magic, she has put so many safeguards in place."

"Has she?" Emily had not been allowed near her husband, at the direct instructions of her mother and her cousin Harold.

Miranda nodded miserably. "He is tied hand and foot, his arm is strapped to the bedpost, there is a guard in the room—and two outside the door of the room in which he is imprisoned."

Emily closed her eyes, picturing him trapped just

like they had hoped to do to Granbury. But it was Granbury who was guilty. Valentine was guilty of nothing but wanting the best for her. She wished, not for the first time, that she had not spoken a word of the elopement.

Her mother might have been infuriated with Valentine if she thought he had been *trying* to elope with her. But her fury that he had succeeded seemed to know no bounds. "Is he being fed?"

"Yes. The cook was fond of him when he was a footman." Miranda smiled. "He always had a way with the cooks at Anderlin, too."

"What shall we do?" Emily felt helpless. But then she remembered her resolution. "No. I know what we must do. We must find the real murderer."

"If there is one," Miranda added skeptically. "Granbury could have staged this whole business just to get rid of a rival for your affections and someone who knows the truth about him at one fell swoop."

Emily smiled, encouraged that Miranda was thinking as she was. "Then we must find him. For no one will believe it until they see him standing before them." The thought of having to find the marquess and manage to bind him for long enough to prove he had staged his own death gave her a headache.

Miranda nodded in agreement, and then said, "But first, we must find Nan."

"Of course." But how? With Valentine imprisoned upstairs there was one less person to help discover where the maid had been taken. One less person to keep their promise to her—to avenge her sister's

death, whether Nancy survived Granbury's wrath or
not.

Oh, well, what was one more impossible task, more
or less?

Twenty-five

The wine cellar was neat, if dark and damp. A tribute to Soames's skills as a butler, Emily supposed. For a moment she did nothing but stand still and silent, holding up the lantern. The glow was not nearly adequate.

The note had said to come alone. The only reason she had done so was the threat to Valentine. The note had said he would be killed if she told anyone.

Trussed as Miranda said he was, he would make an easy target. But though she had come alone, she had not come unarmed. She held the pistol steadily in the hand which did not hold the lantern.

Where was he? The note had to have been sent by Granbury. She knew no one else with such a sick sense of gamesmanship. The question was not where was he, she reminded herself after a moment. No, the question was, where was Nancy? After all, the note had said she would find the maid down here. Was it true?

She moved slowly, swinging the lantern back and forth until she felt dizzy from the play of light in the dark cellar. And then she heard the sound of scrabbling.

She froze and listened quietly. Mice? Loathesome creatures. There was but one way to discover the answer. She moved forward, toward the sound. Rounding a corner of polished bottles resting in their rack, she saw a pair of feet. Small and feminine. Not Granbury's feet.

To her great relief, as she directed the lantern light she found that the noise came from Nancy. The note had not lied. The maid had been tied up and left like a discarded sack of potatoes in the corner of the wine cellar.

But she was alive. "Nancy!"

The girl struggled to sit up.

"Wait!" Emily set down the lantern and the pistol, and hastily untied the maid's bonds. "Come, we must get out of here as quickly as possible. I don't know when Granbury will return."

"Now, my dear." His voice was as silky as ever. She turned to face him, marveling at how calm he could be when he was being hunted for murder. Never mind that most of the inhabitants of the castle thought him dead!

"I knew you weren't dead! I knew it!" Emily reached for the pistol, but he lifted his and pointed it toward her, halting her movement.

"I hope you told no one else your suspicions."

Emily considered that no one could hear her scream down here in the wine cellar. "Of course—I told everyone."

He smiled, as if it didn't matter. His calm demeanor incensed her immeasurably. "Good, then they simply think you mad and will not have believed you."

Nancy stood up next to her and together they faced him, leaning on each other for support. "You will not get away with this."

"Get away with what? The murders of a few poor women who were no better than they should be? Pretending that I have been most foully murdered——by your lover Fenster?" His laughter was full of self assurance. "On the contrary, I will get away with this, and I promise you I will be watching while the hangman's noose tightens around your lover's throat."

"My *husband* will not hang." Emily stood up as tall as she could as she flung the truth at him. If only she could distract him, she could retrieve the pistol and get the upper hand at last.

"Yes, he will, my dear." He blinked at the word husband, but the distraction was momentary and not an opportunity to reach for her weapon. "I will be dancing when he does."

"You are mad." Nancy's voice was toneless. Emily could see that the maid was tousseled but there were no fresh bruises at her throat. There must not have been time for Granbury to torture her—yet. But the girl seemed to have lost her will, judging by the dull look she pinned on the marquess.

He frowned at the maid. And then he smiled at Emily. "So some mundane minds might say. But I know better. And soon, my dear, I hope that you, too, will learn to appreciate my finer qualities."

There was a scuffling sound near the wine cellar

door. Someone called her name. Emily's heartbeat sped up. "Valentine?" As soon as she had called his name, she regretted it.

For a moment she hoped he had not heard. But then he shouted in return, "Thank God I've found you! Emily—are you all right?"

The marquess turned, the deadly pistol in his grip. Emily dived for her own weapon unsuccessfully as she screamed, "It's a trap, Valentine. Run! Save yourself." She knew it was fruitless to tell him to run. But she had to try. "For my sake," she pleaded, "save yourself."

The marquess, seeing her movement, turned back and there was a loud report as he discharged his weapon. Her lantern went out, but she felt no pain. She squeezed Nancy's hand and got a strong squeeze in return. Neither of them had been hit. But the darkness was complete.

"Emily!" Valentine's voice was choked with panic as he hurried past the rows of bottles toward the sound. She could hear his incaution in each step. He had no thought but to rescue her.

Scrabbling along the floor in the dark, Emily tried to find her own pistol. She called out again to warn him. "Granbury is here. He has a weapon."

The shine of a lantern grew brighter as he neared. In the light, Emily saw her pistol and grabbed it. She pointed it toward Granbury, who was crouched, reloading his own weapon. He turned it upon her. A single thought flashed through her mind: so this was what it felt like when men fought a duel.

Valentine's light fell full upon them, illuminating

the stalemate. But, aware of the dangerous nature of the marquess's temper, he halted his forward charge.

"How did you get free? Last I knew you were trussed like a Christmas goose." Granbury's tone was conversational. Pleasant, if she hadn't known he was mad.

"Soames saw Emily going down into the cellar and worried that something was afoot. He ordered the footmen to set me free so that I could look after Emily."

"He dared let a murderer go free?"

"He did not believe your story, Granbury. He believed mine. And he is loyal to Lady Emily, even if the countess is not."

"Loyalty is a rare commodity. So many discard it whenever it becomes inconvenient." The marquess continued softly, "For example, which of you will prefer to die? And which of you will prefer to save the other?" He laughed at the horror his questions evoked. "Or do you both prefer to live?"

"We both prefer to live, of course," Emily said calmly. She gestured to Nancy to leave them, but the maid did not move.

Granbury's eyes flicked nervously from the maid to Emily. "If you wish to live, Emily, then you know what you must do."

"I can't marry you, Lord Granbury. I have a husband."

"I can remedy that," he said, turning his glance, but not his pistol, upon Valentine.

"No!" Emily again gestured for the maid to go.

"Nancy, leave us now. There is no need for you to be hurt as well."

"She can't go. She will raise the alarm before I am ready."

Emily bit her lip and scrambled up from the floor. "If you let her go, I will come with you. I will divorce Valentine. I will marry you." Her voice was deadly calm.

"Emily—no!" Valentine protested.

The marquess's eyes lit with unholy glee. He focused on the maid. "Go, girl. I shall count to ten. If you are gone by then, you shall live—thanks to your lady."

Nancy still did not move. But then the marquess's soft counting began and, with a whimper, the girl dashed toward the end of the row and freedom.

As she reached the marquess, though, her flight ended and she threw herself into him, knocking him off balance. He screamed and they both fell in a tangle. His pistol fell uselessly several feet away.

Valentine and Emily rushed to help the maid get away. To their shock, when the maid was lifted from the marquess, a spread of blood covered his chest.

"What have you done to me?" the marquess whispered, staring only at the little maid who had dared to attack him.

"I stabbed you in your black 'eart, like you deserve, you devil!" Nancy said, and then she collapsed against Emily's shoulder, weeping hysterically.

Twenty-six

"I can have no gowns for the season then?"

"You can have no season." He swallowed hard, afraid to tell her the truth, but there was no other choice. "We cannot afford to lease a place in London, let alone afford the clothing necessary to appear in Society without disgracing ourselves and announcing to the world that we must mind our pennies."

"So it is not that you do not wish to be seen with your infamous viscountess?"

He smiled. "I'm afraid you no longer qualify for infamy, my dear. Your courage is the talk of London." He laughed ruefully. "Of course, even though I am quite cleared of Granbury's first murder, the rumor is that I'm still not good enough for you. But I always knew that anyway. I just didn't let it stop me from possessing you."

She threw her napkin at him. "Rogue!" She dipped her head so that he could not see her eyes. "That is truly a shame, about the season, though. I do not know if I can bear it."

"I wish I could—" He broke off. Taking her hands in his own, he met her gaze steadily. "I promise, no matter what, that you will have a chance to enjoy the London season next year."

"I suppose that will have to do." She pouted. There was just a hint of a smile behind the pout, though, he recognized suddenly.

"Emily, what are you about?"

"It's just that I so wanted to let everyone who doubted that we would have a successful marriage see that I am a good wife."

"And that would be easier this year than next?"

"Certainly! A woman always gains much more sympathy for her sacrifice when she is heavy with child than she does once the child has been born and is lying prettily in its crib, don't you think?"

She was batting her eyes at him so distractingly, that for a moment he did not register what she had said.

And then he replied, with a dazed smile, "I suppose that means I must break the promise I just made then—the budget will not bear both the cost of a season in London and the things a baby will need."

"What a shame." She stood up and covered the few paces between them. As she settled herself in his lap and began to kiss his neck gently, she whispered, "I'm so very disappointed."

Shy Anne Webster's sister has told her she doesn't have to marry if she's not in love, but Hero longs for a real romance. She settles for a little adventure, however, when Arthur Watterley asks her to help him look for a rare edition of *Le Morte d'Arthur.* When they're locked in the bookseller's shop—and found in a compromising position—the pair who have longed for the passion they've found in books is appalled to find themselves married out of obligation. . . .

help him compose courtly letters ~~ ~~s w~~ ~~
his secretly romantic heart made her wish that *she w~~ ~~ ~~ ~~*

__AUTUMN FLAME: The Clan Maclean #2

by Lynne Hayworth   0-8217-6883-2 $5.50US/$7.50CAN

To inherit the Virginia tobacco plantation where he worked, Diarmid Maclean had to wed immediately. Desperate, he buys a British bond slave as his bride. Lucy Graves steals Diarmid's heart and makes him forget his vow to keep the marriage chaste—and temporary. Now the banished Highland warrior must put aside his past . . . before his beloved thief is taken from him forever.

__GABRIELLE: The Acadians #3

by Cherie Clare   0-8217-6802-6 $5.50US/$7.50CAN

From the moment she met Captain Jean Bouclaire, Gabrielle Gallant felt her imagination stirred by the handsome seafarer. And when he swept her into his arms, it hardly seemed to matter that he was a smuggler by trade . . . but now it will take all her courage to risk everything to keep them together.

Thrilling Romance from
Meryl Sawyer